KU-731-702

THE KILLING JAR

Nicola Monaghan graduated from the University of York in 1992, and went on to teach for several years before taking a job in the City of London. A career in finance took her to New York, Paris and Chicago, before she gave it all up in 2001 to return to her home town and pursue an MA in creative writing at Nottingham Trent University. *The Killing Jar* is Nicola's first novel, and is inspired by the lives she witnessed on the council estates where she grew up.

FOR ANTHONY

Acknowledgements

Special thanks to my agent Luigi Bonomi for all his help and advice. To my editor Poppy Hampson and to Jason Arthur, Alison Samuel and all at Random House.

Thanks also to David Belbin, Stephan Collishaw, Georgina Lock, Elaine Palmer, Tim Love, George Szirtes, A.L. Kennedy, James Urquhart, Ross Bradshaw, Laura, Andrea, Maria, Richard, James, Jonathan, Morgan John, Jo and Manny, Mad Kev, Susie, Afshan, Jane D'Amico, and Chris, as well as Mum, Dad, Deb, Paul, Add, Dan, Nat and all my family.

And, of course, to Chad, for everything.

NICOLA MONAGHAN

The Killing Jar

VINTAGE BOOKS
London

Published by Vintage 2007

8 10 9

Copyright © Nicola Monaghan 2006

Nicola Monaghan has asserted her right under the Copyright,
Designs and Patents Act, 1988 to be identified as the author
of this work

Lyrics from 'He's Gonna Step on You Again' written by
John Kongos & Chris Demetrious, as sung by Shaun Ryder
with the Happy Mondays ©Tapestry Music Ltd

This book is sold subject to the condition that it shall not
by way of trade or otherwise, be lent, resold, hired out, or
otherwise circulated without the publisher's prior consent in any
form of binding or cover other than that in which it is published
and without a similar condition including this condition being
imposed on the subsequent purchaser

First published in Great Britain in 2006 by
Chatto & Windus

Vintage
Random House, 20 Vauxhall Bridge Road,
London SW1V 2SA

www.vintage-books.co.uk

Addresses for companies within The Random House Group Limited
can be found at: www.randomhouse.co.uk/offices.htm

The Random House Group Limited Reg. No. 954009

A CIP catalogue record for this book
is available from the British Library

ISBN 9780099496878

Penguin Random House is committed to a sustainable future for
our business, our readers and our planet. This book is made from
Forest Stewardship Council® certified paper.

Printed and bound in Great Britain by Clays Ltd, St Ives plc

ONE

Some people'd say I was destined for all this killing when Uncle Frank came into my life but it goes back further than that. To when my brother was born.

Jon came out wailing like a banshee and didn't stop for months. It were Mam's fault, that. Her bad habits got him hooked on smack and coke before he was even born, poor bogger. She didn't care much that he was screaming. She slept and slept after he was born, and let the nurses feed him from a bottle.

'Your mam's very tired,' one of them told me.

I shrugged. Mam'd always slept a lot and I'd never thought much of it. I looked at the baby, his mouth open and tongue wriggling as he screamed. I noticed he used his whole body to cry with. Looking back now, I wonder why the nurses didn't give him a bit of methadone or summat to help him out but they let him go cold turkey instead. What a way to come into the world. Never stood a chance, our Jon. I walked over to the cot and put my hand on his cheek. He tried to suck my thumb but the nurse told me not to let him cause of the germs, so I tickled his hand instead and he grabbed my finger, clung to it with his whole fist. Can't imagine that no more, Jon's hand fitting tight round my finger, but it used to. I fell in love.

'In't he clever already?' I said to the nurse.

'Don't get carried away. All babies do that. It's a reflex,' she told me.

But I stood there, letting him squeeze my finger as if his life depended on it. I looked up at the nurse.

'Is he brown cause my mam shoots brown?' I asked her.

She clamped her hand over her mouth as if the bad words'd been summat she'd said. I didn't have a clue what were up with her, didn't understand what I'd said. It were just summat I'd heard in a row with a neighbour.

The lady next door, Mrs Ivanovich, was the only reason I wasn't put into care. Mam'd left me at home when she went into labour and walked to the hospital, off her head. Mrs Ivanovich found me sitting in the garden at two in the morning and I ended up stopping at hers. She took me on a bus to visit when the baby'd come and the people at the hospital could tell she was a good sort, thought she'd keep an eye on me. They weren't to know. Anyway, I was glad I was staying with her. I wanted to stay at her house for ever cause even if it were only next door, being at Mrs Ivanovich's was more interesting than being stuck in our house.

She was foreign and everyone thought she was a bit of a nutter, avoided her. She came across like that cause she was old and had her ways, like how she kept butterflies. She had a cage in her back garden made out of a rabbit hutch, the wire replaced with this white gauzy stuff, same as she'd folded into a net on the end of a cane to catch them with. When we moved in I watched her through the hedge and saw how she struggled to get the butterflies out the net. Her fingers were all twisted and mangled.

'Can I help?' I asked. Not exactly out the kindness of my heart, but cause I was into the butterflies. She smiled and gestured at me to come into her garden. She showed me how to take the butterflies out the net without touching their wings.

'You can damage the scales, you see, and then they have trouble flying properly. Aerodynamics,' she told me.

She spoke English perfect, but was hard to understand down to her strong accent. It made that last word, aero-dynamics, stretch and vibrate so's I asked her to say it again. I looked at her, all snot and open mouth. She leaned over and whispered in my ear.

'They're covered in fairy dust. You brush it off and they can't fly anymore. But I can't say it too loud because butterflies don't believe in fairies and if they heard me they'd never take off again,' she said.

I wiped away the snot with the back of my hand and Mrs Ivanovich magicked up a tissue, showed me how to blow my nose.

Ever since then, she let me help her. She gave me the net so I could try and catch butterflies but I never did. I'd run till I fell over knackered, waving the net round and trampling down the tall weeds at the back of her garden, but I still didn't catch one. I asked how come she got so many, when she had to use a stick to walk and couldn't hardly move her hands. She said I needed to be more 'stealthy'. That was the exact word she used, cause she wrote it down for me in this notebook thing what she let me keep. She wasn't happy at all when she heard my mam wasn't sending me to school, and started to teach me stuff her-sen.

I used to love to sit with her in the garden, watching the butterflies stutter and hop between the plants and twigs she'd arranged in the cage. She showed me how to use a magnifying glass so's it didn't catch the sun and burn them, but helped me watch them dead close while they fed. Watch their bubble eyes and the suckers they pushed into the flowers so's they could get out the juice. Aliens in the flowerbed, and fucked up scary ones at that. Mrs Ivanovich had stories about bigger monsters, though, from trips she'd took. She told me she'd worked all over, but was from Russia in the first place. Had come here for her husband's job, then he'd gone and died on her. He'd left her with nowt cept savings back home what she wasn't allowed to touch down to summat legal. Her eyes went all watery and red when she told me that. The Amazon basin was her favourite place, she'd said, and I imagined a massive sink full of the great big insects she described. She told me she used to be an entomologist, another word I made her write down, which was a kind of scientist who studied how insects worked. But it wasn't till I went to stay with her I realised what this meant. When I found her killing jar.

It were the middle of summer, a good few weeks after Jon'd been born. Mrs Ivanovich was in the garden catching 'specimens', as she used to say, and told me to go inside in case I moved too sudden and scared the bugs away. I heard her swear, then she shouted in she needed her other net, and it were under the sink somewhere. I was searching for it when I caught a glint of summat shiny. Kids' eyes are always turned by things what sparkle, especially them as belong to the sorts who've never had owt. I grabbed at the glittery thing and pulled it into the air where I could see it.

The glass was so thick its contents were magnified and distorted. At first glance I thought it were shredded newspaper inside. I looked closer and saw big blank eyes and furry bodies, washed out velvet wings. Moths. Dead ones, sitting on a layer of plaster. I screamed and dropped the jar. The glass was too heavy to shatter, but it cracked round the base and the top section fell on its side. I sat on the floor looking at what I'd done. There was this smell, not very strong, not nice but not rank, only just there so I could of believed I'd imagined it. Mrs Ivanovich walked in to see what was keeping me. She threw the back door wide open and grabbed me, pushed me outside. I saw her sprinkle summat what looked like salt all over what'd spilled.

Mrs Ivanovich made me go through the jitty and in through the front garden. It took her ages to unlock the door and, while she was doing it, Piercey came, his van throwing out a mangled Lara's theme what made my mouth water for ice-cream. Mrs Ivanovich went to the van and got me a ninety-nine with two flakes and that red sauce and everything. That was a big treat for me back then. She took me through to the living room and sat me down.

'Kerrie-Ann, sweetheart, you have to stay in here now for the rest of the day. Those chemicals are strong and if you breathe them they could kill you,' she told me. I crunched through the flake, making sure the crumbs dropped back onto the ice cream.

'Is that why them moths was dead?' I asked her through a mouthful of chocolate. She didn't tell me not to talk with my mouth full like she usually did so I knew summat serious had happened.

She sighed. 'How to explain to a five-year-old?' she said, to her-sen, I think. She walked over and sat down next to me, put her hand on my arm. 'Some things have to be sacrificed so you can do more or know more,' she said. I nodded. 'Those moths,' she said. 'If I can find out what goes on inside them, it helps everyone understand the world better. Like we wouldn't know how to make helicopters if it wasn't for dragonflies. And maybe I'll realise something as important from the inside of a moth.'

'The inside?' I said.

Mrs Ivanovich walked over to the wall unit behind the telly. She pulled out a book and brought it over to me. It were full of dead butterflies and moths, and other insects too. Beetles, ants, teeny creatures called aphids. The little ones were stuck to card and glued down, but the bigger insects were skewered to the page with pins. Then she showed me a wooden box. There was a moth inside. She used a tiny knife and a magnifier to cut it into pieces and showed me its different parts. The heart, the air sacs, what she told me were called spiracles, the nerve cord running right down its back. The exoskeleton. That meant bones on the outside.

'Do you understand now? Why some things have to die?' she asked.

I nodded again but she must of been able to tell I didn't cause she carried on talking.

'Death is part of life, Kerrie-Ann. A very clever man told me that once. A shaman, which is kind of an Indian doctor.'

'Did he wear feathers on his head?' I asked her.

'He wore feathers all over the place,' she said. She stroked my hair and I snuggled up against her. I could feel her ribs dig through her jumper. 'You've got to remember that,' she said. 'Death is part of life, not a bad thing. You must remember it and be strong because I'm going to die soon.'

I bit into my ice-cream and pain stabbed through my gum and jaw.

I didn't sleep well that night. I turned over and over in my bed so's the blankets wrapped me up like layers on a Swiss roll. I dreamed of dead butterflies, and beetles as big as me standing at the end of my bed, goggle eyed, rolling out their suckers into my stomach. I dreamed of Mrs Ivanovich, dead and in the bottom of a jar. I couldn't get the smell from the kitchen out my nose.

Jon got better in the end, and Mam brought him home. I don't know how long it took, it all feels like for ever when you're little. It must of been a while, though, cause by the time they came back to the close nowt ever wiped the dopey smile off his face. It made me think they might of swapped the baby, and looking back I wonder if Mam'd started putting summat more interesting than sugar on his dummy. The good weather had gone on and on that year, an Indian summer they called it, but it wasn't so sunny then, and there wasn't many butterflies around. Mrs Ivanovich was cutting up ants, and it were delicate work so she needed my help more than ever. She swore loads as she tried to get her mangled hands round the tiny knife she used. She had a bath twice a day, and used to send me down the Co-op to get that Radox stuff for her and let me keep the change. Sometimes it took her all her time to stand up or sit down and I'd stay all day bringing her cups of tea. Mam never asked where I'd been. Mrs Ivanovich told me I was a good gell, but she wasn't sure she'd be able to cope with another winter, not with her sore old bones. I should of seen it coming.

It were her daughter what found her, one afternoon. She didn't visit very often and I reckon her mam knew she was coming, set it up that way deliberate. All's I knew was the woman coming out the front screaming, falling on her hands and knees with a screwed up face and shouting 'Mam!' using all the air in her lungs. By the time I got out the house, she was lying on the grass with her head in her hands and wouldn't speak to me. I knew what'd happened. The smell was in the air, kind of nutty, almost not there. Mrs Ivanovich's killing jar chemical.

When you're young and don't know no better, you're fascinated by everything. Apart from insects, the only dead thing I'd ever seen was a bird I found in the hedge, a sparrow or summat. Its beak was jammed open with a bright red rowanberry in it. I knew them berries were poison cause we had a Rowan tree in our back garden and I'd been told never to touch them. I couldn't work out if that was why the bird'd died, or if it'd choked. I couldn't understand why God made owt so red and juicy when they'd kill you if you ate them. God was supposed to be good, but that was a mean trick. I'd never seen a dead person, though, not even someone pretending on the telly. Mam'd sold ourn in the middle of the night when I was three, and Mrs Ivanovich used to let me watch hers but was well strict about what kind of programmes.

I put my hand over my nose to try and block out the lethal fumes and walked through Mrs Ivanovich's front door. Inside, the place had been set up like one huge killing jar. Bowls all over, on the shelves, the 'gram, everywhere, with that chemical shit inside. The fumes'd filled the room, then Mrs I's lungs, then each one of the cells inside her. Pop. Pop-te-pop, pop, pop.

She was sat on the sofa with one eye open and one eye closed, like she was winking at me. The eye what was open freaked me out so I walked over and closed it. The skin on her eyelid felt like cold fish. With her eyes closed she looked better, like she was having a quick nap. I noticed she had summat in her arms then, was hugging it to her like a doll. I pulled it out from under her elbow. It were a butterfly in a smart glass case. Framed to go on the wall, like a picture. Not one like you'd see in the garden, with green-white leafy wings, or even them red velvety boggers you'd see if you waited long enough. This was shiny. Its wings were blue and black and looked like metal. A pin skewered through its body and held it fast against a bit of card and underneath there was some writing. I didn't feel proud of me-sen but I couldn't leave it there for Mrs Ivanovich's daughter to find. She wouldn't know what it were. Wouldn't care. So I tucked it in the waistband of my skirt and pulled my T-shirt down over it, was careful how I walked.

I went through to the kitchen and kicked open the back door before the stuff got to me too. I went out and shoved my find under the hedge, where I could easily pick it up later. I had a thought then, and ran back into the kitchen. Under the sink was a big bottle, the leftover cyanide. I took it, though Christ knows what all I can of thought I'd need it for. I hid it in the same spot of privet as the dead butterfly. I heard noises in the house and backed away from the hedge quick as. I could see the butterfly cage from where I was stood and knew it wouldn't take much of them gases to do for the delicate boggers. I walked over and looked at them one last time. Then I opened the cage and let them go.

There wasn't many butterflies left in the cage, and a couple were dead already. But them as could fluttered straight off. They wouldn't have long, I knew that. Summer was over.

TWO

Morpho Pelaides, that butterfly was called. It said so on the paper underneath where it were pinned. It said it'd been collected from the Peruvian Rainforest by Dr T. Ivanovich in 1965. I didn't know whether that was my dead neighbour or her long-dead husband, cause she'd told me ladies could be doctors too. I called the butterfly Morph for short, like the Plasticene man on the telly who changed from shape to shape. I knew the butterfly had as well. Mrs Ivanovich'd showed it me, let me touch a caterpillar and a pupae. Not a butterfly though, you couldn't touch them or they'd crumble in your hand. 'They dry out, see,' she told me. I couldn't believe this when I looked at Morph. He glistened. He looked like summat you could use to cut skin. He was my lifeline. Whenever I felt crap or worried I'd look at Morph and feel better, remember there was other places away from my house on the close.

It wasn't that long after Mrs I had died when another old woman turned up at our door. Well, she did have grey hair and false teeth, but looking back she couldn't of been much more than forty. People aged much quicker back then I reckon. She was my mommar, Mam told me, which meant she was her mam. Mam made me kiss this lady I didn't really know and told me that Mommar used to take me for drives when I was little, to get me off to sleep, before Jon was born. And it came back to me a bit, the darkness outside, the chugger chug of an old engine, the constant pattern of streetlamps as we passed them, beating a lullaby against my half-closed eyes. I could remember the car too, this bright thing my mam called the Orange on account of its colour. I looked behind the old lady expecting to see it and she laughed.

'Yer mam put paid to the car, ducky,' she said. And I don't know to this day if that meant she crashed it or sold it to fund her habit or what all happened. I could remember a big row though, voices raised loud and slamming doors, and I guessed it were all connected to why Mommar'd been away. She was back now though, and that was definitely a good thing.

Things were all right for a while after that. Mommar was strict as owt, made me sit at the table for my dinner and eat with my mouth closed and say 'Mam and I' instead of 'Mam and me'. But I adored her all the same. I loved Mam more, course. But I didn't know her, not really, knew nowt about what kind of person she was. Having Mommar round to help look after us brought Mam back to life somehow. She was only about twenty-one, and now she had time to look after her-sen she looked like summat off the telly, with all this long blonde hair and smudged brown make-up round her eyes. She wore clothes what shimmered in the wildest colours, vivid fuchsia, and emerald and this blood and gore red what I loved the most. She flitted round the house, and in and out my life, like she was a butterfly. She used to go down to London. She'd be gone for what seemed for ever in kiddie time, and come back with new clothes and perfume so's she smelled of flowers. And these fags what she rolled up. When she smoked them they smelled sweet as the perfume and made me feel happy, cept my mommar used to shout, and flap round at the smoke, shooing me out the room with the other hand. My mommar took care of me, but my mam, well, she took my breath away.

My mommar was a lovechild, as she was fond of telling people when she got the chance. My great-gran's careless-ness with contraception set the tone for my family history. There isn't one gell related to me, at least what I know of, who hasn't got pregnant by accident. Course, when I was little I didn't have a clue what it all meant. When I asked her what a lovechild was she smirked, and said it meant her dad loved her mam a little bit too much. She said we were two of a kind, me and her, I was a lovechild too. But I couldn't work it out. If my dad loved my mam more than he should of, how comes he wasn't round no more? How comes whenever I asked anyone owt about him they shushed me and changed the subject?

My mommar's face puckered up when she took out her teeth and she had to suck on bars of chocolate to eat them. I'd watch when she did this, fascinated with how she could manage not to wolf the whole bar down the way I would of. She was from Eastwood, mining country, and had a broader accent than my mam or me. She wore tan tights and squeezed bread before she bought it to check it were fresh. And she was tough. I saw her take on lads twice her own size, more than once. There's that saying about not suffering fools gladly, but my mommar didn't suffer them at all. I guess I take after her that way, cept she never would of harmed a fly, and that's a big difference. She was the kind of woman who, if she got asked the time in the street, would say summat like, 'It's about nar, if yer got a watch, but seen as you an't you wun't know, wud yer?' All this was great, when she was on your side. But it were terrifying to be a kid round her when you knew you'd done summat wrong. And my mam, she was always getting done by Mommar over one thing or another. Taking a fiver out her purse without asking. Being out all night. And summat else. I didn't know what, not back then, cause when it came up in their rows Mommar backed off, and said she wouldn't talk about 'that thing' in front of 'the babies', which was me and Jon of course.

Mommar took a dislike to this young couple what moved in next-door-but-one cause she thought they were a bit up themselves. It were the way they acted when they moved in set her against them. They came in this huge van and I was fascinated, the way you are at that age. I stood and watched with my mouth hung open as they brought in these big leather sofas and polished up wardrobes and chests of drawers and stuff like that. It wasn't owt like the furniture we had in our house. But the woman came out and shooed me off, like I was a dog making a nuisance of me-sen. My mommar wasn't having none of that. She'd been watching me from the window, the way she often did, and came flying out and down the stuck-up cow's garden path. She knocked dead loud on the front door. No one came at first, so she knocked again. 'Come-ere, Kerrie-Ann,' she called over. I didn't want to do no such thing, but knew better than to cross my mommar. She grabbed me by the hand and yanked me to her side. The door opened with a jerk, as if whoever was behind it was mad someone'd had the cheek to knock. The woman appeared.

'What?' she spat at us. She was seventeen, maybes eighteen, just a gell really. No match for someone like my mommar.

'See this here?' Mommar said, pointing at me. The woman stared all gormless at the pair on us. 'This here's a lickle gell, not some stray what's weeing on yer lawn. She's called Kerrie-Ann and I'd appreciate it if yer could remember that.'

'I were just—'

'You were just nothink. I see yer do owt like that again and I'll tan yer hide, I don't care how big yer are.'

With that, my mommar turned and pulled me after her. I watched the woman as I was dragged off down the path. She looked like she was about to bust into tears. I tried to smile at her but she pushed the door hard shut.

We had our little rituals like every bogger else. My life was quite normal back then, see, you wouldn't of expected it'd go the way it did. Thursday was giro day, and we'd all go down the shops at Coleby like a lot of the families on our estate. Some of them made these huge long lines down the road, a great queue of similar-looking people, and I used to get a clout for staring at them. There was just the four on us, sometimes three on the days when my mam was away or couldn't be arsed to come. I stood on this strip of plastic at the front of the pram. My brother would giggle at me all the way, blowing bubbles out his chubby lips. He was a happy, smiley sod by then, had this cheeky wet grin plastered on his face the whole time.

When we got there, we always went to the same shops in the same order. The post office first, to cash the giros. The supermarket was next door, and we'd nip in and get bread and milk. There was these giraffe and elephant things outside, them rides what you put money in, and I'd nearly always whinge and moan for a go on one and once in a while I'd get my way. The giraffe was my favourite cause I could grab hold of its neck as it moved back and forward. They never did go as fast as I would of liked though. Then we'd go in the bakers, where the adults had a sausage roll each and I got an iced bun if I'd been good and wanted one. More often though, I wanted to go next door to the sweet shop to get a 10p mix, or a lucky bag, or one of them kayli tubes with a liquorice stick. I'd chew and dawdle all the way home, while the two women nagged at me to walk faster or climb up on the buggy board. I couldn't of been happier.

It were that year I started school. I should of started a year before, but my mam hadn't got round to organising it. My mommar wasn't having none of that, though, and got me enrolled at the Catholic school down the road. She was Catholic, see, and said St Teresa's was a better place to go than anywhere else. All's I really knew about it were when she dressed me up in this brown pinafore and made me eat cereal one morning. I didn't want to get up cause Mam was still in bed, and I pulled a right mardy when she tried to get me out the door. But, like I said, my mommar wasn't one to be messed with. She gave me a right clout and dragged me off through the estate and onto Aspley Lane.

It were autumn and there was brown leaves all round where they'd fell off the big trees. I wouldn't look at my mommar cause she'd took me away from my mam so I crunched my way through looking at my feet. I noticed my shoes and tights were the same colour as the leaves and soon that had me so interested I stopped being in a mardy and was talking to my mommar about what'd happen when I got to school.

I got there to find this place where the chairs and tables, even the toilets, were all built at just the right height for me. I walked round fascinated. There was water and sand and a Wendy House to play in, with a toy iron and cooker and all that kind of thing. I was well impressed. There was this woman there, tall as a witch and with this silver hair in a mist round her head. She spoke to my mommar and I heard her going on about how much time I'd missed and the catching up I'd have to do.

Then Mommar left me there. I wasn't impressed about that, not one bit. I curled up in a ball on the carpet and wouldn't move nowhere. The teacher kept trying to come near me and I just screamed my head off. When she tried grabbing me I bit her on the hand. They couldn't ring my mam or my mommar ner nowt cause we didn't have a phone them days, so they just put me in this room on my own till I calmed down.

By then I was dying to play in the sand or the water. But when I was allowed back in the teacher said I had to do some writing. She asked me if I could read and write and I said yes, cause Mrs Ivanovich'd taught me all about letters and words and that, going on about it being a 'crying shame' that my mam hadn't sorted out school. She asked me to write a sentence, 'My name is Kerrie-Ann', and I showed her, printing each letter separate and neat as I could. She took one look at what I'd wrote and took it off the table, ripped it into bits.

'That doesn't say anything,' she said, and then said summat about printing and joining up, and how I'd done it the wrong way.

This was proper confusing for me. Mrs Ivanovich who knew everything in the world, she'd told me this was how to write and now this woman what I didn't know from Adam was telling me it were wrong. I stood up, pushed over my chair and screamed, and shook my leg, and didn't stop till they sent someone to get me out the room. They went and got my mommar then, and she took me away, but not without giving the teacher earache about what'd gone off.

'Our Kerrie-Ann's no bad kid,' she told the woman with the posh voice and the cloud of hair. 'It must of been summat what you did.' That was the great thing about my mommar, always on my side no matter what. Even if it did feel like she might pull my arm out the socket on the way back to our house.

After that I went to the local school on Beechdale Road, where most of the kids from the estate went. I liked that cause I made a load of friends who lived near where I did and we'd call for each other to play. There was these gells called Trace and Jaqui what I was best friends with, and they'd often come round to mine cause there was this park in the middle of the close with swings and a slide, and this bit of grass to play football. It were a good place to live that way.

It wasn't long after that when Uncle Dave started coming over regular to see my mam. He'd bring sweets for me and Jon, and take my mam upstairs for what he called 'a special cuddle'. My mommar couldn't stand him, wouldn't be in the same room as he was and went out visiting or to bingo when he came over. She kept telling me 'he's a bad-un' and 'this'll all end in tears' and other stuff like that, but Mam seemed happy enough and Dave was all right to us as well.

It were the hottest summer in the world and the grass'd charred with the sun. There'd been this plague of ladybirds, landing all over you and flipping from place to place that way they do. It looks more like they're jumping than flying, but if you look careful it's wings they use, hidden under that red and black armour what they have. Kids got all funny when the bugs landed on them, said the boggers stung, but I've never known a ladybird bite no one. There was this one day there was so many it were like a red carpet on the pavement. All summer I played on the park and made daisy chains with my friends. And when it finally rained we all ran outside for a shower, let it soak us right through. It were warm rain, and we stood there till our hair stuck to our faces and our clothes were sodden. My mommar told me off, reckoned I'd catch my death of cold but my mam just laughed at her. 'It's eighty degrees in the shade,' she said. Then my lovely, smiley mam gave me this huge great hug and I clung to her, clamped me-sen on. She spun me round and round and I thought I'd explode with happiness.

Then one day my mommar left us, just as quick as she'd come into our lives. Said she was going out to the shops but she'd been gone ages. I went outside to look for her and waited till it got dark but there was no sign at all.

I ran back to the house and through the door. My mam was sat on the sofa. I tried to climb up and cuddle her. 'Yer hurting me, Kez,' she said, pushing me off.

My mommar didn't come back the next day. Or the next day, or the one after that. I missed her a bit but I loved my mam so it were all right. You don't understand that stuff when you're a kid. My mam said she'd gone to a nice place where it were sunny all the time, which might make you wonder if she'd died but I know now she hadn't.

I don't blame her for running off, not given what my mam was on with, but what I don't get is why she never took us. How could she leave us babies when she knew what my mam was like?

As soon as Mommar was gone, Uncle Dave moved in. He sat in the front room most of the time, drinking beer from a can and watching this portable telly he'd brought with him. He didn't care much what me and Jon did so long as we didn't disturb his programmes. Jon was up and walking by then, and saying a load of cute things the way toddlers do. I loved playing with him. This was a good job an-all cause my mam lost interest in both on us. Just sat there with Dave, or up in her room, eyes misted over and zombified.

Dave was the first in a long line of uncles what came to stay with us. He wasn't the worst by any means. Course, he wasn't really my mam's brother or owt like that. None of them were. I guess she was knocking them off, but that wasn't the main role they played in her life neither.

My mam only had one love by then and it came out of blood-red flowers what grow where it's hot.

THREE

After everything what I've took over the years my head's a mess, and sometimes it's hard to put stuff in order the way it happened. It helps to have Jon to measure it against cause I knew him his entire life. When I look back, I often think 'well that was when Jon was just walking' or 'when Jon started school' and stuff like that. But the best times I remember about Jon are them years when he changed from a baby to a boy.

He was clever, was Jon, I'd been right about that when I saw him first born. He was only a bit more than one when he started to be able to say stuff what made sense, and you could have little conversations with him. Find out what he wanted. Tell him what was good and naughty and check he got it. That kind of thing. I used to help him paint. I could of sat with him all day and night helping him make pictures and listening to him explaining what the different bits were. But my mam'd never let me. She always moaned about the mess we made and told me to clear off from under her feet. I wasn't allowed to take Jon to play out cause he was too little, so Mam just shoved him in front of the telly for a few hours while I was gone and ignored the poor bogger.

When she chucked me out I'd go and call for my mates from school, Jaqui and Trace. They both lived on my estate, and it wasn't that far to walk to their houses, though I did have to cross a few roads on the way and I couldn't help remembering about this gell what'd got knocked down. I remember Trace's mam being really shocked I was allowed out all the way to Bradfield Road on my own but the truth was my mam wouldn't of cared if I'd boggered off out the estate just so long as I wasn't round to make a mess and bother her. Jaqui's mam was more like mine, out all the time and not that bothered what Jaqui got up to so she was allowed to call for me too. When Trace's big sister was around and could be arsed to take her, Trace was allowed round my end too. These were my favourite times. Me and Trace and Jaqui on the park.

They taught me a load of stuff. Like how to put buttercups under your chin to see if you liked butter or not, and not to pick dandelions cause they made you wet your bed. Though you were allowed to pick them later, when they were clocks, and blow and blow till you knew what the time was. Course we made daisy chains, getting the gap under our nails all filled with green as we punched holes in the stems to thread them together. I loved the way it made my hands smell. Jaqui had this idea one day about making perfume and we got hold of a load of bottles from people's bins and picked flowers off the park. Then we filled them with water and waited for them to change cause that was how you made perfume Jaqui reckoned. But we left them in Trace's house, and she had a mam who gave a shit so that was a mistake. Her mam

found them and went on about how it were poison and
we could hurt our-sen and threw them all away. It made
me laugh that. A few flowers and some water, poison. She
should of seen what I'd took from under Mrs Ivanovich's
sink. We never made that mistake again. Whenever we did
owt after 'that we made sure it were at mine or Jaqui's
where our mams wouldn't care.

Course, I did show Jaqui and Trace the poison I'd got.
And Morph, my beautiful, fabulous friend. I told them
the truth about how I got hold of the butterfly too. Jaqui
thought that was well cool, but Trace was all funny about
it at first and threatened to tell her mam, who would of
gone to the police even though it'd happened ages before
when I was just a little gell. But stuff like that's easy to
handle when you're that age. Me and Jaqui just said we
wouldn't talk to her again if she did, and that was enough
to make her shut her mouth.

Uncle Dave left eventually, and we soon had this other
uncle whose name was Bob. He was all right, too, didn't
ever do owt nasty to me anyway. And it were quite funny
to be able to say 'Bob's my uncle'. He would tickle me
for ages till I screamed my head off and my mam told us
both to shut up the racket. He didn't last everso long
though. Must of run out of supplies of the stuff my mam
was shooting up, I reckon, though I'm only guessing cause
I never saw owt like that till a couple of years later.

There were a few more uncles after Bob. I got so used
to the men coming in and out of my mam's bed that I
started to hardly notice what their names were. I noticed
when they changed, and what sort of stuff each one did.
Like Uncle Bob, he liked to go down the bookies and put
a few quid on the horses every Friday when he got his
giro. He'd always come back and put the race on the telly

and tell us which horse and we'd watch with him. If he won it were all ace, and he kissed us and jumped up and down and my mam went hyper. But if he lost his face just sagged, and he looked older, and mam had a go at him for wasting good money after crap horses all the time.

Course the uncles whose habits I really noticed were the ones I needed to watch out for. You know, heroin addicts are not that bad, not in terms of how they'd treat you anyway. It's them what's into coke or drink you have to watch for. There was one what always smelled of booze and I caught him this one time with a tenner and some white powder in my mam's room. It were the first time I'd seen anyone taking drugs and I was too young to know what was going off. But I could tell by the look on his face that what he was on with was summat I wasn't supposed to see. He turned and chased me out the room, and into mine. I hid in the wardrobe but course that was about the first place he looked. He dragged me out by the hair and gave me a right belting. Warned me if I even thought about telling anyone what I'd seen he'd knock me into next week. And he would of. Course, I didn't really know what I'd seen anyway, though I spose I could of described it to a teacher or summat and we might of got took into care. Why that bothered anyone God only knows cause my mam never showed no signs of caring about me now. Maybes I'm being harsh on her there. All mams love their kids, even smackhead ones who can't do much down to their sad little habits.

Them times weren't so bad, with the uncles coming and going. It were before our lives really went to shit. If I did get miserable, there was always Morph to look at so's I could cheer me-sen up, but I didn't resort to staring at him that often. The time I remember needing him was after Mrs Jenkins stopped teaching us and we got Mr Doland.

Mrs Jenkins was the nicest teacher in the world ever, I swear it's true. She was the kind of person what all teachers should be like. She was nice to you if you fell and grazed your knee, and made you feel special when you did good stuff. She made me feel special a lot. She told me I had a high reading age, and explained that meant I could read more complicated books than most children in my class. Cause of the stuff Mrs Ivanovich taught me when I was a little gell, I was well into science and Mrs Jenkins helped me learn more and more. She brought in special books she'd took out the library and helped me do topics on trees, and the weather and that kind of shit. I reckon I learned more in that class than in the rest of my whole school life, if you don't count the time I spent with Mrs Ivanovich which wasn't at no school. But, like I said, it didn't last for ever and then we had Mr Doland.

Mr Doland was the one they sent kids to when they'd been naughty cause he could shout really loud and scare the life out of you. I was never naughty when I was in Mrs Jenkins's class so I wasn't ever sent to see him. When we started in his class, though, he had us all lined up outside and screamed his head off at all on us, even though we hadn't even had time that day to do owt wrong. Jaqui cried a bit and I held her hand and squeezed so's she wasn't so scared. He clocked me.

'What's your name?' he boomed at me. And I told him. My voice wasn't steady, I'll admit that, but when he asked Jaqui she started crying. That was the kind of voice he had. After he'd got our names he screamed at us that we were in the juniors now and not babies, and that we had to stop acting like babies and doing things like holding hands and putting fingers in our mouths. Then he looked at me again, and brought his head up close to me. There was this look of disgust in his eyes as he looked real close at my hair, and picked bits up with his fingers.

'Kerrie-Ann Hill, your head is crawling with lice.'

The class was too scared to even tease me, but I went bright red as you can go. They wouldn't be allowed to do stuff like that to you in school these days but back then the teachers could of done pretty well whatever they wanted. The class wasn't so scared about teasing me on the playground at break and dinner for the next few days. Course, I wasn't the type who was going to just stand for that shit, and I gave a couple of them a right pounding when they called me nithead. And when this happened, it were Mr Doland what I got sent to. He screamed in my face and made me stand with my nose against the black-board for three breaktimes running, and even rapped my knuckles with a ruler this one time. And yet the whole fucking thing was his fault. But that's the kind of tossers what become teachers too. In my experience of school, there was more tossers than good ones like Mrs Jenkins, but then I don't know about schools all over. Just our estate. And who'd choose to work on our estate? They'd have to of had a heart of gold or be so crap they couldn't of got a job anywhere else, I reckon.

Jon was growing up this whole time. By the time I was in Mr Doland's class he'd just turned three and was bright as a button. He liked to run in a circle round the living room, and spin round and round and round till he fell over sick, that way only little kids do. He had this little boy energy what never ran out and you ended up catching when you were with him. With Jon next to me I could run and run and play dobby till I fell down knackered. I could play the same game over and over like three-year-olds do and not get bored of it cause of how much fun he was having. And the things he said. Stuff you wouldn't of thought to say for yer-sen. Little kids have this no bull-shit take on the world you can't never ever quite get back once you've grown a bit bigger.

I was growing up too, and so were Jaqui and Trace. We were getting into all sorts, like kids do on estates like ourn. There was these lads came on the park, only a few years older than us, and they'd got hold of some bottles of Thunderbird, nicked them from the offie on Bradfield. Looking back, I don't know why they nicked the Thunderbird. I mean you'd only buy it cause it's cheap and you'd nick summat better, but they were young so I guess they just didn't know. They sold it on by the mouthful, underneath the climbing frame. Jaqui and me knew better than to ask our mams for money for owt, but Trace got pocket money. She didn't want to spend it on the mouthfuls of Thunderbird at first, but we said we wouldn't talk to her if she didn't, so she changed her mind.

Trace went first, cause it were her money and that. She coughed and spluttered all over, and said it burned. Jaqui did the same. When it were my turn, I stood there under the bottle and let the kid pour. I was determined not to cough or owt. As the liquid hit the back of my throat I understood what Jaqui was going on about. It felt like I'd spilled chemicals in my mouth. I didn't cough though, I'm stubborn like that. I just held it in and my face went all red and that. We kept coming back and getting more and more of the hot nasty liquid. I swear it tasted like summat you'd put under the sink.

All's I remember about what happened next is feeling

happy but a bit sick with it. I reckon you can tell when you drink that you're taking in poison. I could anyway, and I didn't like the feeling, the sicky part on it anyways. We were high though, running round the park playing dobbie and laughing our heads off. We went on the swings then, but that made me feel well queasy. Jaqui shouted that we should go on the witch's hat, and I didn't think owt on it so we all climbed on. This lad started pushing and pushing the roundabout. I realised I was going to puke my guts out but he was pushing it so hard that I couldn't get off. I could see that Trace felt the same by the look on her face but Jaqui seemed all right. Then Trace did chuck up, and the carrot soup what she spewed out flew all over, landing on my arm and in a big splodge at the top of my skirt. I couldn't stand it no longer so I jumped off, even though the roundabout was going well fast.

I landed awkward and gave me-sen huge grazes on my arms and legs. I think I might of sparked out for a minute but I don't know. I didn't split my head open or owt like that, didn't need the hospital, which was just as well cause my mam didn't come running out the door to see what'd gone off. I felt even sicker when I got up, and threw up all over. I kept sicking up for hours and hours and the whole thing put me off drinking for good. It's never been my thing, booze.

We'd seen lads and gells older than us sniffing glue on the park, and giggling their heads off, so we wanted to be grown up like what they were and do it our-sen. Jaqui got hold of some glue from her house and we found a shady spot in the park to have a go in. We'd seen kids with plastic bags over their heads doing it but Trace wouldn't let us do it that way cause her mam'd always said you shouldn't put a plastic bag over your head. This was the thing we did that could of worked out worst, I spose. I look back now and it makes me laugh how stupid we was, but at the same time it scares the shit out of me. Well, course, what Jaqui'd got hold of was some kind of Pritt Stick or water based stuff, nowt what you could of got high on, and it must of been funny to watch us. I mean, we were sniffing at these glue stick things, smelling glue I guess you might of called it, and not even the right stuff.

Anyways, we gave up on the idea of glue after we met some real sniffers and found out what it could do to you. It wasn't on the park on the close. We'd wandered off right up over to Strelley Rec. None on us was really allowed there, but we didn't think we'd get caught up like we did. There was this bunch of lads sniffing near the parkie's hut and after we'd been on the swings for a bit they came over to talk to us. This one lad made a beeline for me. I remember he was wearing these real tight jeans what clung to his crotch and I didn't like it. It gave me the creeps. He sat on the swing next to me and started talking about dirty words and if I knew what they meant. I didn't. I mean, I was only about nine, the pervy bastard.

The other two gells were getting all nervy, and I don't blame them neither.

'We better go,' I said. But this lad grabbed hold of my arm.

'You better not,' he said.

I looked him in the eye and all's I could see there were this cold thing. It scared me.

'Yer mates can clear off,' he said.

Trace and Jaqui didn't need to be told twice. They was off quick as he gestured at the gate with his head.

I stayed sat on the swing, and the glued-up lad pushed

it harder and harder. I talked with him, all gentle, and he told me he'd got a knife. I was scared shitless, I don't mind telling you, but somehow I just talked and talked. I knew if it were Trace stuck like this, that sooner or later her dad'd come looking for her. She'd told me that'd happened once before when she was ten minutes late back for her tea. But I didn't have a dad. My mam'd never of come looking for me and it wasn't like either of the gells could tell anyone I was in trouble without getting done themselves for being on the Rec.

Lucky for me this park keeper bloke came back to lock up and he wasn't having none of it. He made the lad clear off, then walked me back to the edge of the estate.

'Yer too young, gell, to be walking off up here on yer own,' he said. He touched my arm and gave me this smile. One of them smiles what are all thoughtful and full of the weight of the world. I'd never thought before about what it would of been like to have a dad but it struck me then. I cried about it all the way home.

Things weren't ever the same with Jaqui and Trace after that. I couldn't really forget that they'd left me on my own with that nob. I couldn't get it out my head what could of happened if that parkie bloke hadn't of come back. After that, whenever I had kiddie fantasies about having a dad, it were that parkie's face what came into my head. He walked up to the door on the close to claim me and smiled that weight of the world smile as he told me why he hadn't been able to be round for me before. And I ran up and wrapped me-sen round him, clung on like a fucking limpet as he took me away. His lovechild.

FOUR

It were a good job I had Morph to look at when Frank moved in with us. Or 'Uncle Frank to you thanks very much Kerrie-Anna', as if that was ever my name.

Uncle Frank was loaded. He bought me my first bike, a pink thing with white handlebars and a basket on the front made of woven plastic, a leather saddlebag on the back. He'd got me wrong with the pink, but the bike was shiny and oiled, and moved lovely. Some of the kids on our close had bikes, but not many, and them what did had pockmarked rusty old things, nowt like the one I'd been bought. Frank seemed all right at first. He was nice to Jon and me, bought us sweets and stuff, and my mam was much happier with him round. He had his own business, Mam said, and he needed me to help him. He'd pay me, and I'd be able to use my new bike. I had to work with these two boys called Mark and Jason. They were all right, and after I met them two I pretty well stopped calling for Jaqui and Trace. I saw them round the place, and talked to them at school, but I had new mates now from round the estate and I still hadn't forgiven them for leaving me with the glued-up nutter boy.

Mark and Jason and me agreed our job was much better than a paper round, cause our packages were much smaller and didn't weigh too much. The newspapers have all got bigger since, but the Sunday bundle already weighed heavy, even back then. I don't know how people find enough time to read all that shit in one weekend. Mark and Jason had bikes too, nearly as shiny as mine and just as new, cept they'd rode them over Cinderhill tip a few times so they'd gone all dusty. They both called this 'scrambling' but I knew scrambling bikes had engines and were ridden over hills and rocks. Cinderhill tip was just a pile of pit dust and manky old fridges. But I didn't point this out cause I was scared of Mark and Jason. Their dad was also called Mark and was Uncle Frank's business partner. Cause he had the same name as his dad, Mark used to get called Little Mark by adults, which he hated. Jason called it him when he was trying to wind him up, but Mark had a great big temper and used to hit his brother round the head hard, like he was trying to do proper damage. So I said nowt about the 'scrambling'. Even though I was scared of Mark, I fancied him. He looked totally different them days, with all this floppy blond hair what kept falling over his face and a look in his narrow grey eyes what bothered me. I used to practise writing my name with his surname: Kerrie-Ann Scotland. It made a good signature. He looked down his nose at me back then, though, cause I was still at primary school and just a kid. Didn't take long for that to change. Cause I fancied Mark, I showed him my secrets, like the things I'd stole from Mrs Ivanovich. The poison first, cause I knew he'd like that. Dug up from where I'd hid it at the bottom of my garden and covered in sandy mud, the skull and crossbones moulded into the glass and the other warnings. Flammable. Toxic. Volatile. Fucking exciting words when you're ten and fourteen.

'Put it back down there Kez and sit on it. Better keep that hid,' he said. I shoved it back and covered it with soil, put the plant pot back on top. He smiled at me. 'Good gell,' he said. After that I was brave enough to show him Morph, even though I thought he might laugh. He didn't though. He touched the glass case and stared at the butterfly.

'This neighbour-a yourn sure had some treasure,' he said.

Our job was also better than a paper round cause we got paid a lot better. The packets we delivered looked like 10p mixes or lucky bags, but inside they were full of stuff what looked like sherbet kayli. It wasn't sweet though, I once put some on my finger and licked it. The stuff tingled in my mouth but didn't taste very nice at all, and I felt dizzy after. I asked Mam what was in the packages and she laughed and said it were happiness. She said Uncle Frank's business was selling happiness and I'd understand when I was bigger. The happiness was sometimes brown and sometimes white and the people we delivered it to certainly looked happy to see us, and sometimes gave us a couple a quid for our trouble. We thought that was dead good. Mam was happy too. We'd done about words for happiness at school, types of happy. Joyful, elated, ecstatic, thrilled, blissful. All slightly different, like felt tip pens in a fifty pack. It were good we'd learned them words, cause I needed them to describe all the different types of happy what came over my mam from time to time.

It were Mark started using the stuff his-sen first. He opened up one of the packets of white powder and dipped in his finger, rubbed it in his gum. He held it out for me and Jason to do the same and he called us babies when we said no. He said he'd seen his dad do this at a party a couple of weeks before and'd tried his-sen after. Then he was talking loads all of a sudden, but not normal at all, dead fast, and it were hard to get a word in. He was talking so fast he kept tripping over his words and stuttering, then laughing like there was some secret joke only he knew about. His eyes looked frightening.

My first pay packet was twenty quid for a week's fetching and carrying – more money than a ten-year-old can cope with. Enough to buy a whole load of fresh cream cakes and as many bars of Galaxy as I wanted, which I did. I also bought a big shiny book about the rainforest. It had bright glossy photos of insects and snakes, orchids you could almost smell. Lianas, them things what Tarzan swings on. I didn't read it much cause it were too full of long words and stuff I'd never heard of. It were good enough to look at the pictures and imagine me-sen in them. Touching the waxy leaves, swinging on the vines. Canoeing down the Rio Negro. The name meant black river but the water wasn't really black, the book said. It looked like tea.

I bought a Barbie doll too, I don't know why, it just caught my fancy. It meant Uncle Frank got this idea I specially liked the things and he bought them for me all the time. After five or six of these presents I hated Barbie, her nylon hair and plastic tits. I remember one day I was sat on the landing pulling off dolls' heads and bouncing them like balls, throwing them down the stairs. I heard Jon whinge one'd hit him on the head. I stopped, not cause of his moaning, but cause all the dolls were headless. I was bored, and crawled across the floor, pressing my ear to Mam's bedroom door. Her and Uncle Frank had been in there ages and I'd had a little listen before, and heard frightening noises, like Mam was in pain or summat. I knew better than to interfere though. I'd had a clip round the ear-ole for that before and one time Frank'd made me stay in the room and watch what they were doing. Education, he'd said it were. I'd rather of had the belting and that's for sure. I had to look at Morph for a long time after that, to rub out all the pictures from my head.

This time though, I heard them talking.

'I'm not sure, Frank,' my mam said. 'What if she got caught?'

'They won't catch her,' he said. 'And even if they did, she's too young for them to do her for it. It's perfect like that or's I wun't be suggesting it. I need Jason or Kez cause they could get Mark if he's carrying the stuff.'

'But she's me baby.'

'She's hardly a baby, love. She's a little sod most-a the time. Bout time she brought some decent money in, earned her keep.'

My mam didn't say owt for a bit, then she said, 'And yer sure they cun't do her if they catch her?'

'Too young,' he said. 'Not hat the hage of criminal responsibility.' He added h's all over, dropped from other places, and put on that voice like him and my mam did when they were trying to sound posh. He called it their 'telephone manner' but I'm not sure why cause we never had a phone back then.

'We just have to mek sure she knows not to land us in it,' he said. 'I'll talk to her, mek certain-a-it.'

I heard my mam breathing. Then Uncle Frank said, 'Come here duck, this'll help yer think about it.'

I heard him clattering about with stuff, then the click

of a Zippo lighter. My mam sighed really hard. Then silence.

I went downstairs for a bit. Then Uncle Frank came out of my mam's room to find me. I heard him trip over one of the decapitated dolls I'd left on the landing and swear. He bounced down the stairs, making each one beat like a bass drum under his heavy flat feet.

'Kerrie, duck, there's summat I want yer to do fer me,' he said. I stared straight at the telly, wouldn't look him in the eye. He said, 'It'll pay even better than your paper round.' He always used that name for our deliveries, even though we all knew it were nowt to do with paper.

'We're stepping up the operation,' he said, like he was a real businessman or summat. 'I want yer outside Player and Crane every night a-the week flogging ter the kids as they come out,' he said. 'All right?'

I nodded. He meant John Player and William Crane, the two local comps down the road. I'd be going to Player me-sen from the next September. I stared at the TV as if Uncle Frank wasn't there. It sang to me, stretching the syllables to fit the rhythm. Paint. The. Whole. World. With. A. Rainbow. That was what Uncle Frank wanted me to do, selling his happiness outside school. The kind of happiness what makes people talk too fast and their eyes look scary.

'Is this an okay thing to do?' I asked him.

He gave me his standard answer. 'Owt's an okay thing to do, Kez me duck. So long as yer know what yer on wi'. So long as yer don't tell nobody owt to get other people in trouble.'

'Will I get in trouble?'

'No. Like I say, yer just have ter be careful and mek sure we don't neither. You wun't get me in trouble, would yer Kez?'

I shook my head, but didn't move my eyes from the TV, from the man dressed as a bear explaining to the pink hippo and the big orange grin how to share a cake.

I did what Uncle Frank'd said. It were the middle of winter, so he bought me a huge Parka coat with loads of pockets for me to put the packets in. Jason's mam'd said he couldn't come, so it ended up being just me and Mark. We stood outside school and some of the kids just walked by. You could tell what ones'd do this. They had straight, thick ties done up in huge knots over clean, tucked in shirts. Shiny black shoes. The kids what stopped looked more like Mark. Trainers, and ties knotted at the wrong end so's they were dead thin. They whispered with Mark and gave him money, then I handed over the packets. It were always the same, Mark did the money. I was the only one allowed to touch the stuff cause if Mark got caught for possession he'd end up in Glen Parva.

We'd been doing the job about nine weeks when I found out how things really worked. We were standing on Beechdale Road and it were well cold, it'd chucked it down with snow the night before. I dug my hands in my pockets and stamped my feet so much Mark was laughing at me and called me nesh. We were all early developers in my family and, underneath my Parka coat, I'd been growing up some. I'd seen Mark noticing that, and I was sussed enough, even then, to realise this was why he was teasing me. A tall lad with glasses walked over, and the two of them went off down the road, deep in negotiation. I tried to collapse into my coat. I saw another tall boy, clocked him as a fourth year who'd bought from us before. I looked into the road, assuming he'd go and talk to Mark an-all. The houses were glowing like coals and I wished I was inside one of them, sitting behind drawn curtains drinking hot chocolate or eating soup, giving me-sen chilblains hogging the fan heater. I turned back towards the school and it were like hitting concrete. Like when you're not looking where you're going and slam into a lamppost.

I woke up on the floor, my teeth feeling loose inside my mouth. My face was pleasantly warm, but wet. I lifted my head a bit and saw my own blood, vivid and red and gorgeous as it soaked into the snow, spreading out further, pink, like when you put down salt on red wine. Red was my favourite colour, specially bright red. The same colour as blood from an artery. I pulled me-sen up onto my hands and knees, then fell back into a sitting position. As I landed, pain shot through my bones and joints. My neck was killing me, and the side of my face stung like wanno. The glowing houses didn't look so welcoming now. I knew it were going to hurt worse when I walked into the warm again. I saw Mark laying into the four-eyed lad halfway down towards the shops at Strelley. He was really going for it, arms and legs spinning round like that devil thing they have in the cartoons. He wasn't big, but he was doing the other kid a load of damage cause he didn't let up. I sat on the pavement feeling sore. My face felt like I'd been to the dentist, swollen up and numb. The blood worked like sticky red sweat, evaporating and making me colder. I could hear my breathing was funny, all rasping and nasty.

The big lad with the glasses ran off towards Aspley. Mark pulled his shirt sleeves down and walked back to me, taking big strides what reminded me of his dad. He didn't stop and pick up his coat. He wiped my face with a mucky tissue he found in one of my pockets.

'You all right?' he said.

I opened my mouth to tell him yes but more blood seeped out, muffling my voice. I nodded but it hurt my neck.

'They tek the lot?' he asked.

I'd forgot about my packages. I pulled at my pockets and tried to find them but there was only a couple left. I tried to tell him Uncle Frank'd kill me but all what came out was a gargled mess. And more blood.

Mark tucked some of my hair behind my left ear. He wiped the blood from round my mouth. He looked into my eyes and I tried to focus on his.

'I like you, Kerrie,' he said. Then everything went black.

When I woke up I was in bed at home. Uncle Frank hadn't killed me, and him and my mam were sitting there smoking. Mam stubbed out a fag and lit another.

'It in't your fault,' Frank told me. He had another Barbie doll for me, still in its packet. Horse-riding Barbie. I hated horses worse than Barbie dolls but I smiled as he handed it to me.

'How bad's the pain, duck?' he asked me.

I couldn't speak so I didn't answer. My tongue felt like a huge sponge full of water, swelling and filling up my mouth. I wanted to go and find Morph, stare at him hard till it stopped hurting. But I couldn't move, and Morph was my secret what I wasn't letting Mam or Frank ruin for owt.

'We can't tek yer to hospital,' my mam said. 'They'd tek yer off me.'

I managed to speak then. 'It hurts,' I said. I closed my eyes.

'We'll get yer summat to help wi-that,' Uncle Frank told

me. But I didn't see how he could cause I couldn't hardly swallow my own saliva, never mind water and a tablet. My tonsils were swollen and I wondered how that'd happened, like the lad'd stuck his hand down my throat and squeezed.

I slept for a bit, but kept waking up with pain in different bits of me. I only remembered being hit in the face, but the kid'd done a right job on me once I was down on the ground. My left leg was killing me and it felt like there was an iron bar sticking right through my chest every time I breathed out. I kept dropping off, but my breathing was so bad I snored like someone was trying to throttle me, and this woke me up. When I tried to turn onto my front it felt like I was being stabbed in the bottom of my back.

Uncle Frank came back in a bit. My mam came in with him. I tried to wake up proper, forcing my eyes open as wide as I could before they slipped closed again, no matter what I did. I heard Frank's Zippo lighter, then a sound like a very quiet sigh.

'This might tickle a bit,' Frank told me, running his fingers up and down the bottom of my arm. I felt him stab me with summat small and very sharp. Then a tiny thread of ice snaked up the inside of my arm. I felt like I'd been hit again, punched in the face. No, it were the opposite of that, like someone'd took the punch right back, and all the other hits and scratches ever, and gave me back the wellness I'd had before but times three hundred and twenty-four. My leg and chest stopped hurting. I didn't care about getting hit, or about losing the packets and what Frank might think about it. I opened my eyes and my mam and Frank were there, lovely smiley angels. I didn't need Morph now. I was Morph. Had wings. Could fly.

'Feel better, duck?' my mam asked me.

I smiled and nodded and it didn't hurt no more. Uncle Frank threw his head back and laughed. He was holding a needle in his hand, like the ones they use to take blood at the doctor's. He jabbed it into his-sen. Then my mam took it off him and did the same.

FIVE

One night Uncle Frank didn't come home. He wasn't back by three the next afternoon and Jon and me'd wrote him off as being like the other uncles we'd had. Mam paced up and down the kitchen like she was trying to get the lino to settle. I thought the poor cow must really love him. I was so thick when it came to my mam back then.

This loud banging came on the door and I was expecting someone to shout 'police', the way they do in films. But they didn't. Mam ignored the noise, even when I shouted that there was someone at the door. She kept pacing up and down and smoking so I went and answered it. It were Mark Scotland.

'Pigs got me dad-n-Frank holed up at our house,' he told me. I opened the door and made him come in and tell Mam. She stopped pacing, stubbing out her fag and lighting a next one, then she was off again.

'Mam,' I said. 'D'yer not hear what Mark's saying?'

She turned, looked at Mark dead on and said, 'I need me skag, Mark. Can yer gerrit fer me?'

'I'll try,' he said.

It were the first time I'd heard anyone admit what we'd been handling was drugs. Course I knew, but hearing it out loud made my hands shake as I held onto the door.

'Don't look at me all gormless, Kez,' Mam said. 'Yer not that stupid.'

'Can you help me Sue?' Mark said to my mam.

She shook her head. 'Can't even see straight wi-out me skag,' she said.

'Kez?' Mark turned to me. I was scared, I don't mind admitting it. And I wasn't sure about Uncle Frank. Part of me would of liked to see him in prison. But I liked Mark. His big grey eyes were wide open, his mouth held in a tight little ball like he was trying to stop from crying.

'Dad's not bin out of prison five minutes. Mam sez they'll throw the book at him,' he said.

'Mek-aste,' Mam said, hurrying us both out the door.

Mark and me walked through the slush down Lindfield Road where Mark's dad lived. His mam lived the other side of the estate, on Bradfield. The melting snow under our feet was rank, full of dog's piss and crap from people's exhaust pipes. It were trendy them days to break the exhaust on your car so's it sounded sporty.

'Must be nice to have a dad round,' I said. Mark's parents'd never lived together, but they'd been friends since school. He was way better off than a lot of the kids I knew, whose parents lived together but argued all the time. Or like me, with uncles what came in and out of their lives. He shrugged at me.

'He belts me when I deserve it. Gets me stuff though. Videos and shit, before they come out,' Mark said.

I took all this in and walked quiet for a minute. Mark looked at me and smiled, grabbed my hand.

'I've never met my dad, or my brother's,' I said.

'Your mam's fucked up, Kez,' he told me. He'd said this before, a load of times, and I used to argue. I didn't this time.

'I'll never do brown, will you?' I said. But Mark just shrugged.

Lindfield was crawling with police. Outside Mark's house, specially, and his back garden, but also prowling round the whole terraced row, watching people come and go. In case they go through the attic, I thought, try and escape through one of the other houses. It only came into my head cause of this book I'd read, one of them Narnia ones. The story I remembered got my brain ticking. I waited to tell Mark till we'd walked some way off. My old mate Jaqui from school lived next door but one to Mark's dad. I knew she'd let us in without no fuss, and then we could try getting into Mark's place through the attics. We wouldn't be able to get the blokes out that way, cause there was police outside Jaqui's too, but we could take stuff in. More important, take stuff out. Mark stared at me as I told him all this. When I'd finished he looked different from before. Summat raw set in on his face, animal. It were a look I'd get used to. He told me to take him to Jaqui's.

When we walked back, this policeman asked where we were going. Inside I was shitting it, but I held it together and looked the man in the gun, then in his face.

'Me mate's house,' I said.

'Oh yeah? Who's that then?' he said.

I told him Jaqui's name, and how old she was, and that she was in my class at school. He radioed someone, sierra oscar from this and that and all the rest of that shit the police say. He eyed Mark as he did all this. Mark looked like trouble, even back then with his flicked blond hair. It were summat about the angle of his cheekbones. If he hadn't of been a villain, people would of assumed it about him anyway. I took hold of his hand again, and this seemed to reassure the policeman a bit. When he came off the radio, he let us past.

Jaqui poked her head round the door. She hadn't brushed her hair, and I could see a nit crawling through the lugs while we stood there, but I didn't say. Her brown mouse eyes twitched as I asked to come in. She paused, but Mark pushed past her and I followed.

'We can't have no messing,' he said. He looked at Jaqui. 'You can't be the same year as Kerrie,' he said.

She told him she was. Her voice was as little as her nutty brown eyes. She looked different here, with Mark standing next to her, and it made me wonder why I'd ever had owt to do with her.

'You look like a baby,' Mark said.

Jaqui didn't speak back. She looked like she'd cry if she had to open her mouth. I spose you could see why. There were police with guns all over outside her house and then I turned up with Mark Scotland.

'It's just me and Mark,' I told her.

'We need your help,' Mark said. He took hold of a strand of her dirty hair and wound it round his finger. She pulled away from him. 'You know where the attic hatch is?' he said.

Jaqui shook her head. She let out a sob.

'Your mam in?' I asked her. She shook her head. 'When's she back?' I said.

'Tomorra,' Jaqui said. I could see the tiny muscles round her mouth squeeze hard to stop any more sobs coming out.

'Good,' I said.

We found the attic hatch easy, on the landing where ourn was too. Mark gave me a leg up and I pushed it open. I crawled in through the hatch onto the rafters. Mark vaulted up, one long movement, strong as a gymnast with his arms as he pushed up his body. I have to admit this did impress me.

Mark crawled along the attic floor on his hands and knees. I was taking the piss though, balancing and leaping round like a frigging ballet dancer.

'You'll be through some bogger's ceiling if yer keep that up,' Mark said. I realised he had a point and stopped messing, clambering catlike across the dark space with him.

The attics were all connected, just the same as in the book I'd read. There was a low wall dividing each one from the next. This was the hardest bit to get over without falling onto ceiling plaster. It were hard to tell which house you'd got to cause the dark and the endless rafters sent your head funny.

'How'll we know we're in your attic?' I said.

'We'll know,' Mark told me.

A short while after, I felt a wooden crate in front of me. I pushed it, but it were so heavy it didn't even budge a little bit. I delved into the top and could feel summat cold. Metal. I pulled the thing out and felt its shape.

'Are these toys?' I asked Mark and he told me no. I dropped it back in the crate then jumped back, scared it might be loaded and go off or summat. It didn't. There were two crates of the boggers.

'We got a load ter move,' Mark said.

'Yer not kidding,' I said.

We climbed over the crates and found the attic hatch.

Mark stopped by the edge. I felt his body close and still, began to see his outline as my night vision kicked in. I could hear his breathing.

'What if they think it's the police or summat and shoot us?' he said. I shrugged. I felt for the small square of wood what was our way into the house. I thought of Uncle Frank the other side. I imagined pushing the wood aside and seeing him, but I also thought of sliding one of the crates across the top so's no one could move it ever again.

'We could move the hatch and shout before we jump down there,' I said. But Mark didn't shift at all. I opened the hatch. Light flooded in, making Mark and me look like ghosts and the crates glint like treasure. I shouted Uncle Frank. He came onto the landing, holding a sawn-off the way Mark'd predicted.

'Don't shoot, Uncle Frank. It's me, Kez,' I said.

'There in't none-a-them pigs up there, is they Kez?' he said.

'Just me-n-Mark,' I said, jumping down. Mark followed, and by the time he hit the floor Uncle Frank had me held tight against his big fat belly with the gun against my head.

'It is just us, Frank,' Mark told him. Frank believed him and let me go.

'I'm sure glad to see you boggers,' he said.

'Funny way-a-showing it,' I told him. And we all laughed. It wasn't right, though, our laughing. We looked like a group of evil terrorists from a badly shot old spy film.

Mark and me walked out the back with our arms full of guns. We were shitting it. We didn't have any clue whether the police would be in Jaqui's back garden, lurking in the shadows. We crawled near the ground all the way to the back hedge so's we wouldn't be seen. When we got there,

Mark looked for a hole in the privet. There wasn't one. He dropped his guns, making more racket than he should of, and charged at the hedge like a frigging bull. He bounced back off it and yelped. He'd hit a load of nettles. I rolled my hands along the grass after dock leaves but could only find a couple, and some of the rash was near his eyes, which must of stung like I don't want to know about. I grabbed one of the bigger weapons, a shotgun thing. I rammed it in the hedge and gored out a hole big enough for me to squeeze through. Mark made it bigger by following me through it, making the privet yield a bit more. Jaqui's place backed on to Cinderhill tip. There was no proper lighting, just fallout from streetlights round about. For all the world it looked like the surface of the moon. I stepped out with my guns, expecting to float. I could smell the gone off version of whatever chemical makes your fridge cool down.

We walked to the middle of the tip and used two of the shotguns to dig a big hole. We shoved the guns all down the bottom and left them without filling the hole back in. We headed to the house to get more. As we walked towards the hedge we heard voices. Police. We threw our-sen on the ground right next to Jaqui's garden.

'I'm sure I heard summat,' the first voice said. Torchlight shot across the moonscape, slashing the night wide open. It probed the wasteground, but flicked past the hole without hardly lighting it up. I had a tickle in my throat and had to work well hard not to cough.

'Nah, mate, nowt there. Must-a-bin cats or summat,' someone said. We heard steps getting quieter.

'Think it's a trick?' Mark asked me.

'Don't know,' I said. We lay still for a couple of minutes, listening hard for more voices or steps. I couldn't hear owt cept our own breathing, which sounded too loud. I pushed my head through the hedge. There was no one in the garden and I told Mark so. We shot across to Jaqui's back door, hoping she'd not panicked and shut us out. It were open.

We made our way along the attics again and found Uncle Frank and Big Mark. They were laughing and playing cards as we climbed through.

'What shall we do next? Rest-a-the guns or summat else?' Mark asked them.

'Tell yer what,' Frank said. 'Tek this and go get us all some chips or summat.'

He gave Mark a crisp clean tenner.

'Wun't it be better to get all that shit out first?' Mark's dad said.

'Chippy'll be closed soon,' Frank said. 'I'm starved.'

I thought Mark's dad was right, but I didn't say owt. I didn't mind so much losing my sleep and crapping mesen to help out when it were desperate. But just to get chips was a bit much. I wouldn't of dared argue about it though. Mark and me climbed back up to the attic and made the slow journey back to Jaqui's, where we left by the front door.

We went up Broxtowe Lane and bought chips and pie for four. We went to the offie too, who never would of served me, but didn't hesitate with Mark cause they knew his dad. He bought two six-packs of Tennants and we carried them back. We took one each across the attics with the food balanced on top and it wasn't easy. I let mine drop over the house between, just managing to grab it up before it crashed through the neighbour's ceiling. We got back and shared the chip supper, and had some beer. It made me burp really loud, and the blokes all laughed.

Mouths shining with chip fat and high from beer we weren't used to, Mark and me got back to work. It were quicker then, cause we were a bit hyper and warm from the beer. We finished the guns in two more trips and covered the hole we'd made, stamping on top of it to make it flat as we could. Then we went back to get the most important stuff. Valuable stashes of whizz and coke and brown. We took loads in our special coats and hid it under fridges and cookers what'd been dumped on the tip. It were five in the morning before we'd cleared the lot. I wasn't even tired, just wired by how clever and quick we'd been.

'Get out-a here now, Mark duck,' his dad told him. 'Home ter yer mam's or summat.'

Neither 'Big' Mark nor 'Uncle' Frank told me I could go home.

The three on us left a half-hour later. Frank and me went first, him with one of his thick arms wrapped round my neck, the other held up in a gesture of surrender. He was worried they'd just gun him down, and that was where I came in, he said. 'They wun't shoot at a lickle gell, would they now?' he'd said. He held me tight and 'Big' Mark followed the pair on us. We got handcuffed and bundled into cars. It didn't feel real. A massive policeman with hands on my shoulders and my head, pushing me into a car while I kicked and bucked against him. The cold of metal against my wrists. The warm feeling of blood in my mouth as I bit the tosser.

SIX

They didn't know what to do with me, the police. Them days it wasn't so common for young-uns to be involved in this kind of shit. They even kept me in a cell at the station overnight, though I'm sure that wasn't no way legal. This nicey-nicey policewoman cow kept coming to talk to me. She asked me how I felt about everything, and who'd got me involved in all this. She didn't have a clue. The more she stroked my hair and said 'ah' the firmer my mouth jammed shut. I wouldn't of told the silly cow a bloody thing much as I couldn't stand Uncle Frank after what he'd done. Then this good-looking police bloke came and told me to pack up my stuff and I said ha ha cause I had nowt with me. Mam'd not come to find me or owt, and she admitted later that she'd hid behind the sofa when they'd come knocking to find her. Said after she couldn't stand being inside a police station or nowhere near any police. Selfish bitch. And she would of come running to find me anywhere I'd gone if I'd of had some drugs or money or owt else she needed.

It were a shock after all Frank'd said that they could do owt to me at all. Besides, they never found the stuff Mark and me'd hid, never realised he'd been there. This kid copper told me it were mostly about my own safety they wouldn't let me go home, cause they couldn't contact my mam and she hadn't come looking for me. They were sending me to this place in Loughborough.

The East Midlands Home for Girls it were called. I was scared cause I thought it'd be like prison, though I couldn't of known how wrong I was. They took me there in this van with blacked-out windows. It went dead fast all the way down the A60 and I enjoyed the ride. It made me feel important, like a great train robber or someone famous. Over the top for taking a ten-year-old to borstal. I arrived on the back of sirens without a change of clothes or a toothbrush ner nowt.

They made me have a shower and put this dressing gown thing on when I got there. Then this woman looked at my skin and checked my head for nits.

'I an't got none. I wash it,' I told her, pulling away as she tried to run her fingers through my hair. She held me firm with both hands.

'They like clean hair,' she said. But I knew adults only said this to make you feel better about having nits. She didn't find none anyhow. She took me to what they called a 'cell' but it wasn't at all. It were just a plain room with two beds in it, a wardrobe and an old-fashioned dressing table with a big mirror. It wasn't a bad place at all and bigger than my bedroom at home. Sitting on one of the beds was this gell a few years older than me. Her name was Bek.

'Haven't you brought anything with you?' she asked me.

I shrugged. She walked over to the wardrobe and went

inside. She took out this dress, a denim thing. It wasn't all that but it were much better than owt I had at home.

'This doesn't fit me anymore,' she said, holding it out to me, 'if you want it.'

I took it off her and measured it up against me. It were at least two sizes too big. I was well developed for my age but Bek was a woman compared to me. It were a nice dress, though, one of them what were well trendy at the time with buttons down the front.

'What have you done then?' she said.

'Bit a policeman. And some other stuff what I'm not telling you case you grass it,' I said.

Bek laughed. 'You really bit a pig?' she said and I nodded. 'Did you draw blood?' And I said yes and she shook my hand. 'Want some whizz?' she said. I hesitated then thought, well, it's just whizz.

'Okay,' I said.

She went under her mattress and took a wrap out. 'If I give you this then you can tell me what you did. If I sell you out you've got just as much on me,' she said. I noticed then she had a really posh accent.

I took some of the speed and rubbed it in my gum.

'Bit more than that,' she said, smiling. I took some more. I didn't feel owt at first and wondered what all the fuss was about.

'Don't they look under yer mattress?' I said.

'Nah. They're thick as shit,' she said.

I was laughing and didn't know why. There was nowt funny to laugh at. I was choking on saliva over what Bek'd said. She was killing her-sen about it too. That's when I realised the whizz was working. She'd took some too, and was bouncing on her bed with a huge white grin. Her teeth were well shiny, like summat out of an advert. She was about four years older than me and dead pretty. She told me her mam and dad were rich as fuck and didn't take much notice of her. Let her do what she liked and gave her money to do it. They still gave her money while she was in here, with the nod of the carers, who even took her out to spend it from time to time. That's what they called them: carers, like we were old people or summat. Mostly the time there was the best I'd had but it were shit like that what did my head in.

Bek's mam and dad reckoned the police'd got it well wrong about what their daughter was supposed to of done. This was beat up this gell really bad then take the poor cow's white stiletto off and shove it in her eye. She'd lost her eye, the gell. Bek told me her parents were wrong. She'd done it all right. The bitch had stole her feller and her stash of coke and it were fair enough. An eye for an eye, she joked, and I laughed even though I didn't understand what she was on about. I told her about me and Mark and the rubbish tip. Don't know if it were the whizz, or summat else she'd took, but she thought this was the funniest thing she'd ever heard.

The EMHG was all right. There was a telly and a pool table, and they weren't strict on making us do schoolwork. And Bek always had drugs. Got them in parcels marked as being from her mam what the carers never opened to 'protect her privacy'. What a laugh. I was the lucky one sharing a room with Bek and she was a social whizz head and always shared what stuff she got. I missed Morph, and Mark a bit too and Jon loads, but I didn't miss Mam one little bit. Or Uncle Frank. I wasn't ever going to forgive him for what he'd done to me.

Being in the EMHG was like this. We got up about nine and had tea and toast in the big drafty refectory. Then we officially had lessons but we were all so mad in the classroom the teachers soon cottoned it were easier to sit and have a chat with us rather than try and make us work. Then it were dinner and the food was okay. Better than school muck. Afternoons we pretty much could do what we liked. And what me and Bek liked was taking drugs.

Bek introduced me to all the other gells. There wasn't one as pretty as she was, or what I liked as much. There was Ginny, this skinny thing with a piggy little face, all pink and shiny. I kept expecting her to snort loud in the middle of dinner and it put me off my food. Then there was this psycho bitch called Caroline. She wanted everyone to call her Callie like the pretty gell off Grange Hill. But her name wasn't Callie and she wasn't pretty neither. If you called her owt else she lost it. I saw her smash Ginny in the face till her piggy nose was red as a berry. Then there was Paula. She was different from the rest of us. She'd bumped off her little brother and this made us all mad at her. We'd all done wrong things, but you don't no way hurt your little brother. I loved Jon, and the worst thing about being in the EMHG was not seeing him, so Paula made me sick. She'd put the poor sod in the freezer. The carers reckoned she was a bit slow, didn't realise what she was doing. But I didn't care. There wasn't no excuse for doing that to your brother far as I was concerned.

One time I got Paula on her own. It were in one of the shower rooms. She'd forgot to lock the door, and I was walking in to use the shower, not knowing she was in there. She turned, dog-eyed, her long black hair dripping down her back like oil. I grabbed that hair, took hold of it and slammed her face against the tiles. I saw blood drip down. I loved the colour of the red next to her black hair and the white tiles. She let out a whimper like a dog, to match her big sad eyes.

'You're a fucking bitch, what you done to that lickle boy,' I told her. I don't know to this day what brought out this nastiness. It wasn't like me. I wasn't no psycho like Bek or Mark. Maybes it was being left to fend for me-sen like that, without no one I knew.

She didn't answer, just howled. I smashed her face into the tiles another couple of times. Then the thought of the carers patrolling the corridor made me step out, wrapping my towel round me. I stood outside the shower room like I was waiting. One of the carers ran up.

'What happened?' she said.

'Don't know,' I said. 'I just got here and heard her wailing like some fucking banshee.'

'Watch your language Kerrie-Ann,' the carer said. 'Are you sure you didn't see anything?'

I nodded and she looked in my eyes.

'You're not going to tell me who it was, are you?' she said.

I stared back at her with this look I'd been practising. It were what Bek'd showed me. She'd taught me three different dirty looks.

Bek kissed me on the lips when she heard what I'd done. We all hated that Paula bitch.

The week after I made Paula's blood run down the shower wall, the police came to talk to me. Not about her – they didn't care about that silly cow. They wanted to talk to me about what went off in the house with Frank. He sent his solicitor Tim Hesketh to sort it. I'd met Tim before but didn't know he was a lawyer. He was as dodgy as Frank, into just as much stuff and that was why I knew him. I found out after he represented all the dealers and well dodgy types. That he turned up told the police loads about what I was on with. But they couldn't prove owt. Tim was a tall man with the kind of chest what made you wonder if he had a heart problem. He did and it killed him not long after. They took me into this room to meet with him and the police idiots. He made them go out so's we could have a minute alone. Said I was entitled to that.

Tim had black hair plastered in Brylcreem or summat like it. He sat opposite me and touched my hand, a gesture what made me draw back and shiver.

'Sweetheart,' he said, grinning. His teeth were dandelion yellow and I could smell his breath from where I was sat. 'You mustn't tell them what you was up to with Mark,' he said.

I just looked at him. 'As if I was going to,' I said. I'd started to talk a bit posher, like Bek, and read her books too.

'Oh, you're not going to, are you not, Princess Broxtowe?' he said, pronouncing the o-w-e like no one does and taking the piss. I gave him one of the dirty looks Bek'd been teaching me. 'Aren't you scary?' he said. He grinned yellow teeth at me. 'See yer getting an education in here. Of sorts,' he said. 'No bad thing.'

I didn't answer and he let the other people back in. He put on this professional front then. That made me laugh inside but I was careful to stay looking all stroppy.

The police boss said he was Detective Inspector summat or other. He said all this into a tape, and when I asked why they were recording he said it were for my own protection. Everyone seemed dead bothered about 'protecting' and 'caring' for me all of a sudden. The detective had huge eyebrows what sat on his forehead like two hairy caterpillars.

'On what basis are you planning to hold my client, then?' Tim said to him.

'She bit the arresting officer,' he said. I could see then Tim was struggling not to laugh and I liked him better for that. The detective frowned, and his brows covered up his eyes so's he looked like some freaky animal what'd been born blind.

'And under what circumstances did she bite the officer?' Tim asked him.

'She was being put into the car.'

'Don't you think she was probably scared? You stood outside a house where she was staying with her stepdad and his friend. You were armed with guns, and when they came out you arrested and handcuffed this little girl. And found no basis in the house for your actions,' Tim said.

'You know as well as I do what that pair were up to, Hesketh. And we didn't know the girl was in the house.'

Tim Hesketh leaned over the table. He snarled across at the policeman, showing all his yellow teeth and a pink tongue. 'We could sue,' he said. 'You've put this young lady through all sorts.'

Tim went on for ages, talking all that legal shit and this and that and release dates. Truth was, I didn't care for going home. I was enjoying me-sen where I was. I didn't want to go back to Mam's house on the close and put up with the noises she made with the men she brought back. I didn't want to stand in the cold in front of Player and Crane with stuff in my pockets what made tall lads want to smash my face in. I wanted to see Jon, and look at Morph again, and that were about it.

I went back to my room and found Bek waiting there. She smelled lovely. She'd had a visit too, from her mam, who'd brought her new perfume and some make-up. She was putting it on in front of the mirror. She was beautiful. I stood and stared at her.

'What are you looking at?' she said, catching my eye through the mirror. Then she laughed. 'I've got a special treat for us,' she said. She went into the top drawer of her dressing table and pulled out a wrap. She opened it and I saw white powder.

'I'm bored-a speed,' I said, throwing me-sen on the bed.

'It's not whizz,' she told me. And her grin grew so broad I thought her lips might rip at the edges. She had a ruler on her dressing table and organised the powder into lines. She took the straw out of her glass of water, and shook it dry. Then I knew what the powder was.

'I'm not sure,' I said.

'But you should be,' she said. She snorted two lines and held her hand out to me, pulled me over. She sat me on her knee and helped me take the rest. 'You won't regret it,' she whispered in my ear.

She was right.

I don't remember much about that night cept this. Bek turned her music up dead loud, and no one bothered us – she'd probably paid them off. It were Tears for Fears. We danced to 'Shout', jumping up and down so's we made the record jump too. The vinyl crackled between tracks. Then 'Mad World' came on. 'This is my favourite,' Bek told me. She grabbed me and we danced, slow and close like men and women dance at the end of a disco. I'm not a lesbian or owt, but it felt nice. Then she kissed me, a proper kiss on the lips. She drew back and looked at me. Her face was all smiley and her eyes shone with water. 'You're way too young,' she told me. Then she hugged me tight. There are only a few people in my life I'd count as real mates. People you know'd never let you down. Not like them silly bitches Jaqui and Trace who'd leave you on the park with a psycho glue head, or my mommar, who'd run off and left us when we were just babies. And Mark wasn't much better neither, took me ages to realise it but he wasn't. But Bek was. And Mrs Ivanovich and Jon and that were about it, and Jon doesn't totally count cause he's family and that's the way it should be. I didn't know if Bek was gay, or if it were just the drugs. It didn't matter cause she didn't take advantage.

The next day they came and said I could go.

SEVEN

I'd only been in the EMHG about three months but everything felt totally different as the social worker drove me down the road what led up to our close. As we came near, I saw the houses standing in a circle holding hands, like a ring a fucking roses. I noticed like I'd never before what a shitty brown the bricks were. The council were cutting the grass on the park and the smell got up my nose and down my throat. The social worker cow was going on and on, saying how she was glad I was coming out, how all places like EMHG did for kids as young as me was teach them new tricks. She didn't have a clue what she was taking me back to. I looked out the window and let her drone on to her-sen. We drove round the close and curtains moved one after another, as if a breeze from the car'd made them.

My mam answered the door still wearing her dressing gown. Her hair looked like it hadn't been washed for days and she had blonde stubble above her lip. I saw her the way the social worker must of, and it were a right shock to me. It hadn't took long for me to get used to Bek's standards about things. Mam nodded her head backwards, which meant come in. She walked through to the kitchen and me and this woman both followed. Mam was sat at the table when we got in the room, sucking on a cigarette.

'Fag?' she asked the social worker, who shook her head.

'Wouldn't mind a cuppa though,' she said. She made an effort to talk more like my mam did, and it sounded fake. I sat down at the table and lay my head on it. Mam got up like her whole life was a job she didn't want to do, and pressed down the button on the kettle. The room went quiet then. The kettle shivered into action and Mam banged cups round, threw a teabag in one of them.

'It must be good to be home, Kerrie-Ann. Bet you've missed your mum, haven't you?' the social worker said. My mam sucked her teeth and I didn't say owt.

I walked out and left them to it. Couldn't be arsed with it. This silly cow asking my mam questions and getting one-word answers and a waft of fag smoke for her trouble. I wanted to find Morph. I went up to where I'd hid him, underneath one of the loose floorboards at the back of my room, behind the bed where the carpet didn't quite reach. I breathed fast, crossing everything I had that she hadn't found him. She'd of either smashed him up or pawned him for skag money. She'd not though. He was safe and well, a bit dusted up from not being touched in a while was all.

I pushed Morph back into his hidey-hole and covered him up. I stood up and had a look round. The stupid Barbie dolls were still piled in pieces in the corner. Heads, legs, plastic tits, like a sick open grave from some porno movie culling. Mam'd not become housewife of the year while I'd been gone. My bedsheets hadn't been changed at all and nowt'd been hoovered. Everything was where I'd left it. Cept Jon. I couldn't find him nowhere. I heard the door go, Mrs Self Righteous Bitch letting her-sen out. I went down to the front room, put on the telly.

'Where's Jon?' I called to my mam.

'An't got a clue,' she said.

I stood up sharp and walked through to the kitchen, where she was pulling washing out the machine.

'I beg your pardon?' I said.

'Get you wi-yer begging and yer pardons,' she said, looking up from the washing.

'Jon?' I said.

'Disappeared when I wa-out working late. Looked round but I cun't find-im. He'll come back before he starves,' she said, smoking her fag out the corner of her mouth as she spoke.

I could of hit her and I would of too. Cept I knew from experience about Mam's punch and knew I'd be up for miles more damage than she would. It should of struck me then, what was she doing out working late, but I was worried about Jon so's it didn't. I stormed out, slamming the door on the way. I walked without knowing where I'd go for a minute. And then I realised there was only one place I could be sure of getting some help.

I went to Mark's house, his mam's place on Bradfield Road. I knocked loud on the door. His mam answered it and looked me up and down. She turned and shouted up the stairs to Mark.

'Thank Christ you got out,' she said. 'That kid-a-yourn's driving me round the bend.'

I couldn't work out what she meant, then I saw Mark on the stairs. His hair was all shaved, but he must of done it his-sen cause there were little tufty bits left round his head. He'd gone all skinny, and his cheekbones stood out even more down to this, so's he reminded me of a pixie, a rough-looking one. I was shocked by how much he'd changed, but even more surprised as I looked over his shoulder and saw a little boy following him down the stairs. It were Jon. He'd changed even more. Kids that age grow so quick. I was worried he'd not recognise me at all but I needn't of been. He ran down the stairs towards me with his arms out. I grabbed him and pulled him close. I could feel my face all wet, and squeezed my little brother hard.

'What's these?' I said, pulling on the little dreadlocks he'd grown.

'Mark helped me do-em,' he said. 'Dan, in't they?'

'God, yeah,' I said. I hugged Jon again and leaned over his shoulder. I saw Mark standing there, smiling at me. 'Thank you.' I mouthed the words over and over. 'Thank you.'

'Couldn't hardly leave him out on the street,' he said. But he knew what it meant to me.

Mark's mam went off to make me jam sandwiches and a strong cup of tea. I sat with Mark and he caught me up with what'd gone off while I'd been away. His dad and Frank'd been let out straight away cause they'd not done owt silly like bit someone. Then they'd done a runner, worried the police'd come for them again. They'd got a big truck and took all the stuff we'd hid for them, hadn't been seen nowhere since. Rumour had it they'd gone off to Newcastle to set up there, but no one knew owt for sure cept they'd took Jason with them. Mark seemed all right about it, and I was surprised. I thought he'd of been broken up.

'I've missed yer, Kez,' he said. He put his hand across

the table towards mine, but his mam pushed it away, putting the sandwiches down in front of me.

'She's way too young fer yer,' she said.

Jon ran outside to play, and I asked about my mam, how come she'd managed to lose a little boy.

'She's out-on-it. Back on the game too,' Mark said. That shut me up. I'd never known she'd been on the game in the first place. I sucked my teeth and sat there wondering if mine and Jon's dads had paid for the privilege. And it made sense, fitted with the way I used to get shut up if I asked owt about my dad. The thought made me feel sick and I pushed the sandwiches away.

'Sorry,' Mark said. 'Thought yer knew.' And he grabbed my hand and held it dead tight. I didn't cry though.

Mark and me built up a business of our own. He knew a lot of people, through helping out his dad and Frank, and me and him were 'lickle stars' as far as they were concerned cause of how we'd sorted stuff when the police turned up. We stuck to grass and speed to start with, in the main cause it were easier to get hold of. The clients weren't such psychos neither, not like ones who were into brown. We had a slow start but the cash started flowing when I started at senior school and could work the yard at dinner. My school was called Player like the cigarettes and we all smoked them, and other specials much less legal. Not long after I left, Player was in all the papers cause it came rock bottom of some table or other, officially the country's worst school. They closed it down soon after. I didn't like doing the yard that much cause Mark didn't go to school very often. I was scared some kid'd give me another kicking. Mark said not to worry, that he had plans to deal with all that.

Mark and me kind of got it together too. We didn't go out to the pictures or owt naff like that. It were just a given after I'd got out of EMHG. Mark'd hold my hand sometimes, and kiss me when he felt like it. That suited me. But Mark wanted more than that. Course he did. He was fifteen and more would of been the only thing on his mind.

This one day we were walking through Aspley holding hands. It were a Saturday, and we walked past the church and school yard on Kingsbury. There was some kind of fête thing going off at the school, cept it were dead formal. Everyone was sitting round on chairs outside and watching some kids do a play. The kids were all dressed up in old clothes and we were interested, so we snuck round the back to have a nosey. The acting was rubbish, like people reading from a sheet, the way it is with kids on stage, and the words were all old-fashioned and hard to get a handle on. But the story was great, about two kids falling in love and their families fighting and killing each other off. It were *Romeo and Juliet*, of course, but I didn't have a clue who Shakespeare was, not then. I stood there watching Romeo hold the gell he thought was dead, rocking her, then taking the poison out his pocket. I wanted to shout out to him that she was just sleeping, even though I knew it were a play and there wasn't no point. Then he downed the liquid, and lay back dying, and Juliet woke up, stabbed her-sen.

'In't that romantic?' Mark said. 'Would yer do that fer me?'

I looked up at him to try and work out if he was taking the piss. 'Doubt it,' I said.

'Nice. And I would-a took the poison fer you,' he said. Then he kissed me full on, shoving his tongue in my mouth. He'd tried this a few times before and I wasn't sure I enjoyed it specially. I noticed his trousers swell when he did it, and his mouth fill with saliva. He took my hand and pulled on it. I giggled and followed him. We snuck behind the bushes on the side of the yard and sat down. He pulled up my skirt. He used to do this when we were younger but back then it were just a silly game. I could see from the way he looked at me now it were serious. His eyes were all bright and searching, his hands insistent. It scared me. He looked too much like this dog I once saw, ripping apart a rabbit. I backed off.

'Come on, Kez,' he said.

'It dun't feel right.'

Mark crawled towards me on his hands and knees, grabbing hold of my wrists and pushing them on the ground. I shook him off and scrambled from under him and up, running round back to where people could see me. He followed and didn't say owt. I thought how there were plenty of gells round who'd give him what he wanted, and maybes it were no bad thing if he worked that out too.

It were later that day I found out what he'd been planning to do to make sure I was left alone. Danny Morrison. He was the lad what cracked me one the winter before and Mark'd found out where he lived, up Aspley Lane, cross the road from the closed down cinema.

'We're going-ta pay him a lickle visit,' Mark said.

We walked up the lane hand in hand, like we were going on a picnic. I thought Mark was going to beat him up when we got there, and felt a thrill inside at the thought of it. We walked past these small greens, waste of space places you weren't supposed to play on. A load of kids were ignoring the 'ball games prohibited' signs. There were bushes round the edge of these lawns and I eyed them, worried Mark might try and pull me underneath the holly and privet again. He didn't though.

He took this envelope out his pocket and opened it up, showed me a small tablet. It looked like an aspirin.

'What is it?' I said.

'E,' he said.

I'd heard of ecstasy, course, but we'd never got any round our way before.

'You tried it?' I said.

He shook his head and broke the pill, kissing one of the halves before handing it to me.

'We're drug brothers,' he said. And I didn't correct him that I was a gell. He took a bottle of pop out his rucksack and we washed half each down. Powder from where the pill'd been split in two hit my tongue and it tasted rank, like summat you'd find under the sink. We were used to the quick hit of a mouthful of speed, and Mark looked disappointed when nowt happened straight off.

'Maybes it teks a while to get through yer stomach and into yer system,' I said, thinking about what Mrs Ivanovich'd said to me once when she gave me an aspirin.

'It better be that cause this cost me twenty quid,' Mark said.

We found Danny's house and watched it for a bit. No one came in or out. Mark got up, and he looked that way he did sometimes, so wild for it he scared me. His jaw set like concrete and his face wore a snarl. He walked up to Danny's door and knocked on it. I followed him down the path. Danny answered and I recognised him straight off. He didn't look so huge now me and Mark were bigger. He was smiling as he turned towards Mark, like he'd just heard a joke or been watching telly. When he saw who it were, and the knife Mark'd flicked open as he turned, his smile fell clean off.

'Afternoon,' Mark said, pointing the knife right in his face. Danny moved to slam the door but it were too late. Mark was in and had hold of him. He pulled Danny kicking and screaming into one of the bushes I'd noticed before. No one came out the house looking.

Mark opened up his rucksack and took out another pop bottle, but this one was filled with petrol. He poured it onto Danny. I held my breath. I didn't believe Mark'd do what it looked like he was going to do. He took matches out his pocket. Danny wet his-sen, and was whimpering and pleading. I think that was the worst thing, the way he shivered and stuttered and begged for mercy. Mark was having none of it. He lit a match and threw it. Flames crawled across the surface of Danny's skin. He lit up proper then, and looked like an orange angel. We turned but didn't run, just walked up the road like it had nowt to do with us. There was a smell in the air like bacon on a grill. The drugs were kicking in. My stomach'd gone a bit funny and I could feel my jaw tighten, my face tingle. Mark held my hand, rubbing his fingers all gentle on my palm.

'You are too young, yer know. I should get a gellfriend me own age,' he said. Then he looked down at me and touched my chin, checked I wasn't crying or owt. That was the thing about Mark, he was either a psycho bastard or tender as hell and there was nowt inbetween. I grinned up at him. I couldn't of done owt else cause my face was set that way, and my head was flying. I walked away thinking how pretty the flames looked, how lovely the sky was.

EIGHT

Mark didn't regret the twenty quid he'd laid out for that first pill and we went out and bought a load more in the next few months. It were still expensive even though the price dropped a bit, but back then one or two'd do for a night, so's it still compared well to going out drinking. To me, it were so much better. Alcohol fuzzed up your head and made you feel sick. With MDMA, which were what the pills was made of, you got a clean high. A feeling that all were well with the world, everyone was as nice and shiny happy as you felt. It kept you up all night too, gave you energy from God all knows where cause you didn't need to eat or drink ner nowt.

Sometimes when we took stuff we'd go out dancing. The pills made you want to dance like nowt else I've known – disco biscuits some people call them on account of this. It were a while before the proper house scene came along and the exact right kind of music for them, but everything sounded better on pills. Our favourite place was this club called The Garage over Hockley way. It weren't all lights and nonsense like the other clubs in Nottingham and the music was different too. Dance music from the States, acid house and that kind of stuff instead of layers and layers of cheese. It were there I heard The Happy Mondays and KLF for the first time and got hooked right off. We used to go down most Saturdays. I was only about twelve when I started going but well developed for my age so's with a bit of make-up I could pass for a lot older and got let in. Clubs are always softer with gells that way anyways. This place wasn't a meat market like most of them in town – it were all about dancing – but when men did make moves on me Mark cleared them off. He really looked out for me.

One thing the drugs do to you is make you all touchy feely, and Mark and me snogged a few times. He didn't try to take it no further though. It were like he'd made a promise to his-sen about that. I'd of let him, I spose, so it were good that he'd gone all chivalrous over me. I don't totally buy all that Harry met Sally bollocks, but I do reckon friendships between gells and boys have to go through that stage where sex comes into it, and can come out the other side sometimes and be summat better. And I reckon, back then at least, that were what'd happened with me and Mark.

We partied every weekend and sometimes did what Mark called a 'midweek effort'. My mouth was always aching with the strain of laughing and smiling so much, as well as the jaw lock what went on along with taking ecstasy. That could be a pain. You chewed up your mouth and got sores if you weren't careful but we'd usually have gum or a dummy to chew on and that helped loads. All the missed sleep and chemicals in my body made school hard for me. I wasn't a bad attender, cause going in were a source of income for us, but my behaviour was erratic down to me being sometimes hyper and sometimes tired out and mardy. Tuesdays or Wednesdays were the worst. 'The Tuesdays' they call it now but it wasn't so well known about back then. All's I knew was I felt miserable, and I'd take it out on Mam and Jon and Mark when he was about. And of course the poor sods what had to try and teach me. I got in a load of trouble, and they suspended me a couple of times. Most kids'd of got done by their mams about that but mine didn't give a shit. In her own little world by that stage, and didn't even bother reading the letters what the school sent. Course, when I got the Tuesday blues, Mark'd be feeling the same and we had some cracking rows. It took us ages to work out what was going off. After we did, the rows'd still start but we'd clock our-sen doing it and one on us'd smile. Before you knew it then we'd be laughing and saying in loud voices about how it were Tuesday or Wednesday.

There was this one time we were out dancing when it all came on a bit too strong for me. We'd got these new pills from a bloke down Radford flats. The pills we bought came in different shapes and colours, with different pictures and stuff on so's we called them different things, Mickey Mouses or Mitsubishis or whatever. The ones what made me go funny this time were these red speckled things with a playboy symbol on them. My heart was going like mad and I felt like I couldn't hardly breathe. Mark was distracted by the music and just kept dancing, his eyes all over like he was looking at stuff what wasn't there. I felt like the floor was moving away from me. When he clocked summat was wrong he panicked a bit and was flapping round like a gell. This black bloke came over to us.

'She's just rushing,' he told Mark. This was way before

71

the time of chill-out areas in clubs or Leah Betts-style media panic. The man pulled me off to the quietest corner he could find and sat me down in front of him. He pushed my head and neck forward and rubbed them hard and nice all over. It felt amazing, and all the muscles in my face and shoulders relaxed at the same time. I let me-sen flop forward and enjoy the shit going off inside my head.

'You trying somethink on, mate?' Mark said to the bloke.

He looked up at Mark and shook his head, throwing out this big white grin at the same time. 'No man, I'm just meking the gell feel better,' he said. Mark sat down beside him, just in case I guess. The bloke got up and indicated down at me with his hands, telling Mark to take over. He sat down behind me then and started rubbing, but it didn't feel half so nice. The man stood round, though, giving Mark tips and instructions till he knew what he was on with. Then the bloke was off into the crowd. I never did see him again to thank him for doing what he did, but that's the way shit goes. It wasn't very long before I was up and dancing again, and feeling like I wasn't never going to die.

Mark and me did a pill round at his when his mam were away for the weekend, and decided to have a bath. I kept my underwear and a T-shirt on, cause I didn't want to be locked in a bathroom on my own rushing my head off like I had been at the club but, at the same time, I was too shy to get all naked in front of Mark. I looked like a fully grown woman underneath my clothes and was still at the stage where that embarrassed me. I got changed, and Mark got the taps running and put all these candles round the room. It looked like a grotto when I walked in. Mark was already in the bath, not shy like me but bare as the day he was born. It were the drugs that. They take your inhibitions away as good as owt else. This effect meant it didn't worry me him being naked, though I did stare a bit. I'd never seen a naked man and Mark more or less was full-grown by then. He smiled at me staring but didn't say owt.

I climbed in the bath and sat down. Your skin goes all crawly and goosebumped when you're pilled, and every little touch or texture feels twenty times as intense as it normally would. The drug turns nice into perfect. As the hot water covered my feet and shins it felt like it were honey and I could taste it through my skin. I sat down and the same feeling slipped it-sen all over my thighs and hips. Mark grabbed me and turned me round so's I had my back to him. I sat against him and he lapped water all over my shoulders and neck. I sighed with my whole body and settled into the feelings. All's I could think was about how good it felt. There just isn't a word to describe the way I felt, cept ecstasy.

We started dealing the stuff soon after that. I mean, it were always going to happen cause that was our business. Just as soon as we got a wholesale source it were part of our menu. I offloaded plenty at school, and watched as the classroom manners of them round me went running off into the hills. I spose what we did helped close that school down but, the way I see it, if it hadn't of been us someone else would of done it. We took it to The Garage as well, and sold it to the dancers. We'd already been selling acid there, when we could get hold of it, and the clubbers were into that. But more and more people were looking for pills. It were a risky business, dealing in clubs, and a subtle one at that. You had to try and catch people's eyes. And if they clocked you, and knew how the game worked, they'd give you a certain type of look. It's hard to pin down, the way people show you they're after scoring, but it's obvious once you know what you're on with. Once or twice when I was a beginner I made eyes at other dealers in the wrong way so's I looked like a punter and when we had a chat we'd laugh at the misunderstanding. But it wasn't long before that never happened at all. Mark and me got some regular clients there too, lads most of them, who knew who we were and what was what and passed the word out too. We still weren't exactly bigtime but we were making enough.

We were taking enough as well. We'd graduated to at least a couple or three pills, even on a quiet night. Mark'd often drop four or five, and this one night he took eleven. You couldn't OD on the boggers, it seemed, and it were all good. 'Rolling' we called it, the way you got, cause it wasn't like owt else so you couldn't call it tripping. We discovered there was no such thing as a bad roll. We were high as kites all the time for months on end after that. And best mates who looked out for each other and were never apart. Drug brothers, like Mark'd said when we'd split that very first half. I loved him, even then. I didn't know it, or the danger it put me in, but we'd bonded hard thanks to the MDMA. A chemical bond, you might say. Sometimes we took stuff and went out clubbing, some-times we sat round at home, or danced to our own records. Sometimes we wandered round the estate off our faces, spray-painting walls or smashing things up. Whatever we got up to, the pills made it better, put a rose-tinted glow on it all.

Mrs Ivanovich'd taught me about chemical bonds before I could hardly write. They're the kind of bond you get when you heat the right stuff up together. The kind of bond what needs summat really strong to break it open. But things only bond if they match and are meant to. Sometimes you can mix up the wrong things and everything explodes and makes a right old mess. It wouldn't be long before I found that out for me-sen.

NINE

Phil Tyneside was a right wanker and I can say this with authority cause I've seen him masturbate. He was a student at the university, and his family lived down London somewhere. He was at my school doing some kind of community service, stuff he could shove on his job application forms when he'd done at college. He was helping out in the science department, and I caught his attention cause Mrs Ivanovich's efforts with me hadn't been wasted. I was good at the subject. He fancied his-sen as a poet an-all, God knows why. Maybes all that was just an angle. He told me I was like the bud of a flower, fully formed and moist and fun to peel open but ruined once you had. He said being with me was like walking through wet grass just after the dew came down. And I let him away with all this shit cause of his pretty words.

The first time Phil spoke to me I was trying to set up apparatus to do a distillation. We'd fermented orange juice the lesson before and this was in a jug. I was about the only person in the room took it serious. Some people'd drunk the foul liquid they'd made. Sad, I thought, to be interested in drinking the yeasty juice, even if it did have a bit of alcohol in it. Nowhere near enough to get you drunk anyway. One lad was poking at everyone with one of them tripod things. The teacher was running round the room trying to make sure we didn't smash too much, and no one got cut by anyone. I was lucky really, that this woman even tried to do experiments with us. The sane teachers would never of had it the way we went on. I was also lucky that who I was went before me so's I could take the lesson serious without anyone giving me stick. No one was going to mess with me cause of what happened to Danny Morrison. He was scarred so bad you couldn't look him in the eyes. When I saw him on his own in the yard, it made me feel sorry for him, till I remembered that crack he gave me round the head, and how it felt to lie there bleeding in the snow.

I was bunging corks in the test tubes all over cause I didn't want to lose any of the liquid as it boiled off. I heard Phil come up behind me. He was good looking, Phil, and he knew it. Had the kind of eyes what hit you in the clit.

'I wouldn't do that,' he told me. I turned towards him. My top two buttons were undone, my tie hung low below my open shirt and just above was where he was looking. My skirt was hitched up short too. I was thirteen going on twenty and I knew I was fanciable, had just begun to realise what that meant to blokes. I loved the reflection I could see of me-sen in Phil's eyes right then, but the way he looked at me frightened me as well. Just like it had with Mark.

'Why not?' I said, smiling at him.

'Water pressure'll build up and it'll explode,' he said.

And he leaned over me, his chest against mine, as he sorted the equipment for me. 'You're good to go now,' he said, and he wasn't wrong.

I put on the Bunsen burner and after a few minutes the orange muck made spluttering noises.

'This stuff's shit, what we've made,' I said.

'I know,' he said. We both watched the liquid heat up.

'You work hard Kerrie-Ann, and you can do this subject. You thought about going to college?' he said.

I shrugged. 'Call me Kez,' I said. 'Everyone does.'

'Okay Kez,' he said. And he held me in his smile as the sticky brew began to boil and bubble and the pipettes and tubes filled with steam.

The next time I spoke to Phil was in the yard. I was selling whizz, and kids were walking off looking pleased with their purchases. At school I sold it by the gumful and kept the wraps me-sen. Made more that way. I was rubbing my finger in some kid's mouth when I felt this tap on my shoulder. I thought it'd be another one after a hit and when I turned and saw Phil I froze.

'Naughty girl,' he said.

'Shit,' I said.

His eyes glinted at me, and he didn't move. I knew I'd be out of school in half a minute if he let on what he'd seen. They'd call the police an-all.

'Tell you what, I'll not say anything if I get a freebie,' he said.

I held the wrap out to him. He put his finger in slow, then brought it up to his mouth. He pulled his finger in and then out, pop-goes-the-weasel style, and grinned at me.

'Thanks. But that wasn't what I meant,' he said.

I raised my eyebrows at him but didn't say owt.

'I'll come back for what I really wanted another time,' he said, and winked. Then he walked off.

The next time I saw him was in this crappy little night-club called New York, New York. We only went there if we couldn't get in nowhere else, cause they never checked ID. Mark was upstairs, chatting up some tart a bit older than me who he'd heard would 'go'. I stood at the bar getting a drink. I heard some bloke breathing next to me and turned, and there was Phil.

'Can I get you drunk?' he said. I grinned, then nodded and he gestured to the barman. I asked for a blue drink, said I didn't care what but it had to be blue. He walked off to find summat and Phil smiled.

'I love that, ordering a drink by its colour. You here with Scotland?' he said, looking wary about it.

'Yeah. He's on the pull somewhere,' I said.

Phil stared at me as if he hadn't heard me speak. 'You have amazing eyes, you know. They look like they can see into another world,' he said.

I snorted. 'Yeah, I bet that's what you mean,' I said. He assured me it were, and the barman came back with the loveliest coloured fluid – it looked like summat out of a test tube from a TV version of Dr Jekyll's lab.

'Better than orange wine,' he said. I nodded.

'Just a bit,' I said.

'You're very special,' he told me then, and I snorted even louder.

'Yer don't mean that neither. You just want ter shag me,' I said.

'Do you have a problem with that?' he asked.

I shook my head no. Maybes I fancied him more than Mark, or maybes I was just ready, I was older after all. I wasn't going to risk losing a lad like Phil by holding out on him. His posh voice and fancy manners impressed me, see, and all's I can say about that is I was young. Perhaps it were the blue drink and the small white tablet I'd had before what put me in the mood.

Phil said 'good' and put his hand on my waist, making a clicking sound with his tongue. He pulled me onto the small sweaty dancefloor. His face was wet and shiny under the sticky lights. The music playing was screaming on about acid, a drug I hadn't tried, but the E I'd dropped made me appreciate the beat anyway. I wanted to wave my hands in the air and dance but Phil had other ideas. He put his hands on my arse and pulled me close, as if they were already playing 'Time of My Life' or 'Careless Whisper'. He didn't want to waste his time waiting for the music to catch up with his mood. He squeezed me against his dick and it burnt hot as a Bunsen through his jeans.

'Can you do me a favour?' he said.

'Maybes.'

'I want to be a teacher if I grow up. Can you call me Mr Tyneside like you would if I were your teacher at school?'

'Yes Mr Tyneside.'

I said this in a voice made of sugar, and his head went back. He let out a sigh. 'I have to get you home,' he said.

'Yes Mr Tyneside,' I said, and he squeezed me so tight to him it were like he was trying to hurt me.

My mam wasn't in when we got back to the close. I doubt she'd of blinked twice if she had been. She didn't give a shit. I was some accident what happened when she was with some bloke who'd paid her, or too fucked up to know who she was with or why. Anyway, she'd fed her-sen so many chemicals by now most of her brain'd melted and fused with her skull. She didn't go to bed no more, just stayed on the sofa with the telly on all night. She wouldn't of noticed if I'd of killed someone next door.

Phil sat on my single bed and asked me to take off his trousers. 'Yes Mr Tyneside,' I said. I fished for his belt but it were difficult cause he wasn't that fit, and too spoiled from being well off. His belly oozed out his jeans like slime. I had to dig through layers to get at the buckle.

'Jeez, you're desperate to get that off, aren't you?' he said as I fumbled. He pawed at my top, feeling my tits through the fabric. 'Take that off,' he said. I did as he told me. I was not wearing a bra. 'Gorgeous,' he said. He held both hands out and cupped one breast in each, as if he was weighing them.

I managed to dig out his belt buckle and got it undone. I pulled on the end of his trousers and they slipped down his long legs, snagging and stopping at his knees, then his ankles. He was wearing boxer shorts and told me to take them off too. I did and he lay open in front of me like a soggy pink orchid. I didn't want to touch him but he took my right hand and wrapped it round his dick. I was shaking all over.

'Have you done this before?' he said.

'No,' I said, and he let out a loud sound. 'Am I hurting you?' I asked.

'No,' he said. 'Oh God no.'

Next morning I met Mark on the park before school. We were supposed to be doing a survey of the kids at Glaisdale, trying to suss out if they were worth one of our after-school sessions, if there'd be enough business. It were a dull, flat saucer of a day, manky grey cloud stretching out a long way off in all directions above my head as I walked.

It were the end of September and all the kids at school'd been talking about the fair coming up on the weekend. Mark and me weren't so bothered. We could get our kicks how we liked. I remember it were quiet that morning. Numbed. Like the cloud what stretched all the way over the park was bubble wrap and soundproofed it. There was a distant hum from the motorway a couple of miles off. No voices. No footsteps. Too early for even the nice Catholic kids from Trinity traipsing across the way. A crow jumped from a tree to the ground, but I didn't hear it land. The tops of my thighs rubbed and burned as I walked, but it were a sweet soreness.

I saw Mark, sitting against a goalpost with a lit joint. Legs crossed with his feet flat on the wet grass, body curved and crushed round them like in some fucked-up yoga pose. The air stewed round his face as he breathed. His eyes were huge over his cheekbones, and his lashes shone with what looked like dew, as if he'd been part of the grass before I'd got there.

I walked over and sat down beside him, crossed my legs too. He nodded at me, and waved his joint in my direction.

'What's in it?' I said.

He smiled, that grimace he had thanks to a knife scar, so's I knew it were brown.

'No ta,' I said.

Mark sniffed up. 'What's that smell?'

I stiffened, and uncrossed my legs, pushed them underneath me. This told him everything he needed to know.

'Who?' he said.

I didn't answer. His face turned to stone.

'That teacher dick from school you was talking to last night?'

'He in't a teacher,' I said.

Mark gave a dirty look to the big grey sky, as if that were responsible for his problems.

'For fuck's sake Kez, you're a baby.'

'Din't bother you and that were last year,' I said. The set of his face turned against me now.

'I was just horny. And you were right,' he said. 'Yer too young to be fucking.'

'There's gells at school been up to it for ages,' I said.

'There's a whole load of slags and slappers at Player. Take after their mams and'll be up the duff before the end of the third year. Take after yer mam, do yer Kez?' he said.

'Fuck off.'

'How old's the wanker?'

I looked at the goal line, bottom right-hand corner, the perfect place to sink a penalty. I couldn't turn back and look at Mark.

'Jee-suz,' Mark said. 'How old?'

He stabbed out his doobie on the mud under the goal-posts, on the edge of the area where goalies'd worn a bald patch on the grass. I stood up and so did he.

'Yer gonna tell me or what?' he said.

I folded my arms and looked away. I didn't know what he'd do next, hit me or spit in my face. Douse me in petrol and set me alight.

'Bitch,' he said. And he walked off without looking back. The huge grey cloud hovered like a mother ship, all ominous above his head. He'd of had to walk for ever to get out from under it. I sat back down on the grass and cried my eyes out.

Phil took me to this party in a warehouse a few weeks after

I fell out with Mark. This huge place, with stage lights hung from its high ceiling, set to move round all over, and a couple of strobes going off in the corner. We were both pilled up, and Phil was all touchy feely while we were dancing. E'd got cheaper by then, about eight quid a go, and the rave was like some big experiment of its effect on people. The only danger I was in was of my mouth splitting open with how much I was smiling. My face ached from gurning and grinning my head off. I loved Phil. I loved everyone. Ecstasy makes you fall in love like the world's about to end.

I went to the toilets to get a drink. I splashed my face with cold water and looked in the mirror. The sink next to me was full of vomit, bright coloured and pungent. In that state I thought it were pretty. It looked like a bowl of the multi-coloured shit they used to stuff toys with and I almost put my hand in. I looked out the window to a roof covered in skylight windows. Music was throwing itssen through the door, banging to the rhythm of my pulse.

My favourite track came on and I went back out. 'You're twisting my melon man,' the singer said. 'You're twisting my melon man.' I danced with some bloke I'd never seen before. We both looked cool as shit, waving our arms about through the path of the strobes. I grabbed his hand and pulled.

'Where we going?' he said.

'For a walk on the moon,' I told him.

He trailed me through the toilets, past the sink full of puke and through the window onto the roof. The skylights were like craters. The real moon looked down on us like a huge, bright lamp in the ink black sky. We sat on the roof, side by side, and I leaned against him. It's weird, the shit what goes through your head when you're rolling. I thought about the scars I'd got. A circle on my right knee about a half-inch across, from a scab I kept splitting open when I was eight. My left knee, a comma-shaped patch of skin from a burn of candle wax I dripped there deliberate to see what it felt like. I looked at me and this bloke sitting there, as if I was viewing it from a long way off. I thought it would make a good picture. The gell with matted hair resting her head against the blond man, who was sitting straight and tall as a howling dog in front of the moon. Stuff Disney pictures are made of. We stared at the sky like we'd never seen it before. The moon dimmed as we watched, and the sun rose. The light leaked into clouds of ozone and sulphur dioxide lying low over the city. It burned behind the silhouette of factories and warehouses and silos and hoardings what stretched into the distance. Then it happened. Phil appeared on the roof with this gell even younger than what I was. He was pulling at her clothes and she was going 'Yes Mr Tyneside,' like he'd asked me to. All at once I had a load more scars.

'You're twisting my melon man,' the singer said. He repeated it, over and over, as the record faded out.

Six weeks later, my period still hadn't come.

TEN

You know crap all about owt when you're thirteen. I was so thick. Didn't want to believe I could be pregnant so I carried on with everything as if it were all normal. Dropped pills every weekend. Drank beer, smoked spliff, took the odd bit of coke when I had the money. Put the fact I hadn't had a period for ages to the back of my mind. I didn't get fat, not specially, cause I didn't eat much. One of the things about taking a load of E is you don't get hungry or thirsty or need the loo. Your head feels light as air too, so's it's difficult to tell if you're still alive or a ghost. I thought I'd come on any day cause my tummy hurt the way it does before your period. But I smelled different. My skin gave off summat sweet so's you'd want to lick it. Milk and honey. I was sick, course. Projectile vomiting, lurching my stomach so hard it threw me across the room. But even when I felt the baby move I told mesen it were just a tummy bug.

One morning I turned sideways in front of the mirror and looked at the curve of my belly and it kicked. I saw a foot, the heel, clear as day. Still in denial, I decided to go and buy a test.

I went to Boots on Bracebridge. I hovered round the aisle where they had the Clearblue and own-brand testing kits, the condoms I wished I'd made Phil use, the tampons I wished I needed. I looked round the shop to check there was no one I knew there. Then I picked up the test, quick as I could, and took it to the counter. Even walking over I felt my tummy quiver. I told me-sen it were muscles, a twitch.

The shop assistant looked at me as she scanned it, eyes full of guesses. I gave her a chilly stare but she didn't look away. She must of had kids in all the time giving her attitude.

'What yer staring at?' I asked her.

'Yer too young ter be needing that,' she said, nose half in the air like she was better than me or summat.

'Shows what the fuck you know cause this's fer me mam,' I said.

'And if I knew-er I'd check on that, and mek her wash yer mouth out,' she said.

I laughed at her. 'Like to see yer fucking try.' I gave her a tenner for the test and grabbed it, shoved it in the inside pocket of my coat. I didn't bother waiting for my change.

I made certain Jon and my mam were out before I tried it. She'd gone to her dealer and took him with her. She was getting her drugs for favours now, more direct to seller than before, cutting out the middle man. Skag for a shag, fair's fair and all that. It's not fair till October, she used to tell me when I was little and I moaned about stuff, a sad joke about when the Goose Fair would be round. That was back before I knew what she was, when I bothered to listen. I still want to know when this October she talked about's going to come. A few rides on the Forest Rec didn't make up for all the shit in my life.

I undid the packet in the bathroom and read the leaflet careful as I could. You had to piss on the stick then wait a minute. It showed you pictures of what the panel would look like. Pregnant. Not pregnant.

You wouldn't of thought there was much to think about in a minute. But there is. In my head there was all sorts going off.

'Not pregnant, not pregnant, not pregnant,' I said, like it were summat you could conjure up pulling on a daisy. I must of known deep down I was. I guess I was just hoping.

I waited, looking at the stick the whole time. Not pregnant, not pregnant, not pregnant. I hummed it like a fucking mantra. Tried to charm away what was going off inside me. Course, the panel on the stick turned blue where I didn't want it to.

I'm no pussy, I've had a lot go wrong for me and I don't cry hardly ever. Course, I did then. How could I not? I wasn't stupid. After all the shit I'd done the kid wasn't going to have a chance of being all right. It were just good luck I hadn't killed it yet. I wasn't ready to be a mam. I just wasn't. I couldn't hardly look after me-sen. I wouldn't know what to do with a baby, never mind one what'd gone brain damaged cause of my stupid fault.

Mam came back then, so I shoved the test wand in my clothes and went to my bedroom. I buried my head deep into the pillow and bit down to stifle any noise I would make. Then I sobbed.

I don't know what I expected, but I went to see Phil anyway. I knew where he lived cause he'd took me there once, shagged me over the kitchen table, getting excited that one of his housemates might walk in. I stood ringing his doorbell and saw the curtain twitch. For a minute I thought he might not answer. Then he came to the door, opening it just a little bit and placing his body in the gap, like he thought I might charge him.

'We need to talk,' I said.

'Can you keep your voice down?'

I gave him one of my nasty looks but he didn't even break off eye contact. A term or so at Player'd toughened him up.

'I thought we were sorted, love. You understand, don't you? Me and you,' he gestured, 'we couldn't ever be serious.'

My look hardened and he must of thought I was going to hit him cause he flinched and held his hand in front of his face.

'As if I'd bother,' I said.

He stood up taller then, as if he hadn't just been a total dick, and made his voice go deeper.

'It's not a good time,' he said.

'Damn right about that,' I told him. 'I'm pregnant.'

He stopped talking then, but his mouth carried on moving like he was summat out of a fish tank. After about half a minute he spoke again.

'Is it mine?' he said.

'You tryna say I'm a slag or summat?' I said, squaring up to him.

'Well you didn't exactly put up a fight with me, did you?' he said.

'If yer want ter say I'm a slag you could at least have the balls to come out and say it,' I told him.

He shrugged. 'I'm not calling you anything. I just don't see how you can be so sure it's mine.'

'You're the only bloke I've slept wi-ever. That's how comes I'm sure,' I said.

'Oh for God's sake, Kez. Like you'd even know the way you're off your head most of the time.'

I barged him then, started smacking at him. He was bigger than me though, and stronger. He grabbed my wrists and held me still. He whispered in my ear with a voice like sharpened steel.

'My girlfriend's in there. And her mum and dad. If you cause enough fuss that they realise you're here and why then I'll phone the police and tell them you've been stalking me, won't leave me alone and how I wish I'd never agreed to help out at that school of yours.'

'They wun't believe yer. I'd tell them about this,' I said, and nodded down at my tummy.

'And I'd tell them what I caught you doing in the playground, sweetheart. They'd be round searching your house in ten minutes and where would you be then? Who'd be the one got believed?'

He held me fast by the wrists and our eyes locked. I pulled away and he let me go. He smiled as he closed the door. Thought he'd won. He hadn't seen the last of me though.

Course, any normal gell'd of talked to her mam about it next. But I wasn't a normal gell and she certainly wasn't a normal mam. I knew her. She'd shrug and tell me she'd gone and had me and Jon and that'd worked out right. She'd of not cared less, would of left me to have the bogger in secret, in my bedroom, before she'd helped me sort owt out.

So I turned to the only person there was left. I went to see Mark.

I don't know what I must of looked like, turning up at

Mark's door like that. I'd cried so much the skin round my eyes'd puffed up and gone red so's I had huge rosy circles either side of my nose. The skin felt tender to the touch and heavy. I felt sleepy even though I wasn't tired. I could hardly keep my eyes open. When I saw Mark's face I wanted to fall into him, let him wrap me up away from the world. But I hadn't forgot the last time we'd met up, the way he'd looked at me before he'd walked off. So I was wary.

'What's a matter?' he said, looking me up and down. 'Is it yer mam? Jon?' I shook my head and felt my bottom lip curl again, fought against it.

'Can I come in?' I said.

'Is it that teacher nob?' he said then, and I thought my face would explode at the effort of stopping more tears coming. I cupped a hand round my tummy and looked down. I was beginning to show.

'Oh, Kez.' There was this long pause. 'Yer fucking kidding me.'

I shook my head again. 'Are yer going to let me come in?' I asked. Mark nodded his head back and opened the door wider. I walked through and followed him to the front room.

'How far gone?' he said, and I shrugged. 'Is it kicking?'

'Yeah.'

'Jesus, Kez. It might be too late to do owt.' Then I did cry. I was surprised I still had water for it, but I did. It seeped over my scratched face again and evaporated, making my cheeks sting. Mark sat there, arms folded and miles away on the other sofa.

'No point blubbing about it,' he said. 'Yer need to see what yer can sort.'

I wiped my face with my hands and looked at him. 'I can't do this on me own, Mark. I need yer help.'

'Yer mam should be sorting this wi-yer,' he said.

'My mam?' He shrugged to concede my point. 'You're all I got cept Jon and he's way too young to be doing wi-all this,' I said. Mark made a whistle between his teeth and tapped his foot fast on the carpet.

'I warned yer you was too young,' he said.

'I know.'

'We better get yer ter a doctors. There's some money I got fer yer, owe yer from before. An't bin able to bring me-sen to come over. We can use that,' he said.

I smiled at him and breathed deep. I knew he didn't owe me no money, but I didn't say owt about that. He smiled back but didn't look happy. It were one of them smiles what said a million things, none of them good. I was lucky with Mark. He liked it when someone needed him.

Mark took me to this private clinic where a nearly young as me lady doctor with a posh voice asked me a load of questions.

'What contraception were you using at the time?'

I thought about lying and telling her the condom'd bust but I couldn't be arsed so I shrugged.

'Right,' she said. I'd never heard anyone put so much judgement into one word. 'And which method of birth control are you considering using once you've left here?'

I shrugged again.

'Kerrie-Ann, do you want to end up in this situation again?'

'Course not.' I looked at her through my fringe.

'I'd recommend the coil if you're not too promiscuous. Wouldn't normally unless you'd had a kid but you'll be okay now.' She was scribbling on her pad. I didn't know what she meant by that comment, hardly heard, and looking back I wish I'd listened more. 'How many men have you slept with?' she asked me, looking up from her papers.

'One,' I said.

'This year?'

'Ever.'

She looked so sceptical I could of whacked the cow. But I knew it wouldn't get me nowhere cept thrown out the clinic, and I couldn't afford for that to happen. It wasn't a question, not for me. Round ourn all the young gells tended to keep their babies, but I don't see that. Keep a baby I can't deal with and can't afford to do nowt for and they end up no better off than me. Bring them into drug running and dealing at ten, smuggling guns out of attics for pimps and dealers, like what I was. I didn't want it. I would have kids one day, but it'd be after I'd seen through my escape plan. The plan I had was this. Keep dealing. Save up. Run away to South America and start over again. They can't get you back from there, even if you get found out. That's why that train robber bloke went there. I could live in Rio, like him, and go to the rainforest whenever I liked. Then I'd have babies. Coffee-coloured ones like my beautiful brother with one of them gorgeous local boys. Not now. Not Phil Tyneside's.

They did a scan and measured the baby and said I was only just legal for what they called a 'termination'. A couple more weeks and I would of had to have it.

'You'll have to have a late medical termination,' the doctor told me. 'Do you know what that means?'

I shook my head. No one had never, ever seen Kerrie-Ann Hill so quiet as I was them few days.

'We give you drugs to stop the pregnancy. Then we make your body push the baby out.'

I didn't say owt.

'You need to understand that you'll be aware of everything.'

There were a million questions I should of asked right then about what the silly cow meant by that. God knows why she didn't explain proper. But the questions didn't come. I was just too fucked in the head. She said, 'Are you all right with that?' and I said nowt. She said, 'Kerrie-Ann, are you okay for us to go ahead with the procedure or not?'

I thought then of all the polite words they kept using to put sugar on what I was doing. Termination. Procedure. But I said, 'Yes.' It were the last time I felt anywhere near normal. And I closed my eyes then opened them again. The next twenty-four hours was about to really open them up.

I had a 'late medical termination'. It were the 'standard procedure' at my 'stage of pregnancy' and I would be 'aware of everything'. They reckon people repress things what make them feel bad but I know that won't ever happen to me cause if I could repress owt it'd be this memory. What it all meant, once you'd licked off the sugar, was the doctors induced you early so's the baby was born but couldn't live.

They took blood, gave me a tablet to take. They said I might notice the baby stop moving during the night. I slept in a room at the clinic, and this nurse kept coming in to check I was okay. She was all right, that nurse. She was small, smaller than me, made of tiny bones and not like a grown-up woman at all. More like a doll. Mark stayed with me. He laid his head down on the bed next to me, stroked my hair. Tender Mark again. He fell asleep but I didn't. The baby was still kicking.

'You got a good-un there,' the doll nurse told me when she came to take my temperature. She meant Mark, but at first I thought she meant the baby, and my hand went to my stomach. 'You ready for this?' she asked me. I nodded and felt Mark's grip tighten round me. You could almost laugh at how I didn't have a clue.

The next day they put these tablets up inside me. The doll nurse told me this'd bring on the contractions and that was when I realised what they were doing. Soon after, my tummy started hurting like I'd got a bad period. Mark held my hand and I laughed it off but I knew what was going to happen and felt sick. Bile shot up into my throat and I got up to go to the toilet.

'You're bleeding,' Mark said.

And I looked down, saw a trail along my trouser leg.

The nurse came in then, made me sit down and change into one of them hospital slip things. The tummy ache got worse, till it settled into long grinding pains what might of made a different gell cry. But that wasn't the kind of thing what made me cry.

It didn't take long before the bloody bundle came out through my legs. The nurse grabbed it up before I could see but I sat up and shouted at her.

'Give it me,' I screamed.

'I don't think that's a good idea,' she said.

'It's my baby – give it me,' I said.

Mark tried to calm me down but I'd gone psycho bitch like I sometimes do and there was nowt he could do. I wailed and shouted and water streamed down my face and snot out my nose.

'Why din't no one tell me?' I screamed. The bed was covered in blood and as I kicked and yelled it got all over. My arms and legs were covered and I spread it over Mark as he tried to hold me still.

I ran out of steam and lay still in Mark's arms. I sobbed with my head on his chest for as long as I had energy to. When I'd done, my eyes were bright and red like rowan-berries. Like the blood what was all over the place. When I touched round my eyes the flesh sprung back like rubber against my fingers. Never cried like that before or since.

We sat there then, me and Mark, quiet as you like, blood all over us. That picture says it all about me and Mark and where we were going from there. Says too much.

ELEVEN

I **once** saw this accident where a lorry driver slammed on his brakes too quick and jack-knifed, sweeping the motorbike what was overtaking up then underneath him. After my 'late medical termination', my head was more of a mess than that. Summat went with that baby, a part of me what couldn't be replaced. I got all snappy with Jon, and that really wasn't like me. I couldn't stand being with my mam, and Mark wound me up even when he was being all nice to me. My birthday came and went but I refused to do owt about it. When people asked me how I was I said 'all right' and 'okay', like what you do. But there's a difference between all right and okay. Things were sometimes okay after my baby'd gone. They were never 'all right'.

The crunch came, though, when I was supposed to be meeting with some of the lads from the Medders and I didn't turn up. Mark went, so it wasn't a disaster, and he said I was poorly so's they didn't feel skanked. We'd arranged to meet them down Hockley to discuss who'd deal where in town, cause Mark and me didn't want to tread on no one's toes. That was the easiest way to get a gun in your face. We couldn't of had a more important meeting and I could of died that I'd missed it. I thought Mark would give me a real hard time about it but he didn't. That made me feel worse.

'It dun't matter,' he said. 'Yer not right at the minute.'

'There's nowt wrong wi-me,' I said. I kept saying that to him. I didn't want to admit it to me-sen.

'Come on, Kez. Yer don't have ter be perfect all the time. Yer not right and that's that.' I shut it then, didn't bother fighting cause I knew it were true. I sighed deep and looked at the floor. 'What about we get away somewhere, go ter Skeg or summat?' he said.

I felt the muscles twitch in the bottom of my face but I was determined not to let me-sen cry. Instead I forced a smile, and said, 'Yeah, that sounds nice.'

We borrowed a car from this bloke I knew and Mark drove us to the coast. The winding country roads we had to go along made me feel sick. We'd rented a caravan on Golden Sands in Ingoldmells from one of our mates, whose mam owned it. Let us have it for next to nowt as well. We could of gone abroad I spose, to Ibiza or summat, but we weren't so bothered. I just needed a break. It were busy as we approached the town, and the cars were queuing to get in Butlins. Mark didn't feel like waiting behind them so he mounted the pavement and drove us past. We got dirty looks from some of the pedestrians but it made us both laugh.

It were raining by the time we got to the caravan park. I tried to work out the map we'd got to take us to the right van and we giggled as we got lost over and over. We found it in the end, though. Mark unlocked the door and we brought our bags in. The caravan was all right. A sofa curved round the front window and the small curtains were made of the same material as the cushion covers. There was a tiny shower room and a bedroom with a double bed. Mark said he'd sleep in the front room if I wanted, on the pullout. I smiled at him and said I wouldn't mind a cuddle when I was going to sleep if that was all right with him. He smiled back and you could tell it were. We'd been shopping before we left Nottingham, and I put tins of curry and Fray Bentos pies in the cupboard while Mark sat at the pull-out table and had a smoke. I could tell from the smell he wasn't smoking hash or weed. I didn't like it that he smoked brown, but I couldn't stop him and didn't see no point trying. It would of only meant we'd argue.

'Are we far from the sea?' I asked him.

'Nah, not at all.'

'You want to go and see it?' I said. Mark shrugged, but picked his-sen up and put on his coat. He'd grown some in the last year or so, and it surprised me how near the ceiling his head was. He slouched his way to the door and I followed.

Mark pushed the door to and locked it. We walked down the muddy soil path and followed the signs to the small beach what sat by the caravan park. The sea boiled in the distance, brown as mud from the shit they throw in it from open sewers. A couple of miles away I could see the roller coasters on the main beach at Skeg. Drizzle misted over the scene and the sea looked as far away as Skeggie did. They should put this on postcards. I remember when I was little, coming here once with Mam and Uncle Summat or other. I thought it were great then, that I could walk from one town to another all the way

along the beach. Me and Jon sang 'Ingoldmells, Really
Smells' for ages in the car till Uncle Bill or Paul or whatever his name was got nasty and gave me a clip round the
ear-ole.

'Chips?' Mark said. And I nodded. I couldn't think of
a thing I'd like more in the world.

There was a chippy on site, so we walked over to it.
Mark got some beers from the shop next door. I got us
fish, chips and peas twice. My mouth watered as I ordered
it so's I couldn't get the words out right. We walked back
to the van without talking. Mark ripped a hole in the
packet and pulled chips out, flicking off paper and shoving
them in his mouth. We got back to the van and ate the
rest quick, washing them down with beer. When we'd
finished, Mark burped really loud and we both laughed.
We did some speed then, and Mark said, 'Let's go to bingo.'

We walked over to the bingo hall arm in arm, pretending
to be two old ladies. We talked about the price of eggs,
and how the bread at the Co-op wasn't ever fresh no more.
When Mark said summat funny I'd laugh, and before I
knew it I was laughing my head off and'd forgot all about
the stuff what'd gone off recently. I walked along like that
for a bit, happy as you like, then pictures of the red bundle
in the nurse's hands snuck into my head, making me
breathe more heavy.

'Gi-me some more-a that speed,' I said to Mark, and he
held out the packet to me like it were a 10p mix he was
sharing. I took a good fingerful of the white powder.

'Tek it easy,' Mark said, and I shook my hand, sprin-
kling a bit back into the wrap. I rubbed the stuff in my
gum and waited for it to make me go all hyper again.

We went into the bingo hall. We were laughing as we
walked in, and I was leaned against Mark. Pairs of eyes all

over turned towards us, and there were a couple of loud tuts, a deep intake of breath somewhere behind us. That only made us laugh more. We found our-sen a table and Mark went to buy some cards. We sat with our pens and blotted at the numbers. Neither on us won owt. We couldn't hardly keep up with the caller, and whenever we looked at each other we'd giggle again, so loud at one point that the table next to us asked the caller to repeat some numbers. Then this security bloke came over and asked us if we'd leave. We didn't care.

We walked past the site club on the way back to the van. There was a buzz coming through the door. I knew what it'd be like inside. Full of women in stonewashed jeans or leggings, fat slipping out the top. Their blokes, huge tummies what they looked proud to balance a pint on. There would be the odd slim woman dressed in tight black trousers or a dress. They'd dance round, wiggling in a way what made you know how much they thought of themselves. The men always went for them types, though, no matter how cheap they looked.

'Want ter go in?' Mark said as we passed.

'Nah, not in the mood.'

We went back to the caravan and Mark let us in. It'd been raining all night, and it were cold inside. I put on the heating and the telly, and snuggled me-sen into a ball on the sofa. Mark brought some beers over and sat down next to me, put his arm round me. I lay back into him, tried to dissolve. I heard the rain pitter patter the roof, and there was some thunder. It felt good to be cuddling up in the warm, in front of the glow of the telly, with the weather up to all sorts outside. Mark kissed me on the top of my head and I snuggled into him, nuzzled him like a dog. We sipped the beer. *Blind Date* was on the telly.

Mark took the piss out of the cheesy crap they all said, the way they were trying to be clever with their answers. I fell asleep. Mark was talking to me, but I don't know what he was saying. He picked me up and carried me through to the bedroom. I felt him do it, but was too far gone to even wake up enough to say thank you. He put me in bed with all my clothes on and got in beside me. I could feel his legs next to me, hear the rustling denim of his jeans. He stroked my hair and I woke up. It were raining heavy now, and the caravan roof turned the raindrops into big booming noises as they hit. I lay still and quiet and heard my heart in my eardrum, felt it beat against my breastbone. It were going hard and heavy as the rain on the roof. I made my head sink into the pillow and my body drop into the mattress but it didn't help. I lay awake and watchful for ages after I heard Mark snoring. I heard different groups roll drunk back to their vans. I heard Mark talking in his sleep, but his words blurred into each other so's you couldn't make them out. A bit later, I heard the birds singing.

The next thing I heard was the hiss of bacon being cooked, but I think it were the smell what woke me. It were about ten, and I hadn't had much sleep and felt grumpy to be awake. I was stroppy with Mark, even though I knew he was just trying to be nice. He came through to the bedroom with a tray full of stuff and said, 'Wakey, wakey, rise and shine.' It took all the will I had not to tell him to fuck off. I sat up and he put the tray on top of me, handed me a knife and fork. 'For madame,' he said, and grinned.

I wasn't very hungry but felt like I ought to eat summat after Mark'd gone to all that effort. I nibbled at some bacon, put it down, had a spoonful of tomato. Temper stung inside me cause I felt forced to eat. Course that was just my take on it, not the way it really were.

'I could do wi-a cuppa tea,' I said. Mark grinned. He went through to the kitchenette and brought back a mug. He handed it over and I wrapped both hands round it, let the warmth run into me and through my body. I looked at the liquid in it.

'This in't tea,' I said.

'Oh it is. It just in't PG,' Mark said, winking at me.

I looked at him. 'Shrooms. This time-a day?' I said.

'Why not? They in't no rule about it,' he said. Course, there were a whole load of rules called laws about it, but I didn't point that out. Mark threw me a pixie grin and I couldn't resist his cheek. I sipped the liquid. It were warm enough but tasted sour, like there was metal dissolved in it or summat. I spose normal tea doesn't taste that nice neither, not really. It's just what you're used to. I sipped at Mark's special brew and he had a cup his-sen. I didn't eat much breakfast.

I got up and dressed and we walked to look at the sea. It were still raining, but not hard like the night before. Now it were a miserable sheet of drizzle, ice cold, so's it hit your skin like needlepoints. It were dead stormy out there, and the sea was a long way in, there was only a couple of yards of beach the other side of the wall. Mark said it'd be dangerous to go down. I hoped the weather would clear. I wanted to go rock pooling and collect up shells and little crabs. I would of liked to build a sand-castle too, a big one with a moat. Then me and Mark could of jumped all over it and smashed it to the ground. I was still a kid really.

Mark wanted to walk into town, go to the arcades, but I couldn't be arsed and the weather put him off a bit too. We went back to the van, put on the telly and wrapped our-sen up in a quilt on the settee. Mark put his arm round me again. It didn't feel like the night before, though. It wasn't all cosy and nice. There was this draft coming from somewhere, and Mark's skin felt clammy and cold against the back of my neck. I didn't cotton on but I was tripping by then, and it wasn't a good trip.

Mark was happy enough. He kept giggling at the smallest bits of crap off the telly. Stupid ads what weren't funny. The more he laughed the more he got my strop on. I got up and went to the kitchenette, filled a glass with water and sat down at the table. Next thing I knew Mark was there talking to me. I could see him and hear that he was talking but nowt made sense. He was asking me questions but I couldn't put his words together, make them into owt I'd understand. I couldn't move ner nowt, all's I could do was say no and wave my arm in front of my face. That reminded me of the gell in the EMHG what I beat up. Maybes she was like this all the time, and that was why she did bad shit. I shouldn't of beat her up. And as I realised that, I felt worse, deeper in me-sen. It were like there was this ice barrier between me and the world, and there was nowt I could do to smash or melt it. Then it cracked just a bit.

'It's just a trip, Kez,' I heard Mark say. 'Just a fucking silly little trip.' His voice echoed through the crack in the ice and I knew it were, and that I'd just have to wait for it to end. I let my head fall onto the table and the ice shattered.

Just like that I was normal again. 'Sorry,' I said to Mark. I could see my hand in front of me, shaking. 'God, I'm sorry Mark.'

'No need. S'my fault. Shouldn't of given you shrooms after what yer been through lakely. Stupid-a me.'

Course he was right. I realised that and went psycho gell again. I bashed the table then stood up, thumping at him. He grabbed my wrists and I was thrown back to Phil, outside his house, sending poisonous words whispering into my ear. It were like all the temper I felt towards Phil transferred to Mark then. It wasn't fair at all, but what is at the end of the day? Not October, that's for fucking sure. All sorts of foul language came out my mouth, and things you shouldn't say to no one ever.

After a bit I settled, and Mark grabbed me and squeezed hard. I let him push all the breath out of me, tighten like an anaconda so's I couldn't say no more shit to him.

I sat down. I was freezing.

'Yer lips've gone blue,' Mark said and I shrugged. 'You looked like you was possessed or summat.'

'Your fucking mushrooms, that's all,' I said.

'More-n that and we both know it, Kez.' I wouldn't look at him. He grabbed my hand across the table. 'You called me Phil.'

'I called yer lots-a things.'

'Yeh, but I din't mind the other things ser-much,' he said. He did well with that one cause it made me smile. 'Yer know what's wrong wi-yer, we both do. Yer going ter be messed up for good unless yer do summat about it.'

'Like what?' I said, raising my voice. What'd happened had happened, I thought. Nowt to be done about it now.

'Like get yer own back,' he said. Then his favourite word. Revenge. It rolled off his tongue. The way he said it, and his mouth watered, you'd think it were the word for a tasty bit of meat or some nice wine. It were the only word Mark said that made him sound posh.

'Yeah, like how?' I said. Despite all this stuff I got up to, the way I went on with my life, all I was really back then was a stroppy teenage kid and that's what I sounded like.

'Like kill the bastard.' A stroppy teenage kid with mates who said stuff like that and meant it. I went quiet. This was a line you drew, surely. Yeah, me and Mark were kids who crossed lines, but this one? It were too much. I looked up at Mark and saw the set of his eyes. I knew if I gave the okay he'd do it. And the thing was, I wanted to. To stop me-sen doing it, I went inside the tiny caravan bathroom and locked the door.

Mark could of broke the door down. The lock was this flimsy plastic thing and wouldn't of held. He didn't even bang on it though. That was how well he knew me. If he'd of tried to get in, I'd of screamed and shouted and gone more and more against him. Course he left me to it and I stayed in there for hardly no time at all. I looked at my face in the mirror. I was looking skinny. I'd always had cheekbones but now my face looked hollow as a skull. My eyes were sunk and brown all the way round, underneath the lids what they call the whites were hardly white at all. More pink. My lips were still blue like Mark'd said so I looked like some kind of fucked up clown. My hair dripped lank over my shoulders. I looked like a poster of one of them heroin chic models. I looked like my mam. I knew a few drags of one of Mark's special doobies or a shot of what Uncle Frank'd gave me after I'd got beat up would end it all. I'd feel better, like nowt'd gone off with Phil Tyneside or the baby. But I also knew the effect'd last five minutes. Then I'd need more and more and more till I dropped down dead. Seen it with my mam, the way she was going. I vowed again I'd never do brown, not even one little drag of it.

I came out my hidey-hole different. Like Morph must of felt the first time he unfurled them shiny blue wings.

'I don't want ter kill-im,' I said. I paused. 'But yer could hurt-im a bit.'

Mark looked up at me, half smiled. 'No, Kez me duck, no. You can do it. It's the only way it'll do the job, see.'

'How?'

Mark held summat out to me: a small embossed pill.

'Don't be fucking stupid, Mark. Yer can't hurt a bloke wi-just E,' I said.

'Look at it close,' he said.

I took the pill off him. It were about twice as thick as normal. 'What is it?' I said.

'Double stacked. Made of stuff called PMA. Not ecstasy at all,' he said.

'What'll it do?'

'Give it Mr Tyneside. Then you'll see.'

TWELVE

Mark told me it were bullshit about serving revenge cold. 'Get it while it's hot and tasty,' he said, with that wicked grin he had what made you think he was up to nowt more serious than putting a spider in the teacher's desk drawer. He had strong opinions about revenge, did Mark. And three rules he lived by. Do it quick, make sure you see it, make sure they know it were all down to you. So long as you followed these rules, the gospel according to definitely-not-Saint Mark, you could cure owt. At least, you'd believe you could if you rated what Mark said, and I did back then. He was the only person there for me what I could rely on. Jon was too young, my mam was too fucked, my mommar long gone and Mrs Ivanovich, who might of watched for me, was far too long dead.

A few Saturdays on, with my blood still bubbling hard and hot about what Phil'd done to me, I went with Mark to The Garage. We knew Phil went there most weeks cause so did we by then – it were part of the territory we'd negotiated. 'Two birds, one stone,' Mark said as we set out, loading up the hidden pockets in his denim jacket with pills and wraps. 'Business and pleasure.'

'Just mek sure you don't mix owt up wi-the special pills,' I said. And Mark twinkled, held up a moneybag full of double stacked, shook it. The pills hit each other, making a sound like plastic against plastic.

The Garage was heaving, like it always were of a Saturday. Mostly student types like Phil. We'd paid off the bouncers so's they'd let us alone. We weren't risking no trouble, not that night. We paid our dues then launched our-sen across the dance floor to where we knew we'd not be filmed by the CCTV. It were crowded, but most people knew who we were and the room split open to let us pass. I saw this gell make eyes at Mark. She had hair straight as owt, shiny, and her skin was shining too. Like Bek from the gell's home. Someone who'd had the best of everything her whole bloody life. She had a stud in her nose and I could tell by the sparkle in her eyes she was pilled already. Gells like her often looked at Mark. He brought out summat in them. Problies they thought he'd be a nice rough shag. This gell looked that type. The sort who'd had to be daddy's little princess all her life till she went away so now she plays the dirty little slut with a glint in her eye. I pushed between her and Mark as we walked to our spot. If he noticed me do that, or even noticed the gell at all, then he was bloody good at hiding it cause he didn't even blink. But then it were my night, and he wouldn't of spoiled that for owt, least of all for a shag with some posh slapper.

We'd not been standing there long before some blokes came over trying to score. It were almost always the blokes, the ones who approached us. I hated to think the gells were too pathetic to buy their own pills and I don't think that's what it were anyways. I think the lads took over.

Summat primeval. They want to go hunting and come back dragging a huge hairy mammoth behind them. It's funny how these things don't change that much. The bloke what spoke to us was tall, skinny, wouldn't of made much of a mammoth hunter. He looked nervous. He turned to Mark with a bit of a grin and said, 'What yer got?' Mark half nodded and showed the bloke a handful of bright coloured pills.

'Eight quid a pop,' he said. The bloke got out a twenty and held up two fingers. Mark gestured he should hand the cash to me. I gave him change and he walked off with two yellow tablets.

'Don't forget to drink water,' I called after him and Mark laughed.

'Yer don't have to mother-em. They're big boys,' he said.

'Bad choice-a-words,' I said, and I looked at the floor. Mark rubbed my back and said sorry. Held his arm against my shoulder and tried to find my eyes with his own till I looked back up at him.

'It's all going ter get much better soon,' he promised.

I looked round the room but I couldn't see Phil. I was worried he wouldn't come but we were dead busy and I didn't have much time to think about it. It were money here, pills there, the odd wrap of coke. It wasn't really a skag kind of place but some clubbers bought a bit on the way out, summat to bring them down on the way home. They always called it brown, and I heard a couple of them talking once, arguing about what it were made of. They didn't know it were heroin and I couldn't believe it. Fancy taking summat if you don't even know what it is. Mark reckoned half the club types were the same. Didn't even know that MDMA meant ecstasy ner nowt. Street drugs don't come in a nice little box with the active ingredients in a list on the back, I know that, but you'd think they'd of showed an interest in finding out. Money and powder and pills changed hands without explanation and they stayed ignorant. Mark's pockets were emptying fast and mine were filling up. I made him check he'd still got the double-stacked PMA stuff. I would of hated to give it someone by accident. Course he had it, and he told me off for fussing.

At long last I saw Phil across the room. He came in looking like he was trapped inside a bubble of happiness. Some gell close to his own age was wrapped on his arm and they kept smiling and pecking at each other. I guessed this was his fiancée. I wasn't sure then how we'd do it. Didn't know what to do if he wanted pills for the both of them. How was I going to make sure he took the bad ones? She wasn't exactly going to make my Christmas card list, Phil's woman, but I didn't want to do her no harm. She'd done nowt to me.

Phil made straight for us. You'd think he'd of had a bit more decorum about it, given what'd gone off with him and me, but he was such a tosser he didn't care how I felt. Just so long as he got his disco biscuits. He spoke to Mark, course, didn't dare look me in the eye. I wanted to make sure of who was going to take the pills so I interrupted.

'How much you want? And what you prepared to pay?' I asked him. I felt my jaw stiffen, like I'd done some E even though I hadn't. Mark'd stopped me taking owt, reckoned it were important I kept straight that night.

'Just a pill. Usual kind of money, eight quid or something,' Phil said.

'What about yer gellfriend?'

'Julia's strictly a cigarettes and alcohol type.'

I snorted. 'Julia is, is she?' I said, making fun of his accent. 'Ten. Special stuff. Show-im Mark.' Mark took a pill out of the money bag. 'Look, it's thicker,' I said. If Phil'd been owt like me, the sort who worries about what he put in his body and checked it all out, then he might of guessed this was a dodgy pill. But he didn't. He just nodded. One of them knowing movements. I'm summat special. I know what I'm doing here and I'm getting a good deal. The kind of way people like Phil who've never had to worry about owt move in these situations. I wanted to bust out laughing when I saw it but I didn't. He would of worked it out then. I just gave him my curt Broxta nod and took the poor sap's money. Couldn't help but feel glad I was taking his cash and giving him summat to make him sick. Double whammy. Couldn't help thinking that I'd took pills, all them months ago. Pills what'd killed the tiny little baby growing inside me.

I sipped my Bacardi and Coke. It were a novelty for me, alcohol. I didn't usually drink when I was on stuff, so hardly ever. I watched Phil walk off. The way he swung his feet like the big 'I am'. First I thought what a tosser he was, then another feeling came, summat I wasn't expecting. I was sorry for him. I looked at his face as he made a fist round the pill and went to get a drink to wash it down with and there was a knot in my tummy, worse than when the baby was there kicking and moving about and making me sick. I made for the dance floor to follow him. Mark grabbed my arm.

'What yer doing?' he said.

'This in't right,' I said, turning to look him in the eyes.

'It's the right thing for you,' he told me. I shrugged. 'It's up ter you then. It's your problem,' he said.

I shook away from Mark then and caught up with Phil before he got back to his gellfriend.

'What you doing?' he said as I grabbed his arm, echoing Mark a minute before. 'Can't you see Julia's just over there? She'll freak.'

'Tell her yer dropped summat. Thought yer were supposed to be clever. Surely you can blag it?' I said. He didn't say owt to that, but stood there blinking at me, glancing over his shoulder and back again.

'What d'you want?' he said.

'To know yer sorry,' I told him. My jaw tightened even more then and if I hadn't been sure I would of sworn I'd had some E. My throat contracted and I squeezed my whole face in. With all this effort, there wasn't no tears.

'For what?' Phil said, raising his voice and pulling an ugly face. 'For shagging you? You wanted it as much as I did.'

'I'm a kid. I don't know owt.'

'You didn't seem like much of a kid then. Or now. Look at you, dealing in the corner. Not exactly kids' stuff is it?' he said. I could of walloped him one – he had this smarmy, I've-had-you-don't-want-you-no-more grin plastered across his face and I just wanted to smash it to pieces.

'I got pregnant. Had ter have an abortion.'

'Well then, you'll remember next time to take your pills,' he said with this sarky tone to his voice. And with that Phil turned and brushed me off him, like I was muck on his collar. And I thought, yeah, you'll get pills, and walked back to Mark.

'Well?' Mark said, and I knew what he was asking.

'Let's mek-im really sick,' I said.

It wasn't long before Phil stomped back to us to complain.

'That was a dud,' he said to Mark. Not to me of course. 'I'm not up at all.' I had to work at not smiling.

'Sorry mate. I knew there was a few bad-uns in that batch but there's no way to tell what's what,' Mark said.

'What you going to do about it, then?' Phil asked him.

'You can have another one, on me,' he said.

Phil puffed up then, like a boxer who'd just won a big bout. Mark handed him another dodgy pill and he strutted off.

'Tosser,' Mark said and he was spot on. I couldn't believe Phil's conceit. I mean, he could of saved his-sen a load of trouble if he'd of thought straight instead of being so up his own arse. What sort of drug dealer can you complain to and get a refund or replacement? None I've ever met and that's for sure. Anyone ever gave me owt for free and I'd cotton summat were up. That's the problem with kids like Phil. Had too much handed to them on a plate. I can almost feel sorry for him when I think about it now. Back then though, I felt summat swell inside me. The whole room pulsed and looked beautiful. My face grinned without me trying. If it wasn't for the fact I couldn't get into the music I would of sworn I'd had a pill. It were sweet. It were as hot and tasty as Mark'd said it would be.

Mark and me made a few more deals but it got quieter. I danced a bit. Then I went for a wander. Mostly I wanted to check out Phil, see how fucked up he was getting. That was when I realised how thick he really was. He was drinking pints of beer. He didn't look high, just a bit drunk, as he swayed and grabbed his gellfriend's shoulder to stop from falling.

Soon after, he was back complaining to Mark about the second pill. His words were slurred and his face red as owt. I thought about how hard his blood would be pumping, cause that's what PMA does for you and not much else.

'I'm sorry mate. I really don't know how you could of got two suckers in a row. That's fucked up,' Mark said. He let Phil argue for a bit, so's it didn't look totally obvious. After Phil'd ranted for a while Mark said, 'D'yer fancy doing a speedball, to mek up fer it?'

A speedball's only a step away from Mrs Ivanovich and her cyanide, about the stupidest thing you can put inside your body. I could tell by his face Phil didn't have a clue what it were. Mix up heroin and coke and inject them. Coke speeds up your heart and heroin slows it down. Take them both at once and your pacemaker doesn't know what's hit it. It were the same shit what made River Phoenix drop down dead. I knew then Mark was pushing it. I'd told him. I didn't want to kill the fucker, just make him sick.

'It's the best rush ever,' Mark told Phil.

'Course,' said Phil, blinking again. Just goes to show how bullshit can kill you.

'Come on then,' said Mark, gesturing towards the toilets. Phil looked like he was going to bottle it for a minute. I doubt he'd realised a speedball was summat you inject for starters. But he wasn't going to lose face, specially not in front of me.

'You'll love this better than fucking young pussy,' Mark said, and the two of them laughed. See, maybes it were cause I knew Mark, or cause I wasn't so fucked up as Phil, but it were obvious to me Mark was having a dig when he said that. Even more obvious by the way he laughed after that he didn't find owt funny. There was no lightness to that laugh. It were more like summat out a horror movie.

*   *   *

It were about two in the morning when Phil collapsed. First I knew about it was his gellfriend freaking out. The clubbers round him drew back like he was throwing out a wind what'd blew them away. Julia was flapping and screaming and shouting for help. The way she was reminded me of Mrs Ivanovich's daughter, all them years back. I came over all dizzy then, a bit too much Bacardi in me, and had to go outside. I came out the door and stood on the Hockley pavement. People buzzed round me, some of them shouting or swearing. There were a couple of lads braying for a fight a bit further down the street. I leaned against the wall and closed my eyes. I stayed still but the world span round me and I thought I was going to fall over. I didn't like this feeling, being drunk. Couldn't see or think or walk or talk proper. It wasn't nice at all. Mark should of let me take some ecstasy. My head would of been much clearer if he had.

I opened my eyes and stared hard at the sky. The world stopped spinning as if my eyes were holding it still. I gritted my teeth. The sky was hardly dark at all, more of a blue-grey colour, washed out by the lights in town. There wasn't no clouds and the stars winked at me like they knew what I were on with. I could see the whole of the moon and it were that clear you could see craters and all that on the surface. It looked like it were floating, like I could reach out and pick it from the sky, take it home with me. It struck me then that it were a pity I wasn't pilled, that I'd appreciate it all a lot better if I'd got some MDMA pulsing through me. It struck me as dead weird that most people went out every Saturday with the sole aim of feeling like I did then, sick and dizzy. To make everything blurred at the edges.

An ambulance turned up then, filling everything round

me with the squeal of its siren. It were like slow motion. The paramedics must of been rushing like mad. They must of ran into the club but it all slowed down when I watched it, six-million-dollar-man style. They came out a bit later with Phil on this stretcher and his woman following. She had her hand on her chest and was jabbering, just kept going on to her-sen about how it'd be all right, he was going to be okay. But it wasn't going to be all right. Nowt'd been all right for ages, not for me. There wasn't no reason Phil should walk away from that scot free.

The ambulance swallowed the stretcher, then the gell-friend, then wailed into action again, swerving off down the street. That were a job, I thought, driving one of them fuckers. I wouldn't mind doing that at all. Being allowed to drive fast as you like and everyone having to move out your way. When the ambulance was far enough away so's I couldn't hear its siren no more, I breathed in deep. I let me-sen slide down the wall to the floor and sat on the pavement. Then I was sick all over my legs. I curled up in a ball and saw Mark coming out the club, striding towards me on a mission.

THIRTEEN

Phil was in a coma for months. When I saw them stretcher him out the club, I'd assumed the speedball'd done for him but it wasn't that. Mark hadn't even given him a speedball. He'd melted up a couple of them PMA pills and injected them.

I went to the hospital to see him. This was Mark's idea, like everything else. Told me I should go and tell Phil how it were me what did it. Else it'd all of been a waste of time. So I went to Queen's and lied my way into the ward, saying I was Phil's little sister. It's not like they were going to ask for ID or owt. I stood round and waited, watched his mam and that Julia go off to get some coffee or dinner or summat, and made me move. I used her name, Julia's, mentioned I'd just seen her walk off with my mam. Made my voice sound posh as I could and got away with it.

I walked over to the bed. It were surrounded by machines and stuff beeping and ticking, just like they show on the telly. I thought for a minute about switching off the machines but knew straight away it wasn't worth the hassle I'd get. I could see just looking Phil wasn't going to get no better. His face, pale as the wings on a cabbage white. Blood was dripping from his nose, there was a dribble at the corner of his mouth too. I whispered summat in his ear. Told him what'd gone off and that he wasn't waking up. When I moved my face away there was blood coming out his eyes like he was crying it. I took this as a sign he'd heard me. Bright red it were, the trail it made down his face. Against the pale as corpse skin, the red looked so pretty. I didn't cry. Not this time. I'd spilled enough of my own blood and tears for this nob. I hadn't meant to kill him, that was the truth. Mark'd gone too far. I wouldn't say I was glad Phil was dying, but I wasn't sad neither. I can't lie about it. Seeing him lying there on his way out wasn't exactly the best high I'd had for ages but it were comforting. It were justice.

I turned then and saw Julia at the door. She looked tired, and twice as old as the last time I'd seen her. Her face was mottled red so I knew she'd been crying loads.

'Who the hell are you?' she said.

'He used to teach me,' I said. 'I lied to the nurse so's I could say goodbye proper.' Course, she didn't know what I meant by this so her face softened. 'Sorry,' I said.

'Don't be. That's sweet. Good to think Phil's life had an impact on people,' she said.

I could of bust out laughing then, it were so full of crap our conversation. Yeah, Phil's life definitely had an impact on me.

I felt sorry for her though. Not cause she'd lost Phil. He wasn't worth owt to no one. But cause of what she thought she'd lost, this bloke what was worth having and ever so nice to her and with all this good stuff going off in his life. It made me sad that she didn't know the first thing about him. But I felt a twinge of jealousy too. To live like that, not knowing, she'd been lucky. Phil'd loved her enough to lie about stuff. That sounds crap but it's true. The way he was so honest with me wasn't a nice thing. 'I better go,' I said. I made for the door but she was standing blocking it and didn't move.

'He's drowning in his own blood,' she said, staring past me at the mess what used to be her boyfriend. 'Sick bastards fed him too much E and look at him.'

'It wan't ecstasy,' I said, before I thought about how this'd sound and could stop me-sen. Julia's eyes opened wide as they could. 'I just mean it cun't of been. It dun't do that to yer.'

'Do you know something?' she said. I just looked at her. It almost made me laugh that she thought I might admit owt if I did. 'If you know something you should stay and talk to the police.'

I made for the door then, the minute she said police. She tried to block my way but I pushed her hard. I heard her yelp as she cracked her head against the door frame. I didn't run. That would of been the easiest way to get me-sen stopped. I walked double time and dived into a lift as the door snapped shut, making the woman inside tut loud. I gave her a right filthy look and she recoiled like I'd put a hand up to smack her. I was getting good at them looks.

I went outside and stood calm as you like at the bus stop. If anyone was looking for me they couldn't of expected me to do that, stand like nowt'd gone off waiting for a bus, cause I wasn't approached. I got the next bus into town and went to score some pills.

Phil's death made the papers. There he was, under the headline, staring out at me like some perfect version of a human being. They'd chose a photo what glowed full of the potential they said'd been cut short by the evil of drugs. It made me laugh. They said ecstasy'd killed him even though the post-mortem couldn't of found nowt of the sort inside him. They didn't know fuck all about what they were saying. One paper printed all this shit called 'ten things you should know about ecstasy'. I wanted to scream at the paper, shout about how stupid they were and how wrong they'd got it. I wanted to cross out the headline on every bloody copy and write in huge red letters across the Council House that Phil would of been right as rain if he'd had proper MDMA, what good Es are made of. How I knew people who took four or five hits of it regular and it didn't do them no harm at all.

The whole fuss hit our business, specially being as it happened in Nottingham. People were scared off and we couldn't do nowt to talk them round. What would we of said? That we knew Phil didn't take E cause we'd given him summat else instead, deliberate? That'd hardly help them trust what we sold was safe. So we kept quiet and went with the lull. Sold other stuff instead, speed and acid and coke. Made me laugh, that. People taking these drugs instead of ecstasy like it were safer or summat. The whole thing did me and Mark's reps some good though. People in the know, the other dealers and them off the estate, they knew what'd gone off. They knew me and Mark'd done for Phil and they knew the tosser deserved it. That, put with the Danny Morrison campfire, made us untouchable. No one would of dreamed of trying it on over owt.

It were good, to feel that safe. People crossed the street when we were walking towards them, stared at the concrete like the secret to life, the universe and everything was written on it. We were everyone's favourite horror story on the estate. When I was little and Mam gave a shit, it were the ten o'clock horses she used. 'Go asleep or the ten o'clock horses'll come,' she whispered, brushing hair back off my face. When I asked what the ten o'clock horses were, what they'd do, she'd hush me and tell me 'just go asleep'. There was no story, nowt I was told to make me afraid of them horses but that frightened me more. Like it were too bloody nasty to speak out loud what they'd do. So it were with me and Mark. Rumours spread fast as water fills a hole you've dug on the beach.

In the papers there was this quote from the police chief, David summat or other. He said he was 'pulling out the stops' to find the 'evil dealers who are preying on our kids'. It made me laugh cause what they should of known was about Phil. Talk about preying on kids, he'd teach them a thing or two. I knew they couldn't prove nowt about us and Phil dying.

For a bit I thought Mark was a total genius cause I did feel better. Not just better than I'd been since the abortion but better than even before. Better than I'd ever felt. Like I'd had a shot of everything in Mark's pockets, one after the other. Like I'd grown wings and flew off to suck nectar from flowers. Caterpillars have to lock themselves away in a dark sticky shell before they can bust out looking all beautiful. And I came out like a butterfly, going out loads, taking E or speed. I raved till the clubs closed then flew off to illegal parties in warehouses or on farms. I'd sit in the street E'd to the eyeballs looking up at the sky, talking it all through with Mark, everything that'd gone off. I was full of it. Phil'd done me wrong and I'd sorted it. It made me feel like nowt bad could ever touch me again. It made me feel tough as you like. Invincible.

Phil even made the news on the telly, which was as

wrong about what'd happened as the papers were. They called him a 'promising young student' and said 'he was a thoughtful and loving young man who even carried out voluntary work in the local community'. They said, 'No one will ever know why he decided to take drugs that night,' like it were a one off and Phil'd never took owt before. They said his funeral'd take place at Wilford Hill that Friday, but it'd be a private affair for family and friends only. I figured that included me. I was the mother of his only kid for fuck's sake.

FOURTEEN

I held back from the funeral procession. It wouldn't of been good if Julia'd recognised me and started asking questions and mentioning the police again. I put on this red dress, the brightest bloodiest red I could find in the shops. Wilford Hill really is a hill and I walked up it fast, ending up breathless and wheezy at the top. I chose a grave at random and put flowers on it, tidied it up. Watched Phil's friends and family commit him to the earth a dozen or so plots away. Julia leaned against some other young bloke and I wondered if he was just a mate, or if she'd found a replacement for Phil already. If he was just after a shag and'd use her upset to get in there. I liked that idea. I didn't really wish her no harm but thought it'd serve Phil right if someone did that with his woman. Phil's mam was sobbing and clung to his dad. His dad was more dignified and held his head up strong, even though I could see, far away as I were, red in his eyes and damp on his cheeks. I felt bad then, I spose. For doing summat that'd made these people so gutted. But there was nowt

I could do. They were upset cause they had no clue what Phil was. Specially Julia. If she'd of known his secrets she would of never gone near him.

I saw the priest bless the casket. People threw in soil and trailed by. Sobs got louder. And then they were gone. As the group trailed down the hill and turned into a black smudge by the gate, I went over to Phil's grave. I took a bit of soil from the edge and chucked it in. Then I found a stone and wellied it one at the casket so's it hit with a right crack. I'd attracted attention then but didn't notice. I leaned over the grave and spat in it. My own special Kerrie Hill blessing.

'Oi, you! That's sacrilege,' came a voice from behind me. I turned and saw a man running at me with a shovel in his hand. One of the diggers. I strode over the gaping mouth of Phil's grave and made a run for it.

I pegged it down the hill, gravity throwing me out of control past the graves and flowers and memorial benches. My arms and legs were light as air. It felt like I was flying. I ran through the gates and cut a line through the funeral party. I look back now and think of how it must of looked. This flying bit of red shooting through the black smudge like a knife was slashing into someone's sleeve. I wish I could of watched it from the top of the hill.

It were a few months after that when I caught my mam sneaking out the back door with a packed bag. I was fifteen and three months old. She looked like a kid who was running off. It reminded me of a story Mark'd told me, about how he'd fell out with his mam when he was ten and said he was going to leave home. She'd laughed at him and said, 'Go on then,' thinking he'd bottle it and storm back up to his room. He'd got a pound his uncle'd given him, and he'd spent it all on 'Lucky Bags', them things what you used to get with sweets and a toy in them. That was what the row was over. So he'd filled a carrier bag full of clothes and took his Lucky Bags and stood waiting on the road outside his front door.

'What yer waiting for?' his mam'd asked him.

'A taxi,' Mark'd said.

We'd had a right giggle over this story when Mark told it me, that he'd thought he could pay for a taxi with a quid's worth of Lucky Bags or summat. But it wasn't funny finding my mam stood there in the back doorway, clutching a filled-up bin liner with a sheepish expression all over her sickly-looking mug.

'Where the fuck you going?' I said, blocking the door in front of her. I was on my way in from a rave and it showed how much notice she took of my comings and goings if she'd not been expecting this on a Sunday morning. She was out on it.

'I've got ter go, Kez. The police is after us. They'll have me up fer stuff you lot've done,' she said.

I rolled my eyes. I didn't know where she could of got the idea the police were after her and I said so.

'I just know it Kez, I can feel it in here,' Mam said, touching her breastbone. I would of been tempted to believe her if I thought she had owt resembling a heart where she was pointing. I faced up to her and made me-sen big as I could, blocking across the door so's she couldn't go nowhere. Gone were the days when I was scared of the back of my mam's hand. She could only just about hold it still long enough to melt down her smack and inject it, and that was the truth.

'Yer fucking paranoid,' I said. Mam flinched away from me but didn't say owt. 'Who's going-ter look after Jon?

He's just a lickle kid and I'm not sixteen yet or owt,' I said.

'You're owd enough,' she said. I looked in her eyes, tried to see if there were owt there for me. If she gave a shit at all. The sockets were sunk and empty, like she was beginning to turn into a skull. All's I saw was hunger. She was a junkie first, not a mam. 'Yer killed that bloke,' she said. 'The one what wa-in the paper.' Then I realised. It wasn't no police she was scared of. It were me.

'Do what yer want,' I said.

She held out a twenty to me then. I looked at it like I'd never seen one before, didn't know what it were for. 'To tek care of yer dinner for a few days,' she said. I smirked and flicked her hand away.

'No, ta,' I said. She wasn't buying me off for a twenty. I moved out the way of the door and let her go. I could of stopped her. Mark would of helped me persuade her, promised to keep her lined up with everything she needed and all that shit. But I couldn't be arsed. She wasn't exactly much use to us, state she was in. I was well past caring. I watched her walk off, dragging this black bag after her like Dick Fucking Whittington. She was skinny as owt cause the only thing she got hungry for them days was the poppy. She made a right sorry sight walking up Whitwell Road like that. I almost felt bad about it.

So there I was. Still at school and not even sixteen with a lad of ten to look after. I wasn't even that much older than him. Don't get me wrong, Jon wasn't hard work, never had been, not since he was very little anyway. And I'd always done a lot for him being as my mam was such a waste of space. But being all he'd got, just like that without no warning, that wasn't easy to get my head round. For starters there was the small problem of school. He was due to go to senior school the next year but with Mam not round there wasn't no one to register him. If I went down they'd work out she'd gone and left us and then they'd put Jon and me in care cause I wasn't sixteen yet. Then there was the house, the rent to sort with the council so's they'd not notice she'd gone when the DSS stopped coughing up. We had to make sure they never found out she wasn't there no more and threw us out. Worst of all there was letting Jon in on it all, what'd happened, that his mam'd just walked out like that cause she didn't give a shit. I would of rather she'd of died and made us both orphans. That's what I'd tell everyone, I decided there and then, that we were orphans. That we'd always been. All this stuff went through my head as I stood there watching Sue Hill walk off, so's I got all dizzy with thinking and had to go and sit down at the kitchen table and rest my head on it. I was still a bit pilled to be totally honest, and I'm sure that didn't help.

Jon didn't get up till about ten, and I told him straight away. He looked up with them big brown eyes he'd got. I thought he might of cried or summat but he was well brave. He looked straight back at me and asked if he could go out and play football. I said okay, and he ran off out, and even though he didn't show it and Mam wasn't worth it, I could tell he was sad. I watched him go and meet his mates on the grassy area of the park. He was kicking the ball about but his head was down. He was a good footballer, moved dead natural. I was keeping an eye on him, though, but not just cause of Mam. He'd had some problems the last few weeks. It all boiled down to that he was the only mixed race kid on our close and there were no black ones at all. Some of the kids'd been calling him names – nigger, black bastard, and even Paki cause his skin was that coffee colour. Then they started chucking stones at him, which was going way too far. Mark'd lost it and went and waved a gun at the little shits. They didn't do it again. Now they ran round Jon like he was King of the World. That was okay, I spose, but I did give Mark an earful about the whole thing. First, you don't go waving guns at kids. That's the sort of stuff what gets you the wrong kind of attention. But mostly it were that Jon didn't need his sister's mate to go wading in. He needed to take care of his-sen, or he'd never learn how and that wouldn't of been no good.

Next thing I knew, me and Mark'd got it together again. Anyone could of seen it coming, I'm sure. We'd been getting closer and closer, then Mam left and I needed someone. She was a pile of crap as a mam and there was no way I wanted her back but it still left a space in my life. It's hard to explain. I didn't feel sad and wasn't scared neither. It were more like summat'd been moved from the back of me, like a shield'd been took down so's I could of got hurt or summat. And Mark was tall and warm and tough enough to make me feel protected.

He came round that afternoon after Mam'd walked off. I was still sitting at the kitchen table, drinking a cup of tea and staring into space. I couldn't get my arse into gear ner nowt. He came in and must of seen summat was wrong cause he sat down opposite me and didn't say owt, just took hold of one of my hands. After a few minutes just holding my hand, he touched my cheek.

'What's gone off?' he said.

The words came out like water from a tap, and I told him about my mam running off and everything I thought about it. Mark stood up then and came round behind where I was sat at the kitchen table. He rubbed my shoulders and I leaned forward to let him. Let it ease off all the hassle. Then he pulled me up to my feet and tried to hug me.

'I don't need no cuddles,' I told him, pulling away. But I did, see, and he knew me well enough to know that. He pulled me into him and was a load stronger than me so's it wasn't much use resisting. At first I felt suffocated and choked by being squashed against him. Then I let it all go. Relaxed and let him hold me. Let him try and make me feel better. I had a good sob too, which I'd been resisting, but after it felt like summat'd gone, flown off into the wind. My whole body felt lighter, better. I knew it'd be all right with this big, strong man on my side. He'd take care on me, that were obvious.

Over the next week or so Mark held me a lot and I didn't resist no more. It felt good to be cared for, to be close to another person. I'd missed that. My mam and mommar had given it me when I was little, and I got it from Jon if he was in the right kind of mood, but this was different. I was falling in love with Mark. I noticed my skin tingle when he came close, and I realised that if I thought about him when he wasn't round it sent shivers all over me.

It were about a fortnight later when he kissed me proper for the first time in years. I guess what'd happened between us before made him hesitate, plus he knew my head was all messed up from that shit with Phil. We were rolling on pills when it happened, like that's a surprise. Dancing in my front room about four in the morning, with 'I Got The Power' turned up full. We were going mad and waving our arms in the air. Then he grabbed me and it were different. He pulled me close. Then he kissed me.

We were soon in bed together. Before I started going with Mark, I'd never realised what sex could be like. With Phil it were all just clumsy tumbles, stuff what'd got him off and not me and I didn't know no better to suggest owt else. Mark wanted the first time between us to be extra special so he got some powder. Pure MDMA, cut with nowt I can tell you from the way it sent us. He drove all the way down the A1 to this place in Essex to pick up a batch, get some to sell on too. The pills we were getting them days weren't so good as they used to be. It were really hard to get proper decent stuff, what sent me and Mark hyper. We were too used to pills and, yeah, you could double drop and all that, but some of the things the pills were cut with made your tummy go funny. Mark laid a gram of the powder out on the dressing table with a big bottle of Lucozade Energy. We thought you'd take it the same way as cocaine, given it were powder, so we sorted it into lines like we'd both seen other people do. Then Mark tried to snort it but that hurt, so we dabbed big fingerfuls on our tongues and washed it down quick as we could cause the taste was nasty. Mark reckoned he'd burnt his tongue on the shit.

We laid down together and talked for a bit, waiting for the powder to kick in. Mark played with my hair, flicking strands up so's they tickled my neck and shoulders. We talked about my mam and Jon, stuff we needed to do about it. Course, the inevitable happened and we were soon loved up, our jaws clenching and our heads filled with happy thoughts. Every inch of my skin tingled and his fingers felt like silk on my arms and legs. Sex is great when you're rolling. You're really up for it and have a load of energy so it gets pretty frantic. And your whole body feels orgasmic anyway, so sensitive and full of pleasure that trying to cum becomes a bit of a nonsense. And it's more than just sexy. The pair on you move together, think together, and it's all sweet as owt you could ever think of. If Mark and me'd of been pissed we might of forgot to bother with condoms or summat. But our heads were clear and sharp as normal and we were well careful. The first time we made love it were with me on top. And it were making love, not like when most people use these words. So much love neither on us knew what to do with it. Mark's hands swept over my skin, making swirling patterns I could almost see. The path where his fingers'd been tingled, the feelings they left behind dissolving into me like sugar on a hot plate.

It's too easy to fall for each other when you both use MDMA. A month on and Mark'd moved in.

FIFTEEN

When Mark walked up my path with that big suit-case it changed my life completely. His mum'd been dead against it, said I was too young for him and all that again. But Mark told her he was old enough to make his own decisions and there wasn't much she could do about it. She could of gone and told the council that my mam'd ran off but she wasn't no callous bitch. Besides, you did stuff like that round our way then people set against you. They broke your windows and phoned for cabs or pizza what you hadn't ordered in the middle of the night. So she tried to persuade Mark not to move out but when she realised he was set on it she kept her mouth shut. The few months after that were the best in my life. It were like having a proper family for the first time. Mark was always there, and doing stuff round the place. He put up shelves, and mended Jon's chest of drawers what'd been broke for as long as I could remember. Me and Mark and Jon, we were always together, a nuclear unit what no one could break up. Mark took much better care on us than anyone I'd ever known.

Mark and me cooked dinners. He knew how to use a pan and taught me loads about how to make stuff. Spaghetti bolognaise, chicken curry. His mam'd trained him well, I said. He made lasagna too, baked it in the oven with meat and cheese sauce. It makes me laugh to think of it now, how I'd never tried owt like that before. I thought it were the most delicious thing I'd ever ate. Mark told me all the best chefs were blokes so's it wasn't women's work at all. He wouldn't wash up though. And I wasn't having none of that, I was no one's slave. We bought a dishwasher so's we didn't argue. It felt like we were a normal family. Cept of course we made our money a bit of a different way compared to most people.

We sorted the stuff we needed to. We didn't tell the council Mam'd gone but searched out the rent book and made sure it always got paid in cash. Same with the bills. We didn't have no money worries, not in our line of work. Don't get me wrong, we didn't make as much as you might of thought – we weren't exactly big fish. But we were comfortable, could afford nice stuff. We got a Playstation and a load of games, the best video player we could get hold of and a big telly. Jon had all the best stuff to play with, and the right trainers with the right name on them an-all. It made me proud to be able to get him them things. And living on the estate was ace. I liked the way people looked up to us, knew we weren't to be messed with. I liked the park, right in front of the window so's I could watch Jon play. It were other things too. Like the time Mark'd come back with a car he'd bought.

'What d-yer want a car for?' I said. It were a right old banger too, this green Datsun Sunny shit thing. I don't know what he'd paid for it. 'When do we use a car?' I said. Mark shrugged. He knew I was right. We didn't move

from the estate as such, spent all our time round our
house or at friends, or in the club at Six Ways. We went
into town from time to time, usually more for work than
for play, but more often than not we could get someone
to give us a lift and, if we couldn't, there wasn't owt wrong
with the buses what went from the end of Lindfield. Thing
about round our way was you could swap stuff quite easy.
It would of been a right pain in the arse to have to adver-
tise the shitty car Mark'd bought in the *Post* and have
people come by and look and tut and try and get you to
put the price down. But by the end of the same afternoon, Mark had it swapped for a karaoke machine what
we all loved, and it were fun to play when you'd took
summat. Money wasn't the only currency where we were.
And we had plenty of currency to get any stuff we wanted.

That was a good summer. Maybes not as hot as the ones
when I was a kid but the sun came out loads. I guess I
looked on any bad weather we had with a light heart,
thanks to being so in love at the time. So it were raining?
I could stay in with my man, get trashed and make love.
The rave scene got huge that year and they called it the
second summer of love. It were my first though. Mark and
me got up in the morning and drank real coffee, ate them
French chocolate bread things. We had barbecues and
invited over our mates, cracking open beers and charring
meat on the grill. Mark bought steak, which he made us
eat rare. I didn't like it at first, the blood seeping out
when you cut it with a knife, but I got used to it. Like a
lot of stuff, it were an acquired taste. Sometimes me and
Mark sat on chairs in the garden and sipped wine like we
were a normal, middle-class couple.

Mark gave me a family life, summat I'd never had. In
lots of ways I can look back now and say we were kids

playing at mums and dads and there's some truth in that. But it didn't matter. We were happy. Even when we hadn't took pills or owt we acted loved up like we were on one. I'd be loading up the dishwasher and he'd run in like a little boy and grab me, start biting at my neck. Or I'd see him playing Mortal Combat and I'd jump on him and we'd be snogging like crazy on the floor. It wasn't about sex, none of it, it were kissing for the sake of trying to connect. I couldn't help me-sen when I saw him, I just had to grab hold and he was just the same.

Course, with the rave scene kicking off like it did, there was loads of work on. It wasn't just clubs no more, but huge parties in fields and warehouses. Thousands of people in the same place and all wanting to get sorted. That was my side of the business and I took care on it me-sen. Mark had his own bits and pieces to look after, the more hardline stuff. There were gangs what tried to take over and control all the dealing at the big parties so's I had to be careful. But I was sneaky. Made it look like I was just another raver, in part cause I was. I had all the right stuff too, the long white gloves, a dummy to chew on when my jaw went all funny. I danced and blew on this whistle and had a great old time. Perks of the job.

I had this one close call. This big bouncer type came bowling over to me after I'd given this lad a pill. He thought he was well hard, and I'll bet he was tooled up though he never got out no gun or knife ner nowt. I was quick about it and took hold of this bloke's hand, made out he was my boyfriend. Course, you can do that at a rave. The bloke was loved up on pills and happy to cuddle anyone. The fat bloke left us alone then, said he must of got the wrong idea. I looked young still and I think that helped me. No one really thought a little gell like me'd be dealing. The bloke walked off and I put my dummy in my mouth, chewed on it.

Mark'd been smoking brown regular for ages, in joints and sometimes chasing, but now he was injecting it too. Mixing it with water and heating it on foil or a spoon, sucking up the nectar with a needle and shooting it up his veins. I watched him sometimes and summat weird struck me. The whole thing looked a bit like Mrs Ivanovich's butterflies, the way they got pollen out of flowers. You could see what he saw in it too. The effect was immediate. Everything loosened and he'd slump in his chair, like the way I went if I was pilled and he rubbed my shoulders. You could almost see his cares lift off him and fly out the window. His eyes misted over, pools of rain I could of drowned in. He'd reach out for me then, hold me so gentle you'd think he wasn't capable of hurting owt so much as a little ant on the floor. The way he held me then, I almost got a second-hand hit from his skag. I didn't mind it back then, not really, it were just drugs and that was how we made a living after all. And I wasn't worried about AIDS, despite all the gravestone-falling-over ads what'd been out, cause Mark never shared needles with no one. Thought that was well dirty. I wasn't worried about him getting addicted neither cause it were way too late to be thinking about that. There are better battles to fight, ones you can win. When someone gets into heroin it pushes out their soul and shacks up inside and there's no getting rid on it, not without tearing them apart in a nasty, painful way.

It were that summer I left school. I saw it out right to the end, but that was mainly for the business I did in the playground, I have to be honest. I got a few GCSEs though, which was more than most people at my school did. Biology, Chemistry and CDT. I loved CDT, making real stuff from wood or metal or plastic. Sanding the wood down so's you could run your finger along it without even one splinter jarring against you. Covering it with varnish so's it shone. Melting plastic and bending it into the shapes you want it. I even liked the planning bit, though most of the kids hated that and the class used to go apeshit round me. I let them, sitting with my paper, staring at the blank sheet. It were that moment I loved, the paper in front of you without no marks to spoil it. It seemed to me when I looked at that white space that owt were possible. Anything at all.

I was glad to leave, though. We all were. It were a shit hole, that school, plus the place I'd met Tyneside to the bargain. Mark helped me make hash cookies the night before my last day, another one of his mam's recipes. I gave them out for free to everyone from my class at break time. It were like when you have a birthday in primary school. We ate them in the yard then went hyper. It were the hottest day of the year and the sun screamed down on us. We signed our names all over each other's shirts so's we'd remember them. Then we threw water bombs made from carrier bags all over each other, blurring the autographs before the day was even over. The gells walked round with their bras showing like a wet T-shirt contest. The lads made sure the blouses didn't get chance to dry out.

What it were about that day what I loved so much was we acted five again. Like it were our first day at school and not our last. Before I'd ever gone to school, I'd run free round our huge backyard and the park out front, and even Mrs Ivanovich's garden too like a wild gell. Then they'd made me settle and sit down at a desk. I'd never took to that, not really. I was free again when I got to sixteen, allowed to fly off and be wild. Course, it wasn't like that for any of the other kids. Quite a few of the gells'd left already, stuck at home with kids, just like I could of been. Then there was them from better backgrounds, with proper homes and mams and dads what were behind them. Most of them were going to do the Youth Training Scheme, working sixty hours somewhere for their dole money, a right rip off. For most of them this was their last chance to run round and throw water at other kids. I didn't ask to be dragged into this world what I lived in, selling stuff round the estate and in town, but I have to admit there was some good things about it. It were a right high point, that day in the playground. I'd sorted my weird new family, and was running round like a kid. I was buzzing, but not from any drug. It wasn't even the hash, it were a much bigger high than that'd of given me. Bigger than ecstasy, even the MDMA powder Mark sometimes got for us. It took me a while to work out what it were and when I did I laughed and laughed. I was happy, that was all, simple as that. Best high ever.

The sun beat down. My shirt clung to me, a mess of water and smudged ink. I ran. And ran and ran and ran like I was flying.

SIXTEEN

Feeling wasted became an occupational hazard for me. My job was offloading as much ecstasy as I could and to do that I had to rave my little head off. To stay awake and alert all night I needed at least a couple of pills me-sen. And besides owt else the E-plan diet kept me skinny, the way Mark liked me. All's I wanted to do when I was on one was dance and have sex and stay up till the sunrise without eating owt. I have to admit I ended up snogging other blokes from time to time. Mark would of killed me and the blokes if he'd of ever found out, I know that. But the way I saw it I couldn't help me-sen. You get so touchy feely and one thing leads to another. It were another hazard, that was all, and I'd be boggered if I was going to feel bad about it.

What did bother me, though, was the types Mark was getting in with. People like my mam who'd sell their kids for a hit of smack. Mark never got like that, not when I knew him anyhow, but these types he hung round with were frightening. I tried to get out the house when they were round. When I did stay in I watched them file into the living room like a bunch of ghosts, all pale and skinny so's they didn't fill their clothes. There was a layer of grease on their skin, a yellow pallor what lit up their faces in this weird shit way. And there was summat else. A hunger in their eyes, like they would do owt for their next hit. A lot of them carried knives too and it made me dead nervous. They were the sort of ghosts what you should of been scared of.

This one Monday morning I was sat in the kitchen coming down. I felt hollow inside, emptied out like I was just a shell and a pulse. I felt like shit to tell you the truth. I drank coffee and that didn't help, making me shake and my heart thump hard against my breastbone. When I leaned back against the kitchen chair I could feel the wood vibrate against me. Jon was burning toast and asked me if I wanted some. I didn't feel hungry ner nowt though.

'Can I come out wi-yer one weekend?' Jon asked me.

'What so's you can end up feeling shit, like what I do?' I said. He'd caught me at a weak moment, but not that weak. 'Yer way too young,' I said.

'You was using and dealing when you was my age. Regular,' Jon said.

I shook my head. 'I was meking deliveries, and helping Mark out, but not at shit like raves. And I wan't teking much. Who said owt else?'

'Mark.'

'Well you shun't listen to him. Anyways, you're getting a proper job. Summat what won't get you into trouble,' I said.

Jon sat there, munching his blackened toast and staring me out. 'How do I do that then? Wi-out going ter school ner-nowt?' he said.

'I'll sort you a tutor,' I said.

Jon went out the room then, shutting the door a bit harder than normal on his way. It wasn't a full-on slam but enough to make sure I knew he wasn't happy with that idea. I skinned up a joint. I needed summat to help me chill. Yeah, a tutor, I thought. Then Jon could get some real exams behind him and do summat good with his life. He had some brains, did Jon, like me, and I didn't want him to end up using them the way I'd had to. And I wanted summat to get him out the way from twelve till two. That was when Mark's cronies came over, the half-dead junkies what he based his side of the business on. They used our back room to shoot up that shit. Mark didn't make Jon stay out the room when they were shooting up, though he wasn't even twelve yet. It were fucking me off but to do owt about it'd of meant a big row and I couldn't be arsed with that. It'd just make life easier if there was summat Jon had to keep him occupied through all that. I could afford it easy.

I would of just sent him to school but it wasn't an option. The education welfare sent letters to my mam and I sent them back 'not at this address' which was true. When they came round I made Jon hide behind the sofa and told them she'd gone off to Newcastle and took the little boy with her. I was sixteen by then and might of been allowed to look after him, cept with my history, being in the EMHG and all that, I doubted it. I wasn't taking that risk. Wasn't having him put into care, not for no one.

I heard the door go, saw the back of Jon's head go through the gate. I wondered where he was off to. Probably to cause trouble with some other kids. I remember being Jon's age, the shit we got up to. Writing our names in twelve-inch letters under railway arches. Breaking into people's sheds and nicking stupid stuff out their gardens, gnomes and ornamental wheelbarrows and that kind of crap. We used to go out breaking glass at night. A beer bottle cracking open on the edge of a kerb, a dead sound like someone's skull breaking. A brick through a warehouse window. A stone or boot through a car windscreen, glass cascading and making pretty patterns like you get behind your eyes on a mushroom trip. That was my favourite. It were the sound I liked, the shh, shh, scream as the glass stretched and cracked and flew inside and outside the car. And, if you got lucky, the sudden shout of a car alarm breaking the monotony of the night. Then you were awake. Wide awake.

I wasn't wide awake now but sleepy, coming right down. I dragged me-sen upstairs and collapsed in the bed without brushing my teeth or washing my face ner nowt. As I dropped off I felt empty, like part of me'd floated off through the window. I had that thing going off where you feel like you're falling and jolt in bed. Then I was asleep, and dreaming of butterflies.

We found Robert cause he'd put an ad in the paper saying he was good for English and Maths tuition at all levels. I spoke to him on the phone and he said he was a supply teacher but was looking for summat more stable. I didn't blame him. I wouldn't of wanted to go into them classrooms full of kids who didn't even know me and most of them didn't have much time even for the good teachers. I'd been on the other side of that, and I wouldn't wish it on no one. I put on my best jeans and even a bit of makeup the first time he was coming over. I didn't want to look like a tramp.

We'd arranged that he'd come over about twelve every afternoon, just before Mark's junkies did, so it'd keep Jon out the way. At about quarter-to there was this knock at the door. I checked my hair in the mirror on the way to answer, I don't know why. I opened the door and he stood there, all wrapped up in this suit with a briefcase by his side. I laughed.

'What's funny?' he said.

'You in that get up, round here,' I said. Then I looked at him proper, past the suit. Them clothes men wear are just to hide in. He had a way with him, I could see that even then. He was six foot two with thin blond hair, receding a bit at the temples. He should of been dead good looking cause he had huge blue eyes and lips like Elvis Presley but it didn't quite work out on account of the hairline. Still, the way he looked at me freaked me out, the frown what settled between his big blue eyes, the smile he was showing off. The posh voice, cutting through the air like it meant business. But I'd learned by then. I looked away and shook my head. The only bloke I trusted with my heart was Mark.

I showed Robert through to the dining room, and shouted Jon down to work with him. He slid into the room and it were obvious he didn't want to be there. I'd promised him all sorts if he did as he was told and tried his hardest. Robert took this test thing out and Jon sat and did it. I could tell by the way he screwed up his eyes he was trying his hardest. I chatted to Robert as Jon worked.

'Where you from then?' I said.

'Reigate. It's near London,' he said. I didn't like London. It were full of wankers who thought too much of themselves. He must of seen this in my face. 'It's on the way to Brighton,' he said. I didn't say owt. I noticed his gaze move to my tiny bookshelf above the old 'gram. 'What are those books then?' he said.

I pulled one out. I hadn't looked at them for ages. I brushed the dust off the cover and passed it over. The pictures were a bit dated now, the stuff people were wearing and even the colours seemed to have aged.

'The rainforest,' he said. 'Have you been there?'

I snorted. 'What d'yer think?' I said.

'You want to go?' he said.

'Was that an invite?'

He laughed then, and Jon tutted then shushed us. 'I'm tryna work,' he said.

I didn't take no notice of Jon and sat round and chatted to Robert the whole lesson. I called him Rob after a bit, and he seemed to like it. I read the books about the Amazon with him and sat too close, shifting in my seat at the half smiles he threw round. Just goes to show how young I saw Jon as being, that I didn't credit him with the nouse to notice us flirting, but I was a bit daft like that towards him.

It were after that I started to put money away. Talking to Rob about the rainforest'd set me off and I wanted to see it for real, watch butterflies and swing on lianas. That was why I liked him coming, really, more than owt else. I couldn't talk to Mark about this shit. I'd tried to, but he just lost interest and stared past my head at the telly. I bought this pull-along suitcase thing and started filling it up with cash. Mark'd forgot all about Mrs Ivanovich's poison but I hadn't. It were still buried in the garden, cept I had more idea what sort of stuff I might end up using it for now, line of business we were in. I buried the suitcase next to it one afternoon, while Mark was sleeping off a big hit of that shit he took. It were the one thing you could rely on, that he'd sleep for ages after if he took smack. He only took the very best, nice and pure and white as fresh snow. He kept three stashes, this, and then the ones he cut with other rubbish. I never asked what. Didn't want to know.

I dug up the case every week or so and added more cash. Plan was, I'd fill it so much I'd have to sit on it to close it. Then I'd be able to go. Get my arse off to South America somewhere and leave all this behind. Even then I doubted I'd take Mark cause I knew it were just a matter of time before the junkie in him took over. But I planned to take Jon with me. It would be an adventure we could go on, the pair on us, and look for somewhere we fitted in cept this shithole of a place.

It wasn't just that Rob'd put them ideas back into my head, it were other stuff too. Things with our business were getting hairy then, and I was scared, for Mark specially. Like I said, them as was into brown what he sold, they were psychos. And there was this new toy on the street then, specially treated cocaine what you smoked in a bong. Crack. It's old news now, I know, but it wasn't back then. Mark'd got hold of a load on it to sell, and was using it as well. I didn't like the way it sent people, this drug. They went high enough, but with it came summat else. The animal, like what came over Mark without any drugs from time to time. There were already a few addicts on the estate. They were people your worst nightmares are made of. Werewolves. Bogeymen. Horses what come along at ten o'clock and do God knows what all to the children who are still awake. This one night we'd been on our way home when I got properly shitted up about the situation. All's I saw was this kid running across the road with summat shiny in his hand. I didn't notice it were a knife till the little shit got close and started slashing at my boyfriend's jacket. Mark turned and belted the sod one, left him in a heap on the floor. But his hand was shaking as he unlocked our door five minutes later. His puffer jacket was shredded, the foam leaking out like pus.

The next day we went to this DIY place on Derby Road. 'We need some security,' Mark said, getting out these catalogues. He must of had an idea about all this, that we needed to sort summat out, cause he'd had these books a while and marked them all up. I wondered what'd happened to him before. Anyway, we got this dan video camera what could record hours of stuff. Mark said we could use it to have a laugh too, make a few home videos.

'Some special-uns, maybes,' he said, and winked at me so's I giggled.

It were dead funny to watch Mark struggle with a drill to put the bogger up, a joint sticking out the side of his mouth as he tried to push the drill into the wall. He caught the look on my face and giggled, and then we were both laughing. Soon we were rolling on the grass in our front garden, all over each other, the drill going off by its-sen on the front doorstep, making a right racket. The middle-aged cow what lived a couple of doors down tutted as she passed our front yard but neither on us could of given a flying fuck for her opinion.

It were about a week after when they found that bloke in his own wheelie bin. The picture in the paper looked like the kid who'd had a go at Mark but I couldn't be sure, it'd been too dark that night. Whoever'd done for him was a psycho bastard. They'd stabbed him over and over then tried to cut him all up, so's they could get rid of him I spose. They didn't have the guts for the job, though, so just left a load of holes in him. Nasty bastards.

I know Mark'd gone too far with Phil but this was summat else. Well, it wasn't till much later that I even considered much else about it.

After that wheelie bin thing, Mark slept with a hammer hung on a chain round his neck. It were another thing he'd had on his list for the DIY shop but he hadn't started using it right away. It made me nervy laying next to him with that huge metal bastard hung round his neck like it were some fucked up St Christopher pendant. I watched him sleep, breathing so deep he was almost snoring, and sometimes with his eyes doing that REM thing what meant he was dreaming. And I wondered. What if he had a nightmare and didn't know what he was doing, turned on me with his hammer?

It were round then I found out Jon'd been going to Mark behind my back. I caught them smoking spliffs together and wasn't happy with neither of them. I'd tried to bribe Jon about the lessons, but Mark kept buying him the shit he wanted anyway. Then Jon moaned on and on about having to do the work and Mark told him to shut it. When Jon realised this wasn't working, he tried a different tack.

'I think that tutor nob fancies our Kez,' he said. We were sitting in the front room watching *Eastenders* and passing round a doobie. 'Ooh, do you want to go to the rainforest with me?' Jon said, trying to take off Rob's accent and not making that bad a job on it.

'Shut it,' I said. 'He was just being friendly.' Mark was passing the joint on to Jon and I knocked it out his hand and onto the floor.

'What do yer think you doing?' I said. But he looked straight past me and picked the joint up, passed it back to my brother.

'Maybes I should be asking you that,' Mark said, glaring at me. I didn't like his eyes set on me like that and touched my chest, thinking of the hammer he held next to his skin at night. 'Yeah, I'd whittle, if I were you and I were up to summat,' he said.

'I'm not up to owt,' I told him. But for some reason I felt dead bad about what Jon'd said.

I was extra careful the next time Rob came over. I ushered him through to the back room and shut the door sharp so's there was just him and Jon in there. I walked off but the door opened behind me.

'Aren't you going to join us today?' It were Rob. He threw me that winning smile and I shivered.

'I'm busy,' I said.

'It won't be the same without our chat,' he said. 'Perk of the job.' I wondered what was wrong with me that I always fell for this middle-class charm school shit.

'I an't got much interesting to say,' I said. I noticed I touched my own hair as I said this, like a flirty little gell. I didn't like the way his voice made me feel. Then Jon appeared behind Rob, touching his dreads all effeminate, making fun of me. I could of swung for the bogger.

The next day Jon wasn't even there. He'd sodded off somewhere with his mates and I couldn't find him.

'Well no point wasting our time. Why don't you do some studying today?' Rob said. I laughed all nervous and touched my chest like I'd done when Jon'd tried to stir it with Mark.

'Me?' I said. 'There in't much point in that.'

'I'm sure there is,' Rob said, and he grinned at me.

We sat down at the dining table and Rob got out a couple of books he'd brought to work with Jon. 'These are a bit easy for you but never mind. What's your favourite subject?' he said.

'Biology. Well, entomology really,' I said.

He started then, and looked up at me sharp. He laughed. 'Entomology, huh?' he said with this big thick grin all over his mug.

'Yeah, what's wrong wi-that?' I said.

'It just wasn't the answer I was expecting,' he said.

'Yeah well, we in't all ignorant boggers round here,' I said. And I felt me-sen purse my lips like the middle-aged cow next door but one.

'Entomology, then,' Rob said. And he wrote a test for me on his notepad. It were easy stuff, specially the first few questions. How many legs he started with, and the difference between insects and other bugs like spiders. These questions made me snort out loud and there wasn't one thing he wrote I couldn't answer.

'Do you want to travel, Kerrie-Ann?' he asked me then.

'Yeah, I do, more than owt. I want to go to Brazil,' I told him.

'I'm going to take some time out and travel,' he said. I wasn't sure but the way he said it and how he turned his head, it were like an invite.

Then Mark walked in with this junkie mate of his. I didn't know the bloke's name. I didn't know any of their names, made a point of not talking to them. 'Where's Jon?' Mark said. I didn't know if he'd been on heroin or crack and it were important to suss this, cause it made all the difference as to whether he was going to lose it or not. The way he rolled his eyes and swayed a bit made me think crack, and I hoped not.

'He's sodded off,' I said. 'We're hoping he'll come back.'

'Wanta do some brown wi-me, schoolboy?' Mark asked Rob. He grimaced at the tutor.

'No ta,' said Rob, clearing up his stuff. He turned to me. 'I'd better go, then.' I nodded at him. He picked up his briefcase and walked towards the door. Mark blocked his way.

'It in't time to go yet. And you was staying before I came back,' he said. He turned to me. 'Any truth in the crap Jon was spouting about this nob the other day?'

'Did we look like we was shagging?' I said.

'Yer looked pretty cosy ter me,' Mark said. He turned to his junkie mate. 'Wan't they nice-an cosy back then?' he said. The bloke nodded. Then Mark pushed Rob to the side of the door and nodded his head back towards it. 'Gerrout Kez,' he said.

'I'm not going nowhere,' I said.

'Fine. Then we'll do it in front-a yer,' he said.

Mark grabbed Rob by the shoulders and pushed him over to the table. He was smaller than the tutor but that didn't matter cause he was so psycho and out on it. He pushed the poor bastard's hands down on the table.

'Grab hold on that,' he said to his mate. The junkie bloke held Rob's hands down. It were like summat out of *Reservoir Dogs*. Mark took the hammer from round his neck and lifted it into the air.

I closed my eyes every time the hammer hit. I heard Rob screaming, the sound of bone cracking.

When Mark'd finished, the junkie bloke let Rob go. He wasn't crying, I'll give him credit, but he let out little yelps, like a dog being kicked. He was all dignified though and picked up his briefcase. It were painful to watch, the way he had to grip it with the palms of his hand. His fingers were all swollen and red. I wanted to think they'd get all better in the end but wasn't sure how it worked when your fingers'd been smashed to bits. I didn't want to think about it much.

Rob walked out the door and the bogger smiled at me. Talk about a death wish. He was lucky Mark didn't clock him.

We all stood there in the dining room till we heard the front door click. This junkie mate of Mark's had a sick grin on his mug. I didn't know where to look or what might happen next. Mark came over. He cupped my chin in his hand and made me look into his eyes.

'Don't you ever go leaving me gell,' he said. 'I couldn't handle it.' And he grinned this crackhead grin at me, his eyes all shiny that way coke makes them. Then he winked, like it were all the biggest joke in the world.

He'd said this before to me, about leaving him, used pretty much the same words. But it'd been different then. I didn't know exactly what he meant by it this time, the way he'd said it an-all. But there was one thing I did know. It wasn't good. If he found out what I was on with in the back garden I'd have to run, and run fast.

SEVENTEEN

This one morning we were sitting round getting some breakfast when there was this ringing at the doorbell. It went right through me, specially with all the other stuff what'd been going off. It wasn't the normal time for Mark's junkies to be coming round. We'd been nervous as hell since that shit'd gone down with Rob. He was the sort what might go to the police, even though that'd of been one of the stupidest things he could of done.

'You expecting anyone?' Mark said to the pair on us. I shrugged back and Jon said no. Mark looked at me all intense and I returned the look. The corners of his eyes folded over as he frowned, a cute look I hadn't seen much compared to the animal what set over his face sometimes. He got up and went into the other room, and I followed not far behind. He switched on the telly, turning it to the channel set up for the security camera. We saw a couple standing outside our door, junkie types. It wasn't no one who usually bought from Mark, and I thought they must of been tipped off to come see us. Mark went to answer the door.

'It's for you,' he said, coming back in the kitchen where I'd sat me-sen back down in front of some toast. He nicked a bit, and sat down with the paper.

'Me?' I said. 'Who the hell is it then?'

Mark shrugged. 'Din't ask,' he said, through a mouthful of my toast.

The woman at the door was well skinny, and had that look about her what told me she was a junkie. Clothes what hung from her body, rough skin, pockmarked all over, tracks showing on the bits of arm poking out from under the sleeves of her jumper. I didn't know her so I looked at the bloke she was with. I'd been wrong when I looked at the telly. Unlike the gell, he wasn't a junkie. His skin was nice and olive, shiny, his teeth white. His eyes were sparky, like he was looking round and taking everything in. No way was he into brown or he wouldn't of been so healthy. I didn't know him neither though.

'Can I help you?' I said.

'Kez?' the gell said. She examined my face as if she was expecting me to recognise her. 'It's me, sweetie.'

The only thing left of the gell I used to know was that voice, dripping with money. It were Bek from the EMHG.

'Oh my God,' I said. And I walked out and hugged my mate. I could feel how she was all skin and bone and she smelled a bit like sick, so I soon drew back. 'You better come in,' I said. I stared dead careful at her as she came through the door, trying to see any resemblance to my mate from the gell's home. It were there, the same features, nose and eyes and all that. But her skin was awful. I mean, she would of been about twenty by then, but she looked closer to thirty-five. It were sad to see it.

Bek introduced me to the man who was with her. His name was Duggy and he was her fiancé. He was dressed all street in a hooded top and shell bottoms, and had the bolshy accent like Mark and Jon. But there were summat about him didn't ring true. The clothes were too new, and his voice didn't quite sound right. It were like he was an actor playing the part of an estate kid. But maybes it's just hindsight has me say that.

We went through to the kitchen and I put on the kettle.

'This is me mate Bek from that gells' home I was in for a bit,' I said to Mark and Jon. 'And her bloke Duggy,' I added. Mark nodded at the pair of them. Jon grunted hello. 'Tea or coffee?' I said.

'We got some beer,' Mark said, walking up to the fridge and getting some out, cracking them open as if they was standard after-breakfast fare. He passed cans round and we all took one, even Jon. I frowned at Mark but didn't say owt. I'd never of made a fuss in front of company, not unless it were summat really bad. Mark would of killed me. He was busy producing various packages and laying them out on the table. He rolled a couple of joints. The first he melted hash on and stuck down, handed it to me. I lit it and took a big drag, noticed my hand shaking as I passed it on. It were so fucked up, seeing Bek here in my house looking the way she did. Mark rolled a second joint.

'This one's a special,' he said, winking at Bek. This was Mark's own word for a joint with heroin in it, but Bek got what he meant. Mark lit up and sent it past me to Bek, who took a couple of drags then handed it back to Mark, rather than on to Duggy. He held it out to Jon. That was way past the boundaries of my patience. There was no way I could let it pass and Mark knew it. It were like he was trying to wind me up in front of my mates. I grabbed the doobie from Jon's hand and passed it to Bek.

'You give that ter him again an I'll put it out on yer

face,' I said to Mark, who let out this gruff laugh. Then I turned to Bek and smiled, my mood turning on a coin. 'What you doing here? How'd you find out where I live?' I asked her.

Bek held the doobie to the side as she let out smoke from the corner of her mouth. 'It was Duggy, really. He'd heard about you through some friend.' She waved her hand round. 'You're well known round these parts.'

I smiled at that, wondered if it were good or bad.

'You've done a lot since you left that shithole in Loughborough,' she said.

'Yeah, we've done all sorts. You look like you have too,' I said.

Bek giggled, but it didn't sound at all lighthearted. She flicked her joint in the ashtray and looked away. 'You know me. I'm always after having a laugh, and'll pay what I need to get there. But I hear where you're coming from,' she said.

I felt shitty then. Bek'd been good to me in that place, and I didn't want to upset her now she'd sought me out. 'I have this thing about brown. It killed me mam,' I said. Jon and Mark looked over but didn't contradict me. So she wasn't dead, not so far as I knew, but she might as well of been. 'I like to have a laugh too. Just not brown,' I said to Bek.

'What you into then?' Duggy asked me.

''E mostly. Does more fer me,' I said.

'I see that,' he said. He sat tapping his fingers on the table. Then he said, 'You sell that too?' and I nodded.

'Remember that time you beat up that odd girl, in the home, the one who used to walk round muttering to herself?' Bek said.

'Yeah, that Paula bitch,' I said.

'Those carers were idiots. They didn't cotton on it was you even though they found you right outside the showers,' she said. We both smiled at the memory.

'You want a proper hit?' Mark asked her.

Bek shrugged. 'I've got no money,' she said.

'S'all right for an old mate-a Kez's. On the house,' he said. This was well out of character for Mark, it just wasn't summat he did. It made me wonder if he fancied Bek. Years before I would of bet on it. But by then . . . well, honestly, she looked a right mess. I wondered what he thought he'd get out of giving her free smack. The pair of them left the room, and Jon and me sat looking at Duggy, all uncomfortable.

'Want a pill?' I asked him, more to break the ice than owt.

'How much?' he said.

'On me,' I told him, following Mark's lead. We were selling them for about five or six quid by then in any case, got hold of them for a few quid a piece, so it wasn't much of a cost to me.

'Ta,' he said. And it struck me again he didn't seem quite real.

I gave Jon a pill too. By then he was taking them regular, and I didn't see no point in trying to stop him. It'd be too easy for him to get them elsewhere, they weren't exactly expensive. At least this way I knew he was getting decent pills without no crap in them. I'd educated him too. I'd done a lot of research, after I heard about some gell what died. Sip liquids so's you don't get dehydrated, but not too much cause that'll make you sick too, I'd told him. Isotonic drinks if you can get them, rather than just water. Then you'll be all right. He'd listened. Cause I was giving him a bit of freedom I spose, so he tried to keep me sweet.

That way we both got what we wanted.

Duggy took the pill off me and swallowed it down with a big slug of Lucozade and an exaggerated flip of the head. It struck me as an OTT way to take summat, but all's I thought was that he wasn't used to doing stuff and was fronting it. And that were part of the truth.

Bek and Mark came back then. I looked into my old mate's hazel eyes, the pupils like pinpricks, this glazed expression all over her face. Mark the same. The return of the evil dead, zombies from a crappy horror flick.

'Ever been riding?' Bek asked me. I shook my head. 'Jon?'

He shrugged. 'Spose,' he said. And I turned and glared at him. He shrivelled away from me and looked at Mark. It were beginning to feel like the two of them were ganging up on me.

'Lighten up. All teenagers are into it,' Bek said, touching my arm. She took my hand and led me to the door and I was reminded of that time she'd kissed me, when we'd both had a hit of coke.

We went out then and walked up Aspley, to that same road where Danny Morrison'd lived and we'd set him on fire. Like I said before, there was all these greens inbetween the houses and the roads. It made it easy to take cars from round there. People couldn't park nowhere near their houses and couldn't get out to stop no one if they saw them getting into their car.

Mark examined a few cars, looking through the windows like he knew summat about what he was doing. I could of laughed out loud about this, cause I knew he'd never done owt when it came to joyriding and didn't get why he had to act the expert. Again it made me wonder if he thought summat of Bek. Maybes it were a bloke thing I couldn't understand. Bek was ignoring him, though, doing her own thing. That much about her hadn't changed. Mark was going for the sporty-looking ones what you knew must of belonged to nobs. That was how I cottoned Bek knew exactly what she was on with. She was only looking at the Escorts and Cortinas.

'Easy to get into,' she told me. She looked specially hard at this silver Escort, then took this bit of coathanger out her pocket. In seconds the door was open. I gestured at Mark and Duggy. They were staring in the window of a BMW, looking like right crooks. They came over.

'You know how to trash an ignition column?' Bek asked me and I shook my head. She asked Mark for his hammer. He hesitated, but handed it over to her. She bashed the plastic below the steering column till it split open, then pulled out a couple of wires and touched them together. The engine growled alive and Bek pushed down on the pedal, making it roar. 'Get your arses in here,' she said to us.

We all climbed in the car. I made Jon fasten his seat-belt. He tutted and rolled his eyes at me.

'We're going joyriding,' he said.

'Yeah, well we need to talk about how much yer know on this joyriding lark,' I told him. And I gave him one of them looks of mine and he went all quiet. Everyone did.

Bek made the car fly off. It were the beginning of November and the air smelled sweet with bonfires and gunpowder. As we pegged it down the road, dead leaves shot up and danced round the car in the spinning air. They reminded me of walking to school when I was a kid. Leaves used to line the road and I'd crunch them up, and watch the gells who wore pinafores the same colour as the leaves were. They went to the Catholic school down the road, the one I'd gone to for a few days. When I tried to talk to any of them, they were jolted away by the arm. Their mams made it clear I was different to them.

We dumped the car on Denewood, set it on fire. It spluttered and sparked and added to the smoky air. All's I could think about was how lovely autumn smelled. As we walked home grinning, Bek put her arm round me.

'We got thrown out of this halfway house place, Duggy and me. Got nowhere to go,' she said.

'He's bin in prison too then?' I said, finding it hard to imagine. Bek nodded. I figured I owed her summat, the way she'd looked after me when I was in the gells' home. And I'd not realised till I saw her how I did miss her, even all them years on. 'The pair-a yer can stay wi-us,' I said.

'You sure, sweetie? I wouldn't want to impose.'

I nodded. 'Course I'm sure. Don't be ser daft.' And Bek kissed me on the cheek and I shivered. It wasn't like when she'd made me shiver before, hyper off coke in the EMHG, but cause she scared me to death. It proper creeped me out this gell what used to be so full and shiny and a picture of health could of ended up like this. Sunken-eyed, and bones covered in a layer of skin without hardly any fat. Shrivelled like a mummy. Well on the way to being a corpse. And I looked at Mark and saw he was the same too. That'd happened behind my back, when I wasn't looking. He was halfway dead. I thought about Morph, imagined him sitting on a branch then taking to the air, fluttering through the currents and getting buffeted here and there. I didn't look at Morph often them days. Didn't have to. In the case, hidden in my drawer, he was dead and dry behind glass. But in my head he was moist to the touch and could fly, suck nectar from flowers and land on branches, shutting his wings like he was saying a prayer. He was alive.

I thought about the money in my garden.

When we got home, it were obvious Duggy was tired. He kept yawning, and his eyes looked sore and red. He kept going on about how he needed his bed. I thought it were strange that he should be like that already, when he'd had the same I'd took. I was still in that mode where your eyes feel stuck open like you'll never need to sleep again. Course Bek and Mark were both ready to sleep too, but that made sense given they'd shot up brown. I wondered if Duggy was a heavy user, so's it didn't have the effect on him it used to. But it seemed unlikely, given how much I'd took over the years and I was still rolling. I sorted some bed linen for Duggy and Bek, showed them the spare room and where everything were. We didn't have a proper bed in there, just a blow-up mattress, but they both said they didn't care and that beggars couldn't be choosers and all that kind of thing. I left them to it.

I went downstairs and sat on the sofa. Jon'd gone to meet some mates and I wondered if he was going to steal another car. I could see what he liked about it, I was quite into doing it again me-sen. But I did worry about my little brother. I felt on my own. Not just that I was sitting in that room alone, wide wide awake while they all were snoring, but also on my own when it came down to Jon. Every bogger else seemed to think it were all right to let him go off and do whatever the fuck he pleased. I leaned back, sipping at some pop, and reached behind me, pushing my hand right down the back of the sofa to push me-sen upright. I felt summat small and slippy wedged there.

I wriggled my hand around till I got a decent grip and pulled the thing out. It were an ecstasy tablet, a Mitsubishi same as the ones we were selling at the time. I was sitting where Duggy'd been, so I knew it must of been his. For some reason, he hadn't took it. I wondered why. I thought he must be green as owt, scared or summat. He could of just said, we would of sorted him. He'd been fronting, like I thought. That was why he'd made such a big deal of looking like he was swallowing summat. I put the pill in my pocket. I'd have him about it later, I decided. Find out what he was on with.

Just then the phone rang. We didn't get loads of phone calls, specially not at that time of night, and it made me jump. I picked up the handset. The voice on the other end was all slurred. It were Rob, the teacher with a death-wish, drunk.

'Meet me. Just to talk,' he said.

'You know that in't a good idea,' I said.

'Just come out onto the park and meet me now.'

'Yer on the park?'

There was no sound on the other end of the line.

'Rob?'

'I'm nodding.'

I opened the door, slow so's it didn't creak. I guessed Mark'd be dead to the world but wasn't taking no chances. I walked up the path and crossed the little road. Rob was sitting on top of the webby climbing frame, staring in my direction. I came over and climbed to the top with him.

'I miss you,' he said.

'How did yer phone me from there? On yer fucking Spiderphone?' I said. He waved a mobile at me, which I have to say impressed me. That was back when no bogger had them. It were like a brick, course, the way they used to be.

'Flash bastard,' I said. And he giggled. The way drunks do.

'I miss you. Miss our chats,' he said.

I shook my head. 'You know this in't possible. You know what'll happen if Mark finds yer here.'

'What will happen, Kez? Just what is that bastard capable of?'

I looked at the floor. 'How's yer fingers?' I asked him. He held them out for me to look at. They were healing a bit, but he had problems bending some of them.

'I'm worried about you,' he said.

'I can look after me-sen,' I told him.

He moved his mouth towards mine. I pushed him away so's he had to steady his-sen. He let out a yelp as he had to grab onto the frame to stop from falling and it hurt his damaged hands. 'I just want to help you,' he said.

'Thanks,' I said. We sat there for a minute and I looked round me. The moon and the streetlights were sharp as blades cutting through the dark air. It were beautiful. I wondered if it were really beautiful, or if it were all in my head. I wondered what else was going off inside my head, and how I could tell what was real and what wasn't no more. 'The best way yer can help me is by getting lost,' I said to Rob.

'Fine,' he said.

Rob climbed down the kiddies' plaything. He couldn't make a quick getaway cause his hands held him up. When he got to his feet on the concrete below, he stormed off. I watched him go.

I looked round the park. It were typical of round here, broken glass all over and the swings twisted round and round the top of the iron frame so's no one could use them. I wondered where kids played these days. I sniffed the burnt air and closed my eyes, pretended I was some-where else.

EIGHTEEN

A couple of weeks on and I was thinking about what Rob'd done, the risk he'd took coming to see me. I have to admit, it made me feel good about me-sen. I must of been smiling at this cause Bek clocked me.

'What's tickling you?' she said. And I couldn't help but smile broader thinking of Spiderman with his handheld phone, sitting on top of the kiddies' climbing frame. Come all the way to the depths of Broxta to try and save me. 'Come on, tell me,' she said, slapping me all gentle on the arm and reminding me how we were thick as you like with each other before. So I came out with it, told her about Rob.

'He was nice ter me and had a nice smile,' I told her.

'And what happened?' I felt me-sen cloud over when she said this, and she must of seen it in my face cause she said, 'What happened, Kez? Tell me.'

'Mark,' I said. I didn't elaborate. Didn't need to.

'And he came back?' she said. I nodded. 'Did you sleep with him or something?'

'No.'

We were quiet then. Bek looked at the joint she was rolling, pretended she had to concentrate even though we both knew she could of rolled up in her sleep.

'Do you love Mark?' she asked me, licking at the Rizla. I watched her tongue flick over the edge of the paper, like some creature catching flies.

'Yeah,' I said.

'Then I'd steer well clear,' Bek said, and I nodded.

The door flew open then, Mark appearing in the room. I knew right away he'd been listening in, from the look on his face.

'So you bin seeing that posh nob behind me back?' he said. I stood up and he came over, sticking his chest out towards me like we were about to have a fight.

'He just turned up outside. There were nowt I could of done about it,' I told him.

'But yer went out to meet the bogger,' he said.

I couldn't answer that with owt, cause I had. I never should of been so stupid as to say owt about it, not in the house where Mark could listen in. I didn't know what he'd do next. Truth was, like Rob'd pointed out, I wasn't sure what he was capable of, not even when it came down to me or Jon. He fingered the hammer round his neck. Bek licked her lips and shuffled in her chair. Then Mark turned and walked out. I heard the front door slam.

'Fuck,' I said.

'Fuck doesn't even begin to get there,' Bek said.

I made some tea and tried to watch telly but I couldn't concentrate on owt. Bek tried to help me. She said I should have a puff of brown to calm me down. I said no, but I showed her where Mark's stash was, let her help her-sen. I must of been on a deathwish that night, talking in the house about seeing Rob, then giving away some of Mark's best shit. I felt fluttery, like I got the next day after I'd been wasted on pills. It wasn't a nice feeling. I knew it were a lottery now, how things'd pan out. If Mark'd gone out and done some rock, or been drinking like he sometimes did, I'd be for it when he got back. If he'd had some brown he'd fall asleep and forget about it.

I chewed at my nails. Bek paced about. Jon came in, out on it. I don't know what he'd took cause he hadn't got it off me. Normally I'd of freaked out at him but all's I could think was what Mark'd do when he got in. Jon was so mashed up he didn't notice the mess me and Bek were in.

Mark came back close to midnight and we were all in bed. I heard banging about downstairs and knew it wasn't good. Then he stomped up to our room and stormed in. I could smell whisky coming out his skin. It were like the smell filled our tiny bedroom as he slammed the door shut.

'Bitch,' he said. He knocked some of my make-up and my hairbrush down off the dressing table with a sweep of his hand.

'Nowt happened,' I told him.

'Yer met wi-him. And you would of liked summat to happen, that much were obvious from yer little chat with yer mate,' he said. And he opened up a drawer and pulled out some of my knickers and started pulling them apart at the seams. 'In't much point yer having these, is they?' he said, scowling at me, all animal again. I sat calm as I could cause I didn't want to do owt to inflame him.

'Look what I fount,' he said. He pulled summat from the drawer. It were Morph.

'Fucking put it down,' I said.

'Never had yer down as such a sap, our Kez, keeping summat crappy like this,' he said.

I lost it then, couldn't see owt cept the glint of wings under glass. I launched me-sen at Mark. 'That's mine,' I screamed. I could hear my voice, all screechy like a banshee. Mark held Morph away from me with one hand, and pumped the other fist into the side of my face, catching my eye then my forehead. It were a hard punch and by rights I should of been knocked out. I gritted my teeth, though, I'd took a few punches in my time. I wobbled round like a losing boxer and I couldn't see much, felt sick as owt. I heard a clink as Mark put down my prized possession, then I saw his hand go back again, and braced me-sen for a second punch what didn't come.

As my sight came back to me I saw Mark standing over me with his hammer raised above my head. This is it, I thought. I'm going to die. My boyfriend who I've known since I was nine's going to kill me, wipe me out with a hammer round my skull. But I didn't scream or try and run. I felt calm. I thought – bring it on.

This look came over Mark's face. I can't describe what it were like, maybes I can't remember it proper. I was dizzy as fuck. He dropped the hammer and fell on his knees. 'Jesus Kez, what did yer mek me do?' I could hear my breathing then, in and out shallow and short and fast. 'I'm so sorry,' he said. 'Fuck, I'm sorry.'

You'd think I would of got up and ran off if I'd had some sense, and I can't explain why I didn't. All's I know is the only choice I had was to take him in my arms and hold him close. You can't choose who you fall for, and you certainly can't control the way they behave, specially if they're into the kind of shit Mark was.

'I love yer, yer know that don't yer?' he said. Thing was,

I did. I hate all that, it makes me sound like one of them abused wife types and I'm not. But Mark did love me, in his own way. His own way was a bit psycho, that's all.

We fell asleep like that for a bit, lying on the cold floor, wrapped up in each other. A draft on my neck woke me up though. I touched Mark's shoulder and he jumped up from his sleep, alert and ready to kill if need be.

'S'all right,' I told him. I walked him over to the bed and we both got in. I made him lay on his side so's he didn't choke on vomit. I lay in front of him and he squeezed me tight to him. Too tight. He didn't fall asleep right off.

'I'll never gerr-over it, yer know? It's goin-ter piss me off fer good,' he told me.

'That I went to talk with Rob? Are yer daft or summat?'

'Nah, not that. I know deep down nowt went off wi-im. I'm talking about Tyneside.' I didn't say owt then. What could I say? I just let Mark squeeze me tight as he liked. 'I should of bin yer first,' he said. And things slotted into place. Why he'd gone so mad over nowt with Rob, who must of reminded him of Phil with his posh manners and nice accent. Why he'd took it further and made sure Phil died. It were Mark's revenge, not mine. He'd duped me into helping him, made a prat out of me. I gritted my teeth at this second punch in the face, but this one really knocked me sideways. I thought about the money in the garden. And summat else this time too. The poison what I'd buried there first, all them years ago, and what I could use it for if I was pushed to.

Mark laid his head on top of my chest. I could feel his pulse racing, and the cold metal of his hammer resting next to my bare skin. I was mad as you like, but it were fucked up, cause when I looked at his face, all peaceful with sleep, all's I could think was how I loved him. He'd not hit me before, never, and I was confused. I was a big open cut, the slightest touch making everything hurt and throb, and I don't mean where he hit me, but inside. Your heart, I spose you'd call it if you were a sap and I'm not, but I don't know how else to explain. I let me-sen fall asleep, hoped I'd wake up and find out it'd all been a dream. Not just that night, and Mark's punch, but my whole fucked-up fucking life. Everything since before Mrs Ivanovich'd topped her-sen.

I woke up in the middle of the night with my face throbbing. Mark's head was still laid on my chest, and I got me-sen up from under him and his hammer with more than a little difficulty. I was scared of waking him up cause I didn't know who he'd be. The gentle tender Mark he was before he fell asleep, or the violent drunk who'd stood over me about to crack me on the head with a hammer a few minutes before that. He didn't wake up though. I snuck downstairs and took a bag of peas out the freezer, shoved them on my face. I remembered advice I'd seen on the telly, about how if your finger or hand gets cut off to bring it to the hospital wrapped in frozen peas. It made me smile, in spite on it all, imagining people going down to casualty with fingers wrapped in frozen peas.

Someone was moving about above me, and I held my breath as I heard footsteps on the stairs. But it were Jon, coming into the kitchen, looking half asleep and still out on it.

'What were all that row about last night?' he said, walking in a few steps. He stared at me close. 'What the fuck's wrong wi-yer face?' he said. He came right over then, and I shied away as he tried to get a proper look. 'Jeez–uz,' he said.

'It in't no biggie,' I told him.

'Did Mark do this ter yer?' he asked me. I wanted to lie, but couldn't, not to my brother, so I didn't say owt. I placed the peas back on my face so's he couldn't see, but he moved them away. He winced. 'Was it Mark?' he said again. He took my silence as a yes. 'I'm goin-ter kill the fucker,' he said.

'It in't worth it,' I told him.

He started pacing then, up and down the room. I tried to explain how this wasn't going to be for ever, this shitty house and the close and the stupid estate we lived on. But it were impossible to explain without giving the game away, and I'd learned my lesson about saying shit in the house. He started chucking stuff then, the toaster, and a dirty plate what was sat on the worktop, then all the cutlery out the top drawer. He was making a right racket, and I was shit-ting it that Mark'd hear and come down, then Jon'd go for him and someone'd get killed. But Mark must of been dog tired from our fight and the booze, cause he didn't wake up. Duggy did though, and came running through to the kitchen like we were on fire or summat.

'What's going off?' he said. And he saw Jon reach for the mugs on the draining board, then clocked my face and must of worked it out. Jon kept repeating, 'I'm goin-ter kill him. I'm goin-ter kill that bastard,' over and over. And all's I could see was Jon ending up on the wrong end of Mark's hammer.

Duggy went up to him then, and started saying all this stuff in a soft, calm way. Jon turned towards him, and I thought he'd go all psycho into him, but he didn't. He listened, and breathed more normal, stopped throwing stuff. Duggy put his hand on Jon's shoulder, got him to sit down at the table and talk.

'I hit him too,' I told Jon.

'That really in't the point,' he said. And he slammed his hand down on the table.

'Listen to her, Jon,' Duggy said. He kept using his name like that, and his voice was different to the way it were normally. I looked at him and wondered where he'd learned these tricks. It were, I don't know, professional's the closest I can get to describing it. I looked back at Jon and he was calmer again. Whatever way Duggy'd learned to do this, it were impressive to watch.

'Mark sleeps wi-a hammer round his neck. And don't think he wouldn't use it on yer,' I told Jon.

'Yeah, that's as maybes but d-ya think he wun't use it on you?' Jon said, and he had a point. We all went quiet.

'It's complicated. Things between adults,' I said to Jon.

'Yer reckon I'm a kid then?' Jon said, his face all screwed up and his eyes flashing. 'Bout time yer noticed I'm all grown up over here,' he said.

But I didn't see Jon as a grown up. I spose you could ask who I was to say, given I was just a baby me-sen. Jon might of been six-foot summat and broad with it, but he was only twelve, which is no age at all. He was in this big rush to grow up, but I didn't want him to have to, not like I had. He didn't have a clue how to handle his-sen, not really. Didn't have the first idea about psychos such as Mark.

'Mark's a dangerous bloke,' Duggy told Jon. His accent sounded posher than it normally did and I think he noticed me look at him funny, cause he shot a nervous glance in my direction, then back at Jon, and carried on talking with his normal Nottingham drawl. I didn't know what was going off with Duggy. The truth was, I thought he was harmless, just some posh kid faking it, and didn't see owt past that explanation. Didn't have no reason to. Not at that point.

'Damn right he's dangerous. Please mate, just leave it,' I told Jon. He looked up at me, a frown knotted across his forehead. 'For me?' I said.

Jon sighed and rolled his eyes. 'All right. I'll leave it,' he said. He didn't look happy about it at all.

'Go to bed,' Duggy told him. 'I want ter talk ter Kez about summat.' And Jon did what Duggy'd told him to, just like that. As the door sighed shut behind him, I turned to Duggy.

'Just who the fuck are you Duggy Bryant?' I said.

'Don't know what yer getting at,' he said.

'I think yer do,' I said. And I caught his eyes in mine and held them there. He stared me out and didn't flinch.

'What yer goin-ter do about Mark? Yer can't go on like that,' he said.

'I've got plans,' I told him.

'Yeah plans. How many times do gells like you say that kind of shit?' he said.

'What do you know about gells like me?' I asked him. Duggy shrugged. He smiled up at the ceiling and I could of cracked him one, he looked so fucking cocky. He didn't have the first clue.

I walked out and left him to stare at the ceiling. He could preach to that, I decided. I went into the dining room and slammed the door. I took the rainforest books down from the shelf and leafed through them. How much more could I pilfer into my suitcase before Mark noticed summat? Would I ever get away from this shithole?

I thought about this one insect Mrs Ivanovich had caught. It were this beetle thing. She put it in the killing jar and it took ages to die. She said it were cause the chemicals needed topping up in the plaster, but I'd only just done that and I don't think it were. It seemed like that little bogger wasn't ever going to give up. It flew at first, but kept hitting the sides and being knocked back to the bottom so it gave up on that approach. It climbed the jar walls instead, getting a bit further, then a bit further each time, but always falling down to the plaster in the end. I watched it struggle for ages, and my eyes welled up. I didn't cry though. Mrs Ivanovich'd taught me you don't cry over insects and I always did what she told me. But all that effort, and even if it'd ever got to the top there was a lid on the jar. Course, the poison got to it first in any case.

I sat at the table with my head in the rainforest and I cried. Some on it were for Mark hitting me, and the way he'd stood over me ready to mash my head in with the hammer after. But it were mainly cause I didn't know what Jon'd do next. I wasn't convinced by his promise to leave it, he was a right hot head, too much like me, and I thought there'd be more to come on it. It were other stuff too. The baby what I killed. Mam and Bek and Mark all living dead thanks to the poppy. Phil cold and buried in Wilford Hill.

I thought about how beautiful my brother was and that made me cry too. The mix of race was a powerful thing, he was all muscle and height but with the fine features and high cheekbones what my mam gave to both on us. His eyes were hazel-green, his skin the colour of coffee. When I thought hard about it, he was so beautiful it made me sob, and bring my breath in sharp between. I wondered who his dad was. A dark figure came into my head, summat from my childhood. But with it came another thing, a cold jolt. It made me stop crying and sit up sharp. I couldn't remember what'd happened with this man, or if he was just summat my head made up.

The bogeyman.

The ten-o'clock horses.

The things we put inside the heads of kids so's they'll do what they're told.

I got up then, and went upstairs. I needed to be warm and held tight in bed. Even if it were the worst bogeyman of all holding onto me. Even if I knew that.

NINETEEN

I got woke up the next day by Mark kissing me
all over my back and neck, like I was in some messed up
version of *Sleeping Beauty*. He was picking up my hair and
dropping it and it tickled a bit.

'You awake?' he said.

'I am now.'

He laughed. I turned on my back and looked up at
him. I couldn't help but smile as he looked down on me
with this wicked grin. I mean, I know he loved me. He
kissed me on the lips then, and he slipped his hands
round my waist and pulled me close. His body felt so
warm.

'I'm sorry,' he said. But I shushed him and made him
kiss me some more. We both got a bit hot and bothered
then. A minute on and he was inside me. I looked into
his face as we made love. This was summat what didn't
happen very often anymore. I'd forgot how he could look,
the times when he was really into me. His features melted
into each other and all the animal was sucked out of them.

He looked so vulnerable. Even after all that's gone off, this vulnerable face is the one I took with me of Mark, the way I remember him. His pupils were dilated for a change, instead of the needlepoints they usually were in his scary grey eyes.

We lay there after for a bit. Mark was still touching me but it wasn't the same. His hands were moving faster, and he was fidgeting. Loads of gells moan about their blokes not wanting to sit round and cuddle after they've had sex, but this was different. The problem was Mark needed his next hit. Was desperate for it. The only thing I can compare it to is when you're sat in a bar with a smoker, and there's no ashtray on the table. You can see they aren't with you, all's they're thinking about is where they can get summat to put their ash in so's they can light up. And lying in bed with a junkie who hasn't shot up is just like that. Thing is, I'd give a smoker some slack, me. But not Mark. He was waiting for me to excuse him, to tell him to get up and go get wasted already. But I wasn't going to say that. I was never going to condone his habit. Mark wriggled and struggled with his cravings till he couldn't no more.

'I got-ter gerrup,' he said, launching his-sen from out the covers and onto the rough floorboards.

'Right,' I said.

He stood there for a minute, looking down at me. 'Don't be like that,' he said.

I looked back up at him. He held eye contact for a bit, then turned, grabbed his dressing gown, and made to get out the room. I watched him go and wondered what I was on. I'd been happy to let my mam walk off, never gave her no leeway even if she was my mam. I couldn't work out why I gave this bloke so much more credit. She didn't deserve owt from me but neither did Mark.

I turned over in bed, noticed how grubby the sheets were. I got up, and promised me-sen I would leave, and soon. I wasn't going to be that gell Duggy thought I was. This couldn't be for ever, not after what'd happened the night before. I came downstairs and found Mark in the kitchen, strapping round his arm, needle in. His arm was covered so bad in tracks it would of given Midland Mainline summat to think about. He looked up at me, then his eyes rolled back. He looked back at me again, like he was embarrassed to be caught that way.

'I'm sorry Kez, I really am,' he said. I couldn't work out if he was talking about what he'd done the night before, or his addiction, which he knew I didn't like and'd never wanted. I was sad then. Wondered about Mark. What chance would he have on his tod. He just wouldn't cut it, was too hooked on that shit to make proper decisions, in the long run anyways. What would happen to him if I was gone? I thought. I corrected me-sen. What will happen when I'm gone? Who'll turn him on his side and make sure he doesn't choke on vomit?

Mark started fiddling in the fridge, poured some juice and took out eggs and bacon. He waved the bacon at me. I spose it's how old married couples get, asking each other questions by waving packets of bacon at each other. I smiled at him, which was enough of an answer too.

The smell of bacon and eggs cooking filled the room, cheering me up. I made us both a big, well stewed cup of tea, mashing it for ages and squeezing the teabag so's the liquid was the colour of polished oak, then adding a load of milk. That was how Mark liked his tea and over the time we'd been together I'd took to drinking it that way too. I heard footsteps on the stairs.

'Ey up, smell-a bacon raised the dead,' I said, grinning

at Mark. Jon walked in the door, carrying this dumbbell. I'd clean forgot about my worries the night before. I thought he was exercising, pumping iron, bringing it down with him to show off. I watched him walk over to Mark without thinking much on it till he raised the weight above his head and I realised what he was on with.

'Mark!' I yelled. But I was only in time for him to turn and get the thing right in the face.

Jon shouted as the weight fell onto Mark, telling him he was a bastard and a wanker and didn't deserve me. Mark's face was shocked as hell, like a cartoon version with a big round mouth and exclamation marks for eyes. He didn't fall or owt. I would of thought a blow like that'd knock anyone out, but Mark was left standing. He was knocked sideways but that were all. The pan went flying, and some hot fat splashed on Mark and Jon, and on the floor. All's I could think was I'd better clean that up before one of them slips on it. It sounds daft now but it just came into my head and before I knew it I was down on my hands and knees scrubbing at the hot fat.

Course, Mark wasn't having what Jon'd done. He started laying into him. 'I'll kill yer, yer lickle shit,' he said. That woke me up from my fat-cleaning trance. Next I knew, Mark'd took the hammer from round his neck. He was standing there holding it up, looking Jon in the eye and saying, 'Yer playing at big boys, huh?' repeating it over and over like the psycho he was. I got straight up and stood between the two of them. Mark just stood there, looking at me. He was foaming at the mouth like he had the rabies or summat.

'You'll have ter come past me,' I said.

'Yer think that'll stop me?' he said. And he pushed his face at me, all menacing, and the pair on us danced round the kitchen like prizefighters.

'Gerrout, Jon,' I said, pointing at the door. He didn't go straight off but I said it again, and he must of been scared to death cause he did as he was told.

'We goin-ter have this again, then?' I asked Mark. He growled at me. I swear that's what it were, a growl. I bared my teeth. It shocked me to think how much like animals we were behaving.

'Yer lay inter me wi-that hammer they'll find out. Bout that, bout everything. Phil and the works. Jon'll tell-em if he dun't kill yer first,' I said to Mark. 'They'll search the house. And you'll end up locked away where you can't get nowt to feed yer habit.' I knew where to hit him, that was for sure. He stepped back and sat down with this dazed look all over his face. I sat down next to him. 'Gi-me the hammer,' I said. I took hold of his hands and the blunt end of the weapon, and he hesitated, then let go. 'Yer got-ter stop doing that,' I said. The funniest shit goes through your head when summat mad happens, like all this crap. I couldn't help but pat me-sen on the back, thinking how I was just as good as Duggy at this lark. I didn't need no training to deal with it.

I looked then at the cuts and bruises across the side of Mark's face. They were nasty, and it were a mark of how tough he was that he'd not been knocked out. Mark'd took a load more punches than me. Plus the odd knife attack what he'd managed to fight off. I shivered at the table, all cold and clammy from shock. I thought I might faint, cept I knew I couldn't afford to. Couldn't leave Mark and Jon to kill each other.

'I'll get summat for that,' I said. I took out the same pack of frozen peas I'd used the night before, and put it to his face. He made a sharp sound, more than he'd done when he actually got hit. Then I couldn't help smiling as a thought crossed my head.

'What the fuck's fucking funny?' he said.

I couldn't help it, even though it were winding him up, and I ended up letting out a snort of laughter. I put my hand over my mouth. Maybes it were the shock but I couldn't stop and Mark was getting more and more angry, shouting at me about what I was laughing my head off at given all what'd gone off. I stopped after a bit, and felt my throat tighten. But I wasn't going to cry, not in front of Mark.

'It were just how we match now,' I said. 'An eye fer an eye.' One of the things Bek'd said about what she'd done to that gell before she got stuck in the EMHG. But Mark didn't get the funny side.

I asked Mark to do me a favour and sit still with the peas on his face, so's I could go and sort Jon out. I couldn't help laughing again, at what I'd said about holding peas on his face, it were such a fucked up thing to say. And Mark said he'd sort out Jon if I wanted and I said no thanks. Then even Mark smiled a little bit.

Jon was sitting in the dining room. He still had the dumbbell in his hands.

'Yer goin-ter put that down?' I said.

'Like I'd hit yer,' he said.

'I din't think yer'd be stupid enough ter hit Mark,' I told him.

Jon dropped the weight to the floor and it landed with a thud. He stared up at me, this right bolshy look on his face. It were a good job he'd only caused all this shit out of loyalty to me else I'd of picked up the weight and given him a good crack across the face with it me-sen. He was at that age, was Jon. Thought he ruled the world, just cause he was big and a lot on the kids were scared of him.

'I'm not having this shit. Sooner or later we'll have the police round here cause someone's called-em, then we'll be fucked,' I said.

Jon looked up at me from where he was sat. The know-it-all look slipped away in a flash and he looked like he'd cry any minute. No matter what he said about me treating him like a kid, sometimes I forgot how young he was. I could see the effort he was making holding onto his face. He was a good lad though and he didn't cry. I sat down next to him and put my hand on his arm.

'Mate, you and Mark got ter live wi-each other and just gerr-on fer a bit,' I told him.

'You should get rid,' he said.

I sighed. 'It in't that simple,' I said.

Jon looked at me like he thought it were, and that I was thick as shit for not seeing that.

'I've got plans,' I told him. He was shaking his head at me. 'Real plans. For me and you to get out of here.'

'Like what?' Jon screeched the words.

I put my mouth against his ear. 'We're getting outta here. I'll have-ter tell yer the details some other time. If Mark hears what I'm saying ter yer we're both dead,' I said. Jon looked up at me then. I think he could tell I meant it.

'Promise?' he said.

'I promise. But will yer promise me summat?'

Jon shrugged.

'That you'll stop fighting wi-Mark.'

'Spose,' he said.

'No. You got-ter promise like what I did.'

'All right. Promise.'

And I knew Jon'd keep his word once I'd made him

say promise. It were our code, Jon's and mine, that a promise meant summat. I told him to get his arse out the way while I sorted things with Mark.

I went back to the kitchen where my boyfriend was still sitting with frozen peas pressed to his cheek.

'He were bang out of order,' he said.

'I know. But so was you, last night. What would you of done if some-un else'd left me looking like this?' I pointed at my face.

'I'd want-ter know why first,' he said.

'Bullcrap. Like yer did wi-Danny Morrison.' I gave him this right lairy look then, like I wanted him to drop dead on the spot. Mark went quiet. We both knew he'd gone much further than he should of with that lad, leaving him for dead, burning in the street.

'What d'yer want Kez?'

'Nowt. But you should know – yer do owt ter Jon cause of what's happened today and I'll leave yer. Don't think I won't cause I'm goin-ter. Understand?'

Mark didn't say owt.

'D'yer understand?' I said.

He nodded. 'I wun't do owt ter hurt yer anyways,' he said.

It seemed a bit easy, all that. Mark agreeing to leave it without no fuss. It didn't make sense. I knew how hard Mark held a grudge. There was one bloke with a melted face could vouch for that, and another on Wilford Hill who couldn't no more.

Mark's junkies came over later, walking through the door all twitchy cause they were running out of shit. None of them commented on mine and Mark's matching set of mashed up faces. Maybes they were all too scared to say owt, but I reckon they were too full of poppy-lust to give a shit what'd gone off. I left the zombies to it, and went to sit in the front room with a cup of tea. Jon wasn't nowhere to be found still. Bek walked in.

'What happened to your face?' she said.

'Don't ask,' I said. She didn't say owt more about it; maybe she'd heard it all go off and was just being polite. 'Not going wi-Mark and his cronies?' I asked her.

'Nah. I've quit,' she said.

I snorted. 'Right. And Mark's not selling ner-more neither,' I said. If she was cold turkey she would of been much more freaked than she was.

'It's the truth, Kez. I swear it.' I looked at her. 'I went to the doctor's,' she said. She took this bottle out her pocket.

'What's that then? That methadone shit or summat?' I asked her and she nodded. 'Does it work?'

'I can't say it makes me feel high as a kite, but it staves off the cravings and the fevers,' she said.

I sat there, shocked as Mark'd been that morning when he'd got clobbered by Jon.

'Why yer doing it?' I said. She took her breath in sharp and didn't answer me right off, like she was scared of how I'd react to what she wanted to say.

'It was partly that Duggy persuaded me,' she said.

'How can Duggy preach on drugs? I mean he teks stuff right?' I said.

'Yeah, grass and pills and shit. Nothing heavy.'

And I nodded, but I'd never seen Duggy take a drag of spliff, and the one time I'd given him a pill he'd shoved it down the back of the sofa, pretended to swallow it. It were all hanging together bad now, and my skin prickled at some of the thoughts I was having.

'Listen Kez, I have to say this to you. It was mostly seeing Mark, the state he's in,' Bek told me.

And there it were, truth on a plate. Mark was such a scary junkie even confirmed good-time gell Bek didn't want to be owt like him. It reminded me I didn't neither, and about my escape plan. There was summat I'd been meaning to ask Bek. It were making me more and more nervous, having all that money hanging round buried in the back garden. Too risky. I was finding out what Mark was capable of towards me. I couldn't open a bank account cause that'd mean someone'd come sniffing round sooner or later, wanting to know a bit more about where my income was coming from. I needed some help from someone who knew money, and Bek was the only person I knew who'd ever had much of the stuff.

'If you had a bit-a cash, and yer wanted to keep it out the road wi-out no one finding out, what'd you do?' I said.

She smiled at me. 'You want to hide some from Mark?' she said. I looked through my fringe at her and frowned. 'It's all right, Kez, I'm on your side,' she said. I nodded. I was pretty sure Mark was still locked away shooting up and doing business, but I wasn't going to say owt out loud in case he was outside the door listening. I wasn't going to be that stupid again. Bek took the hint and came right over to my chair and knelt beside it so's she could talk in whispers to me. 'Premium bonds,' she said.

Bek explained that these things were a competition. That you could put your money down, and get it back, cash them, anytime you wanted. And they were wrote in your name, so it were a bit like the cash being in the bank. No one else could get it. She said loads of people had them, and if yourn got drawn out you could win summat, a lot of money sometimes. She told me I could get a few thousand pounds worth in a small bag. When she said that about the bag I looked at her, and wondered if she knew more than she was saying. If she knew summat about the suitcase. And if Bek did, why wouldn't Mark when he was around all the time, watching me and listening in to what I said?

'Where can I get them things from then?' I asked her.

'The post office sells them,' she told me.

I nodded. It made a lot of sense. Then this look came over Bek like her head was full up with worries. 'What?' I said. She shrugged like she didn't want to tell me. 'What's wrong wi-yer?' I asked.

'How far d'you think Mark'd go if someone upset him?' she said.

'You're talking about this, in't it?' I said, pointing to the mess on the side of my face.

'Not really. Just something Duggy said.'

I looked at Bek full on. 'All the way,' I said, quiet as I could.

'Do you really think so?'

I hesitated. The only people I'd spoke to about Phil was Mark and Jon. 'I know it,' I whispered.

Bek shivered. 'That's what Duggy reckoned.'

I did wonder what the fuck Duggy knew about owt and it got all them doubts I had about him raging in my head again.

'What did he say?' I asked Bek.

'Can't remember,' she said. But I knew she could and just wasn't telling.

'Why d'yer ask this stuff about Mark all of a sudden?' I said.

Bek shrugged. 'Just that the way he is scares me.' But she did that thing she'd always done, I remembered it from the EMHG. Bek wasn't a great liar, not when you knew her well. Every time she'd said owt what wasn't true to them carers she'd licked her top teeth and messed with her hair. So I asked her straight.

'Is there summat yer know about Duggy what I ought to know about?' I said.

'God, no. He's just Duggy,' she told me, tongue doing overtime on her teeth, hand flicking at her hair like mad.

I didn't know what Bek was hiding from me, but I did believe she was the sort of gell who was loyal, who'd tell me if she really thought there was owt I should be worried about. She'd always proved that way when we were in the home together. I decided to go softly on it. Wait for her to tell me in her own time, when I needed to know. Thing was, Bek was a psycho too, like most of the people I loved. I couldn't of been sure if I'd of pushed at her that I wouldn't of got a stiletto in my eye.

'Good fer you,' I said.

'What?' she said, screwing up her eyes and lighting a fag.

'Giving up the smack,' I said.

'Yeah,' she said. And she smiled, but not that much.

I looked at her and wondered if she'd manage to kick her habit, and what her body'd do next if she did. Would the way she smelled go back to that musky milky way it used to be? Would she fill out again, into the slim hourglass she was when I first knew her? Would her skin ever get back that glow of good health? Somehow I doubted it, no matter what she did. Even if she did stay off the shit she'd probably replace it with some other obsession. That was the kind of person she was.

I sipped my tea. I promised me-sen again I'd never do brown.

TWENTY

Bek and Duggy came to be part of the furniture round ourn, and didn't look like moving out months and months later. I guess I knew summat was going off with Duggy, but the problem was I didn't take him serious at all. I talked to Mark about it, though, and he said I should threaten him to be on the safe side. I'd never done owt like that before, and I suggested it might be better if Mark did it. But he was having none of that. Said I needed to learn how to deal with this sort of shit. Said Duggy wouldn't be a bad place to start, so I guess he didn't take the bogger so serious neither. And when I found me-sen with him in the front room and everyone else off doing whatever they were doing, I decided to have a go. He was sat picking at his nails, half watching some Saturday morning rubbish on the telly. I stared at him doing that till he noticed. He turned and looked up at me.

'What?' he said.

'What? It's what I asked yer ages ago when yer first got

here Duggy Bryant. Who the fuck are yer? And yer never answered me,' I said.

'Maybes I din't get what yer was going on about,' he said.

'Yer remember me asking then, don't yer?' I said. You would of thought Duggy'd of blushed or looked away at that, but he didn't. I should of known then he wasn't just some kid fronting.

'You know what I was getting at. I want ter know what's going off,' I said.

'In terms-a what?' Duggy said, blinking fast and holding eye contact. He looked like he was thinking about what I'd said, ticking it over through his brain and trying to work out what he could get away with saying.

'I don't know what. That's why I'm asking, see. There's summat going off what yer not telling me about.'

'I don't get where yer coming from.'

'I'll gi-yer an example Duggy Bryant. I gev-yer that pill, that day I first met yer, but yer din't tek it,' I said.

'Din't fancy it,' Duggy said, quick as a flash.

'Fair-nuff. But yer could of just said, instead-a pretending to tek it and hiding it down the back of the sofa,' I said.

'Din't know yer so well then. Was try-ner mek a good impression,' he said. He put it in a way what you couldn't of argued with cept I wasn't convinced.

I slid over the sofa so's I was right beside Duggy. I leaned over him, put my face in his. He tried to push me away but I bit into his nose, summat Mark'd told me to do if I ever wanted to make someone sit still. He'd given me a whole load of tips about this kind of thing, but I'd never used any of it before, never needed to. The heavy shit was all Mark's side of the business. It felt good though, to have this big bloke squirming in pain and scared underneath me. Gave me a real power trip despite me-sen. 'Don't yer move an inch, Bryant, else I'll bite it off,' I mumbled, clinging to his nose with my teeth the whole time, grabbing his hands and digging in my nails.

'Fuck you, Kez, what yer doing?' he said.

I sat astride Duggy. I'm not sure why I did this, it were just what came into my head. I felt his dick harden underneath me.

'Now just what d'yer think you're getting?' I said, moving my mouth close to his ear and letting my hair fall into his face. 'I don't think so,' I said. And I thrust my knee hard into the swelling at the top of his trousers. He let out a mad sound and curled up in a ball, pushing me away onto the arm of the chair.

'Bitch,' he said.

'That's just the start-on it,' I said. 'Yer don't know how lucky yer are it in't Mark having this chat wi-yer.' But I looked at his face and I could tell he did. 'Just watch yer step. Damn well mek sure me-n-Mark have no more reason to suspect owt dodgy's going off. All right?'

I walked out the room, pleased with me-sen. I didn't look back to see what Duggy was doing, how he was reacting. I've learned since then that kind of thing is important. I could of told a million and one things from the look on the tosser's face. I know that now.

It were only about a week later when Bek came to talk to me about Duggy. 'I found something,' she said. Duggy was out with this bloke he'd got pally with, Chris summat his name was. He was one of them people who lived on the edge of my world. I'd known him since I was about six, and I'd had the odd conversation with him, but I couldn't say he was a mate or owt like that. From what I gathered he was a good sort, bought off us from time to time and knew how to enjoy his-sen. I'd felt better since Duggy'd been hanging round with him. It'd put my mind at rest a bit. But that was about to be shattered to bits.

Bek took me up to the box room the pair of them shared. She lifted up the blow-up mattress they slept on. Underneath was this one wonky floorboard.

'I noticed cause I couldn't get the mattress straight no matter how hard I tried. It was getting on my nerves and I tried to fix it,' she told me. She wiggled the board round and it came off in her hand. Underneath there was this big Tupperware box. Bek pulled it out and put it onto the bare floor, re-covered the gap. I pulled the lid off. Inside was all this stuff. Notebooks. One of them small tape recorder things, the ones what fit in your pocket. Loads of them tiny tapes what went inside.

'Yer played any-er them?' I asked Bek, and she nodded. 'Is this what I think it is?' She nodded again.

That bastard Duggy was police or summat. He'd put away tapes he'd made of a load of our conversations. Not just ones he'd been a part of, but stuff he must of listened to through doors, shit about Phil and all that even. No wonder he was so quick into the room when Jon went psycho that night. He was probably recording us, listening in with that crappy little taping machine. No wonder he'd been so good at calming Jon down. I'd been grateful for it at the time but I realised I should of seen through him there and then. I wondered how I could of been so dim and not realised what he was.

Inside the books were notes about me and Jon and Mark. He'd got Mark sussed, that was for sure. Said he was psychotic and'd do owt if summat got in his way. His notes didn't implicate Jon. I was glad about that at least.

They said he was a normal, well-adjusted boy considering. That he'd not been involved in any of the shit Mark and me were on with. But it were what he'd wrote about me I found most interesting. He said I had a 'borderline personality' whatever that meant. Said I'd not been treated well, that I'd been brought up this way and didn't know no better. Said Mark'd manipulated me.

There was part of me thought about letting Duggy do what he liked with all that shit. They'd of put Mark away for good if he'd took that back with him to wherever he'd come from. Me, I'd get ten years tops, out in six for good behaviour. And Jon'd be all right. He'd get help to reha-bilitate, they'd make him get some direction or summat. All this went through my head, weighed up and consid-ered in the minutes while I waded through them books and Bek played the tapes to me. But I was a loyal kid and you couldn't change that. Duggy was right that Mark'd manipulated me. But he'd took care on me too. I couldn't just stand by and let him go down for life, not without warning him. I stopped the tape Bek was playing. I'd heard enough.

'We got ter tell Mark,' I said.

'Mark'll kill him,' Bek said. She didn't mean he'd just go mad, the way most people would of if they said this. She meant he'd kill him.

'It in't a choice,' I said. And I got up and walked out the room. Bek followed me.

'Be a good gell and put that stuff back. We don't want him to work out he's bin proper fount out,' I told her.

'You can't let Mark kill him,' Bek said, following me into my bedroom. I turned to face her.

'What yer suggesting? That I just lerr-im run ter wher-ever he's come from wi-all that shit he's got on us?' I said.

Bek walked deeper into my room. I prickled and stared at her. 'C'mon, Kez. I've told you about this. I didn't have to do that. I could've kept it all to myself.'

'Then Mark'd of killed you too,' I said.

'That's not why I told you and you know it.'

There was a stand-off then, me staring at Bek and her staring back.

'It in't a choice,' I told her again. I went in my top drawer, looking for the address book. I knew Mark was at this bloke's place, someone who'd got this dodgy batch of pills to sell us. He was talking to him about a deal, in spite of me saying I wanted nowt to do with snide pills. He'd given me the bloke's number. It were on a piece of paper I'd put inside my address book. I wanted Mark back, helping me sort out what to do about this.

Bek walked over towards me. 'Please, Kez. I love him,' she said.

'He's a liar and a treacherous bastard. For fuck's sake, I can't believe we've bin putting the tosser up all these months and we've never asked for a penny from the pair on yer.' I paused for breath. 'How can yer love-im?'

'I fell for him before I knew all about this. You can't control someone you've fallen in love with,' she said, hitting a chord and she knew it, cause I'd said the exact same thing to her about Mark at some point.

'Can yer come up wi-any other way?' I asked her.

Bek looked round the room. 'You could just get rid of all that shit he's been collecting on you. Burn it or something,' she said.

'He'll have more stashed other places. I'd put money on it,' I said.

'Couldn't you just blackmail or kneecap him or

something?' she asked. She was clutching at fresh air and we both knew it.

'And how's that goin-ter look to whoever he's working for?' I said. 'Nah, there's only one answer.' I turned to look at Bek. I thought she was about to cry and I held my hand out and touched her arm. She pushed me away. Then she launched her-sen at me. Like I said before, Bek was a psycho bitch when it came down to it.

We were biting and scratching at each other, and I'd threw a few punches, though Bek fought like a typical gell, all teeth and nails. Things'd reversed and I was bigger than her, and stronger, but she was out of control. Then the worst thing happened what could of. Morph was still sitting on my dressing table. Bek flung her-sen round so much she ended up knocking the dresser, and Morph flew off the side of it.

I heard the frame scrape across the wood of the table and looked down. I saw Morph flying across my bedroom, headed to the floorboards too fast and heavy for me to stop him before he hit. I was no better at catching butterflies than when I was five and ran round Mrs Ivanovich's garden with a net. The glass round my butterfly smashed to pieces, making a harsh, musical scream what tore my nerves out. I saw it shatter and rain over the manky floorboards.

I turned away from Bek and bent down, grabbed at the butterfly. I touched him and he crumbled in my hand, just like Mrs Ivanovich'd told me he would. There was this long shard of glass lying near him. I picked it up.

'You bitch,' I said to Bek. She looked scared then, like she thought I could of stabbed her or summat. I threw the shard on the floor and it shattered into smaller pieces, making a sound like water. I looked away from my friend, disappointed over what she thought of me.

'Get out,' I said. I meant get out the house and don't come back. I was so mad over her breaking Morph. Bek didn't know I meant that but she still left the room quick as a dart. I sat down on my bed and looked at the mess on the floor. It sounds stupid, getting so het up over a butterfly in a glass case. It wasn't about what it were, though, but what it stood for – getting away and all that. And more. It were all I had left of Mrs Ivanovich. She'd gone, but she'd left this beautiful thing. Bottled a bit of where she'd been. She'd clutched it to her as the cyanide fumes got stronger, then knocked her cold, then stopped her breathing. It were like she'd left a bit of her-sen for me to keep. I'm sure she did it that way deliberate, so's I'd find Morph and could keep summat of her with me. And now Bek and her psycho tendencies'd messed that all up. It were all Duggy's fault, I decided as I sat there. If it wasn't for Duggy, Bek and me'd never of had a fight like that and it'd never of got broke. He was going to pay for what he'd done.

I stared into the mirror. Watched my eyes blink. Followed the line of my cheekbone round and then down. I thought about Bek, going mad at me. I thought about what she'd told me. She'd tried to do the right thing and she didn't deserve to get her boyfriend killed on the back of that. But I couldn't see Mark settling for owt else. It were too dangerous. For starters, Duggy knew about Phil. I shivered at the thought of what we'd need to do. I decided to go down and talk to Bek, see if she had any bright ideas about other ways to deal with it. Maybes we could sort it, and wouldn't have to say owt to Mark at all, though I didn't think I'd be able to keep such a stonking huge secret from him.

I walked in the living room. Bek was there, shooting

up. She gave me that same look Mark always did when I caught him in the middle of using, all sheepish and embarrassed. Like you'd caught them having a wank or summat. I spose it's the same kind of self-indulgence is what it comes down to.

'That's a big shame.' I pointed at what she was doing as if she might not know what I was talking about. 'It won't help owt yer know, not in the long run,' I said. She smiled, kind of, and looked up at me.

'It's hard enough as it is, without all this stress,' she told me.

'Blame Duggy. He's the wanker what dragged you into all this,' I said.

'I'm not sure it's like that. I don't know what's going on with him but I don't think it can be the way it looks,' she said.

'Course it's the way it looks. They in't nowt cept the way things look,' I said.

I sat down for a bit. Bek didn't seem to have any more suggestions. I got up and went over to the 'gram. The lid was padlocked down, and I took out a key and undid it. I lifted the lid and delved inside the part where normal people kept their records. Course, we weren't normal people and kept different stuff in there instead. I took out a hundred in cash and a few wraps of Mark's best heroin and gave them to Bek.

'Tek this and gerr-out-er here,' I said. She looked up at me all gormless. 'Mark'll want you out the way as well as Duggy. Best you run off now so's no harm can come ter yer,' I said. I bit my lip. I didn't want Bek to go.

'When d'you want me out by?' she said.

'Go now. Get yer-sen upstairs and tek what yer need and just gerr-out,' I said, waving my hand at her. She got up, slow, and walked over to the door. She stood framed in it and flashed me a look, and for one moment I could see the gell I'd met all them years ago at the girls' home. Then, quick as you like, the junkie was standing there again. Then she was gone, out my life for good this time. I held my head in my hands and breathed deep. I'd been right on Bek, she was a psycho but she was loyal as they came. I was going to miss her.

I sat round then, waiting for Duggy or Mark to come back so's we could start sorting things. I kept thinking of how to handle it but it all came down to the one thing Mark'd be prepared to do about the situation, and I wasn't much more comfortable with that than Bek'd been. I thought about telling Mark, how I'd have to find the right time to do it, when he was in a good mood so's he didn't go psycho on me. He could go mad, given Bek was my friend and'd brought Duggy here. And I'd let her go, with our money and some of his smack. It'd not go down well if he worked that out. Why did Duggy have to go and turn out to be a copper? We were all having such a good time an-all.

It were that Judas traitor bastard who turned up home first. He walked in the door all cocky and on one cause of summat he'd been up to with Chris. I looked him up and down.

'What's wrong wi-you?' he said.

'Nowt,' I said. But I wouldn't look him proper in the eye so he knew there was.

'Where's me gell?' he said.

'Gone.'

'What d'yer mean gone?' he said.

'Ran off. Yer know what these junkies are like,' I said.

Duggy sat down then, drifting slowly back onto the sofa

like he was full of air and it were leaking. His eyes'd took on that dizzy look what people get when they've been in an accident or seen summat nasty. It seemed he did care for Bek, was totally bothered she'd gone. He wasn't just using her to get at me and Mark then, after all. There was more to it than that. I almost felt sorry for him. I remembered what he'd wrote about me, in one of them notebooks of his what was causing all this trouble. Borderline personality, he'd said. I wondered if that was why I could always see two sides to things, like the way I felt then, even feeling sorry for someone like Duggy who had it in for me and the people I loved.

He held his head in his hands and cried. I don't like it when men cry so I left him to it and went upstairs.

TWENTY-ONE

Mark was mardy for about a week after Bek went. I think he missed her too or maybes it were that he'd lost a punter. Maybes he was missing the heroin I'd let her take. He asked me a couple of times why she'd done a runner, but I said I didn't know and Mark believed me cause he knew what junkies were like. He even said that, which made me glad I was looking after me-sen and Jon. It were clear we couldn't count on him being round for good.

This one night we were sitting round and Mark was sober. He'd had a couple of spliffs but nowt to send him OTT, no crack or coke or booze or owt like that. He was in that silly phase, when you've had a bit of puff and you're giggling and messing and can't take stuff serious. We were sat in the living room and Duggy was out, and Mark was tickling me to death, so's I couldn't hardly breathe, the way men like to do to women sometimes, God only knows why. When he stopped and I was laying there, my head on his knee, tired out and grinning my head off, I remembered I loved him. All the shit he'd done recently and it were gone, in a flash, just cause he was in a good mood for a change. I thought about what I needed to tell him, and it wiped the big soppy smile off my face. Mark noticed straight off.

'What's a matter?' he said, sitting up.

'I fount summat out. About why Bek ran off,' I said.

Mark screwed up his eyes then, and sat up straighter. 'Go on.'

I explained what was hid in Duggy's room. I left out the bit where Bek'd showed me, and we talked about what to do, and how I helped her sort things so's she could run off. I took him up to Duggy and Bek's room and showed him the loose floorboard and the stash of notes and tapes Duggy'd hid there. He asked me how comes I'd found them, and I said I'd been suspicious for a while, told him about the pill Duggy didn't take and how he'd calmed Jon down, all professional. 'Bek running off crowned it. I knew summat was up so I came and had a look for me-sen,' I told him. Mark nodded, and held onto his chin and looked all thoughtful and serious as I told him and showed him everything I knew.

'How long yer known bout all this?' he said.

'Since last night, when Duggy was out,' I said. He screwed up his eyes at me then, as if he knew I was lying. I wondered if I'd done summat to give me-sen away, like the way Bek played with her hair and licked her teeth. If he had his suspicions then he didn't say owt, so maybes it were all in my head. He walked up and down the room looking deep in thought, and I got all nervy thinking I hadn't seen owt of his reaction, not yet. He sat down on the mattress and crossed his legs.

'Well he'll have ter go, won't he?' he said and looked

up at me. I half nodded. I knew he'd say this but it still sent sparks down my neck then through my body. At least he wasn't going psycho or blaming me. 'Can yer see any other way?' he said to me, as if he'd read my thoughts about it. I shook my head. I'd been through it with Bek. 'Right. You better think-a summat yer can do then. Summat careful so's it looks like an accident, like what happened wi-Tyneside,' he said.

I looked him up and down and laughed out loud. 'Me? Why me?' I said. I thought he was having a laugh.

'I did Tyneside for yer.'

'Yeah, you did that fer me,' I said, in this sarky tone of voice.

'What yer try-ner say?' he said.

'Nowt,' I said, and started stomping towards the door.

'Kez,' he said, all soft, calling me back. I hated that. I hated the way people used the different ways of saying my name. How they called me Kerrie-Ann if they wanted to lecture me, specially the teachers at school and older people like Mrs Ivanovich and my mommar. But if they wanted me to do summat for them it were 'Kez', or 'Kezza' or even 'Kerrie-Anna' in this teasy way. That bit more friendly, creeping round me so's they could get what they wanted. I hated most of all that it worked on me. I turned back.

'C'mon, have a seat here a minute,' he said, tapping the space beside him on Duggy's mattress. I sat down.

'My hands are dirty with this Phil nob, and I did it fer you, no matter what yer think. Do us a favour and help out here. Yer need to learn how ter deal wi-this side of the business anyways,' he said. He put this as if bumping someone off was just one of them things you had to do in our line of work, like how divers have to go underwater, and electricians to the top of huge cooling towers. It made me wonder what'd gone off behind my back. It sounded like he'd already learned to 'deal with this side of the business' on a regular basis.

'I don't see why,' I said.

He kissed me then, on the lips. He held my face with his two big hands and pulled away, making me look into his eyes, 'Just trust me, Kez,' he said. And that was the thing. I didn't trust him. I might of loved him, but trust was a different thing altogether.

'Yer got ter be careful though,' he said.

'How d'yer suggest I do it then?' I asked him.

He took this as me saying I was in, and patted me on the back and called me a good gell. 'Tek him joyriding and mek sure he gets threw out the car or summat. Mek it look like a good, old-fashioned road crash and cover yer tracks,' he said.

'Okay, that's easy then. I'll just steal James Bond's car wi-an ejector seat or summat, shall I?' I said.

Mark laughed then, and I half smiled, and he nudged me like he wanted to get me to laugh again, but I ignored that. 'Yer'll think of a way,' he told me. 'Clever gell like you.' He put his arm round me then, squeezed me tight. His skin was warm and nice next to me, but I shivered. It'd struck me, you see. How clever he was when it came to killing. And I'd took the money off I'd saved, a bit at a time, and bought a load of them bond things Bek'd told me about. If he cottoned what I was up to then it wouldn't be no trouble for him to sort me out. Jon too. He'd do it in a flash and make sure no one knew it had owt to do with him.

'You cold?' he said, noticing me shiver.

'Someone walked over me grave,' I said.

'Yer'll be alright,' he told me, and I guess he thought I was worrying about Duggy. 'Besides owt else, yer a better rider than me. Yer'll have more chance-a pulling it off, not being nasty,' he said.

He was right. We'd took to doing a lot of joyriding since Bek'd showed us the ropes. If we fancied going somewhere, we'd sort out an old car off the estate and use it, bring it back to where we found it. We'd never properly steal from them like us on the estate, see. But we would from the nobs who lived up Aspley and Wollaton. We'd take their posh cars without giving it much thought, drive them round fast as we could. Prang them sometimes, if we felt like it. Sometimes we'd take them back so's the owners didn't even know they'd gone. Mostly though, we brought them back to the estate and torched them, made a little bonfire to amuse our-sen. It were better than being bored.

We'd took to racing too. Stealing the fast cars, which were much harder to get into and wire, then doing the circuit round Ilkeston and Stabbo and the back end of Kimberley. That was the best thing. We'd always drop some speed or ecstasy before we did, so's our hearts'd be racing fast as the engines. Nowt felt better, I swear it didn't. The drugs could of been designed for it. I won a few of the races. Jon went faster but he crashed a lot, and Mark was rubbish. I reckon the amount of smack he'd always got in his system slowed all his reactions down, and made it so's he wasn't as bothered as the rest of us about going fast.

But even though I was good at driving cars fast and crashing them without hurting no one, we did it for laughs. I really couldn't see how I could turn these skills to killing, not without taking me-sen out too. I wondered if that was part of Mark's plan and looked him in the eye to see if there was a shred of guilt about him. If there was, then he hid it well. But he noticed me looking and stared back at me, all quizzical.

'You alright?' he said. And I nodded.

I wasn't all right, though. I couldn't of been more stressed about what Mark wanted me to do. It did my head in. Mark was out on it all the time, the few weeks after I'd told him about Duggy. For the first time in my life I was jealous of his addiction, wished I had somewhere to turn the way he did, summat I could put inside me to take all the worries away. I remembered what it felt like. I wasn't stupid, I knew the stuff Uncle Frank'd given me that time I got beat up was smack, probably shitty stuff too knowing that wanker. I could recall like it were yesterday how good it'd felt, though, how it'd took all the pain I could of ever had and lifted it, made it float off. I liked my chemicals, speed and ecstasy and stuff like that, but all they did was get you up and going. They weren't painkillers, not like what Mark had.

This one night, a couple of weeks on from me telling Mark about Duggy, Jon wanted to go raving. I still wasn't comfortable about him doing that kind of shit on his own. Besides owt else, I knew what kind of rubbish other dealers were selling them days, in the name of E. It were more than just pills cut with other stuff by then. Some on it just wasn't MDMA at all, but other nasty chemicals what you wouldn't want no one to take. I wanted to make sure if Jon was taking stuff, that he should get summat decent. And I fancied it me-sen to tell you the truth, getting out of my head and dancing the night away. It were summat I hadn't done in a while.

'I'll come wi-yer,' I said. And Jon didn't argue, maybes cause he wouldn't of dared, but maybes cause he knew I had the best pills in town anyhow, and he wouldn't have to pay for them.

The rave was on a farm the other side of Strelley. Some local farmer who was a bit of a hippy'd set it up, given over his land in the name of peace, love and under-standing. This was what you got out of MDMA, I spose. I know we never had no trouble at raves, not unless there was alcohol round as well. Not like you got downtown in Nottingham. Jon and me walked through Strelley Village, downing pills and water as we strode past the church. I'd walked through there at night before, a load of times, with Mark. Phil used to bring me down the village to get up to stuff, when he couldn't at his flat cause his gell-friend was staying. It'd always seemed a friendly place before, even with all the graves and the old, quiet church. It didn't this time though. Shadows danced round the churchyard and it seemed like they was taunting me. We know what you're on with, they said, peeping from behind the oldest headstones, the ones so black with what the rain'd left behind you couldn't read the names no more.

'Hurry up,' I said to Jon.

'Where's the fire?' he said. He smiled. 'The field'll still be there in five minutes.'

'I'm cold,' I said, and shivered to prove it.

He looked at me funny. It were midsummer night and the air round us was warm as a bath. Then he shook his head and laughed. 'Sometimes I just don't get yer, Kez,' he said. Jon wasn't after owt when he called me Kez. He always called me that, whether he was mad with me or wanted summat or was trying to give me a lecture. It were just my name to him, not summat he used to get his own way. To manipulate me, as Duggy would of put it. I looked at my not-so-little brother and felt a surge of love for him. Not like the way I felt about Mark, that black keening love you feel for a boyfriend when things aren't quite right. But summat stronger. Summat thicker than water. I put my arm in his and he smiled down at me. We skipped along the road and I didn't feel cold no more, had forgot about the graveyard.

By the time we got to the farm, we'd come right up. The pills we'd took were strong as you like, needed to be to be any good to me them days. We were grinning our little heads off. I looked at everyone gurning round me. It were ridiculous to look at, like summat was wrong and everyone was trying to smile anyway. Cept their eyes were wet and haunted with it, and you could tell people were gritting their teeth that way you do on E. The farm was the prettiest thing I'd ever seen, at least, since the last time I'd been E'd up to the eyeballs. Fairy lights'd been strung over the hedges and dry stone walls what lined each field. The place was full of people, all young and beautiful and as full of it as me and Jon. Huge great speakers were made tinny by the sheer size of the venue, couldn't compete with the open air and the sky what went on for ever and ever. I looked up and loved the stars. I hugged and kissed Jon. We went and danced to the empty music. In the fields it were like the light breeze was blowing the sound away, but we didn't care.

Some bloke I'd never met before grabbed me from behind. I giggled. I turned and kissed him. Then we were snogging like there was no tomorrow. I turned back to my brother, who was looking a bit put out. I smiled at him, and brushed my hand down his arm, flirty almost. I let it hover near his hand, just touching his skin. His skin was so beautiful. So smooth and unworried, such a rich chocolate colour in the moonlight. It felt silky under my hand and I told him so. Before I knew it he was hugging me, then this bloke what I'd been snogging a minute before. That was the way it worked, see. You couldn't get mad with no one, not for more than a minute, even if you tried your hardest.

'Look,' some gell said, pointing up. The sky was amazing. It were like the sun hadn't completely gone down that night, and there was some of its red light leaking into the darkness like blood over leather. It looked like summat out a science fiction story, all smoky and industrial. God knows what made it look that way, maybes summat from the power station a couple of junctions down the motorway. Or smoke from the Player's or Boot's factories, not far away in the Rylands. I was staring so hard at the sky my neck started hurting. I tried to lean back and go with it, and lost my footing, started falling. I laughed. I was scooped up by Jon before I hit the ground and then we were both laughing. Laughing and laughing so's we couldn't stop. I'd forgot all about Duggy. I couldn't of remembered about him if I'd had to.

We didn't stay for sunrise in the fields, with the speakers not strong enough to make headway against the midsummer air. We walked off, and headed back towards home. We walked towards the motorway, but hadn't remembered the right route from the farm and found our-sen a long way from the bridge. I was walking towards it, and Jon came up behind me, ran into me and dug his hands into my ribs, tickling me like mad. I couldn't hardly stand it, but I giggled again. The muscles in my cheeks, at the corners of my mouth, well they were hurting like mad I'd laughed and smiled and gurned so much.

'There in't no one on the motorway. It's quiet as owt,' he said, turning me to face it.

'Yer mad. Tockally, utterly mad,' I told him. But he just kept saying look, look, look, and the pair on us kept falling into each other, and laughing again.

We stood on the edge of the huge road. Jon was right, there wasn't much traffic at all. Occasionally a huge truck would lumber along past us, whistling away, up to Leeds, going faster even than our hearts were. God it were beautiful.

It made me think then. There I was, standing beside the ugliest road in the world, watching big monster trucks shudder past, shooting out spent diesel. I even liked the way the diesel smelled.

Jon took my hand. 'Close yer eyes,' he said. I told him he was mad again, but he shushed me, and we both laughed. Then we ran into the road like we had wings on our feet, eyes still closed. But I could hear summat coming, a massive vehicle, a truck or lorry. I squeezed Jon's hand tight. I could hear both our breathing, made faster by the running, as well as the drugs. We were running flat out, hands squeezed tight into each other's, eyes closed fast. I didn't know whether we were running into the path of the truck or away from it. I just went with it. I heard brakes squeal, and the screech of a big suspension trying to adjust as someone made it veer quick to the left. What the fuck was he doing in the fast lane anyways when they wasn't owt else on the road? We fell into the central reservation and lay on the grass. All's I could hear was our breathing. We were alive. It sounded so beautiful. There it were, that word again, the b word, kept making its-sen heard inside my head over and over. Beautiful this, beautiful that. Like owt, it lost its resonance repeated like this over and over.

It didn't mean owt no more. All's it meant was I'd had some pills.

We made it safe across the other carriageway, to our side of the motorway. Thing was, we had to walk over to the bridge to get back to Strelley anyway, so it'd all been a stupid waste of time. A very stupid waste of time in hindsight. It's the things you do on drugs what makes them dangerous.

We walked through Strelley, still on one. We made our way across Wigman Road. Even that looked frigging 'beautiful' through my E-coloured specs.

We went into Strelley Park. Jon smiled at me and squeezed my hand. We'd been like Siamese twins since we'd crossed the motorway together and we'd both done another pill on the way back. The sun was rising. Midsummer dawn. We lay down on the bowling green. Now that was beautiful. The grass was wet and lush, thick and even as if it were fake and made from fabric. You could feel the love put into it as you laid against it, the warmth came up to greet you. Course, the parkie would of killed us if he'd caught us laying on it.

The sun rose, casting more blood and pus into the mucky air up round the clouds. I grinned my head off. It were beautiful, I knew that. I was at least using the word proper then. Jon was gorgeous, lit by the yellows and reds and what was left of the moon. We laid there, and birds started to sing, and we could see the grass was green again, and that our jeans were blue, not black. I hadn't noticed before that instant that everything was black and grey and mud brown at night, even once your eyes got used to the dark and you could see.

'Happiness is cheap in the East Midlands, Kez, me duck,' said Jon. I looked up and saw the sun, a broken yolk in the egg-white sky. He was right. Two quid wholesale, them pills'd cost us, and here we were laying on grass and in love with the light.

I was eighteen years old and I was invincible. That morning everything was amazing. The light, my brother, everything. Amazing. Ecstasy does exactly what it says on the packet.

TWENTY-TWO

The council estates at Broxtowe and Aspley are laid out in ever decreasing circles. I am an authority on this cause I have floated above them, listening to them sing and vibrate.

I don't know the technical details of what ecstasy does to your brain, cept the papers say it leaves holes when it's done. What it does to me is this: I talk all posh, use long words I've picked up from books. Jon was always telling me I read too much, but specially when I was E'd up to the eyeballs. And everything makes sense, life and death and fate and collective unconscious and all that shit. The whisper-thin layer between body and soul goes permeable for an instant. I slip through it, easy as water. And I remember stuff I've not thought about for years. Like how my great mommar ran off aged fifteen and a half, carrying her cousin's birth certificate with her to Gretna Green so's she could get married. That my mommar was there at the wedding, curled up like a ball inside her mam, but it wasn't ever legal. Mommar'd told me all this before she

ran off and I'd forgot all about it. It's like the pills connect
things up in your head, get the electrics working, fire up
the synapses. Anyone who tells you they're just about happiness and dancing is missing the point.

Pills are good for happiness and dancing though, and
for staying awake. The morning after that rave, me and
Jon lay in the park with our eyes glued open.

'Got any more pills?' I asked him. I didn't want to come
down. But he didn't. 'We could steal a car,' I said to him.
'Go riding.'

'You shun't drink and drive,' he said, swigging water
from a bottle, and we both laughed.

We walked down Strelley Road towards home. We
wouldn't be stealing a car from round there, not for proper
riding when you might wreck it. You didn't do that, shit
on your own doorstep. People on our estate didn't always
have insurance, so it wasn't fair. As we walked past the end
of Coleby Road two men shot out in front of us on kids'
scrambling bikes. This wasn't that surprising in its-sen
cause people round our estate didn't exactly keep normal
sleeping hours. But it were Chris and Duggy, and that was
a shock to me. A damn lucky break, too, I thought, remembering what Mark wanted me to do. I waved at them.

'Hey boys,' I shouted. 'Giz a lift.'

'Course, darling,' said Duggy, pulling over. Chris
stopped behind him.

'Where you going to?' Duggy asked me.

'Down Aspley skanking cars,' I said.

'You should do Wollaton. S'better,' he told me. I climbed
onto the back of the scrambler.

'Yeah, Wollaton,' I said. Jon climbed onto Chris's bike
and the back dipped like the end of a seesaw. Chris looked
worried to death.

'It's too heavy wi-us both together,' he told Jon.

'It's too heavy wi-just you. It's a kid's bike,' Jon said. Chris shrugged and the two of them wobbled off, the bike revving full throttle.

'Fast as you can,' I told Duggy.

'Hold on baby,' he said.

I was skinnier than Jon and so Duggy's bike flew off much quicker. We caught up and overtook the other two after a couple of minutes. By the time we got back up to the new road near Strelley we were miles ahead. Duggy didn't give way at the junction and we got beeped at by a small white van. I stuck two fingers up at the driver and squealed with delight. I loved it when we nearly crashed. Life's not worth a toss if you don't know how easy it is to lose it.

We headed up Bilborough Road and on to Trowell, up to the posh houses with the fast cars. Most of them'd have alarms, I knew that, but there would be some what didn't or what hadn't been switched on. People didn't learn. Then I saw it. A yellow Boxster. Cake and custard, sitting there on the road. The tosser hadn't even garaged his car, too pissed to manoeuvre it through the doors when he parked up the night before, problies. Duggy pulled up and we checked it out. It had an alarm but I knew the owner hadn't switched it on cause the light wasn't flashing.

'You sure?' Duggy said. I knew Duggy had a flick knife so I asked him to give it me. I hacked at the soft top, then peeled the car open like it were a can of sardines.

'Jump in,' I said. Duggy hesitated so I went first. The alarm didn't go off. 'Told you,' I said. Duggy jumped in. As he landed soft on the seat the plush interior took a deep breath. The smell of cut leather was everywhere. Chris's bike stuttered up beside us.

'Nice wheels, baby,' he said.

'You coming for a ride, sugar?' I asked him, one hand on the huge steering wheel and one on the door, lips squashed in a moist, round pout. I was imitating the prostitutes in American movies.

'Nah,' Chris said. 'Once I get this bogger off I'm happy wi-the bike.' And it were like it couldn't of worked out better if I'd planned it with Chris and he knew what I was on with. Jon muttered summat under his breath and got off the bike. It rose up from under him and bounced. I could see the springs in its suspension. He vaulted over the side of the car and into the seat beside Duggy, all Starsky and Hutch.

'Ow,' said Duggy. 'Yer too big for tricks like that.' Jon was wide eyed as he jumped in the car. I was laughing. I didn't know how many pills he'd took but it must of been at least three or four cause he was really fucked up. There was a steering lock on the floor, summat else the owner'd forgot about. I picked it up and smashed it round the ignition column till it came off. I used the knife to tease out the right wires and connect them up. I heard the engine spark alight like a struck match. I pressed hard on the gas pedal and made the car growl, then jammed the accelerator to the floor.

I took the car out down the A610 at record speed. There's nowt like doing a hundred and ten on pills. It's like being on the Space Shuttle. When we were past Kimberley and Eastwood I veered off onto the country roads. I turned the stereo up loud as it went. Its owner'd left a Mondays CD in it, like he was cool enough to know summat about this music. Jon and Duggy were dancing in their seats.

We passed one of them signs what are a picture of skids.

I booted down then, flooring the gas pedal. We were heading straight at some fluorescent arrows and I yanked the wheel left at the last minute. I saw the cats' eyes wink at me from the middle of the road. I saw how fast we were going, via the picture in the wing mirror. We all screamed like we were on the Corkscrew at Alton Towers. This was better though. I was a great driver.

I glanced sideways as I spun the car round another mad bend. Jon's seatbelt was done up virtue of all the times I'd bullied him about it. My seatbelt was done up cause I knew what I was planning. Duggy was crouching over the handbrake like he was about to give birth.

'You should be up n-dancing,' I screamed in his direction but the words got picked up by the wind and buffeted down the road miles behind us.

'You should be up n-dancing,' I told him again, but this time I whispered in his ear so's he heard. He turned and grinned at me. He stood up, straddled between my seat and Jon's, and bounced from leg to leg, looking at his feet the way the bloke does who sings that song. As we flew at the next hedge, I slammed the brakes full on. I saw Duggy's face as he realised what I'd done. I looked him in the eye as he caught on where he was going. And I smiled. He clocked me smiling.

The Mondays blasted out from the speakers, turned up so high we couldn't hear the tyres squeal. You're twisting my melon man, the vocalist said, cool as shit. You're twisting my melon man. Whackah, whah, whah, the guitars ground notes, close to feedback, the drums rattled and I was fourteen again, waving my arms and swinging baggy jeans against my shoes on a packed dance floor.

TWENTY-THREE

Jon was curled up like a foetus on the seat beside me, sweating and shaking. I was driving fast, back down Trowell Road to get Duggy's bike. When Duggy was thrown from the car, Jon totally whited-out on me. I loved Jon but he could be crap like that, no good in a crisis.

We reached the place I took the car from. There was no sign of life in the house. The Porsche's owner was probably snoring upstairs in his big posh bedroom, dreaming about fucking some gell from the movies, hand on his dick. Saddo. Didn't know what living was. I opened the boot of the convertible and checked it out. It were empty and looked big enough to fit the toy bike. I pulled on Jon's arm and shook him.

'I need you to help me lift this thing,' I said. I gestured towards the scrambler and he walked over as instructed, head in front of his body like a gell I used to know at school who'd got tunnel vision. We both grabbed an end of the bike and lifted. It were heavier than it looked. 'Hold up Jon,' I said. I wheeled the bike over to the boot and told him to lift again. We scratched the car as we hoisted the scrambler in, but that wouldn't matter later. I heard more scraping as I slammed the lid down on top. It reminded me of men getting rid of bodies in gangster films. The boot closed and was tight shut.

We'd pulled Duggy's body from where it landed, and left it somewhere behind a hedge near Moorgreen. I'd walked over and checked his pulse, just for Jon's sake, but it wasn't really necessary. I knew he was dead. Had made sure of it.

It were weird the way he'd left the car. I'd imagined he'd fly up into the air and fall a long way but it wasn't like that. He shot straight forward and flew down the road, scraped against it like a plane crashing. I don't know if he screamed or not cause I wouldn't of heard his voice above the roar of the engine as I revved the car. I put my foot right down then and let the clutch out. Jon was looking open-mouthed down the road. And that was when I did the worst thing. I booted down and ran him over, to make sure. I had to make certain, see, cause nowt would of been worse than him waking up at the Queen's Med and telling them how he'd ended up left half dead in the middle of the countryside.

I maxed-out the car on the way back. I didn't think much about the vicious thing I'd done. I couldn't. I had too much to do and I'm like that, the kind of person who'll forget about stuff till I get the practical shit out the way. Then it hits you twice as hard.

'For fuck's sake slow down,' Jon screamed as we scraped past a hedge. His cheek was bleeding, but it were just a scratch.

I found the stretch of road where it'd happened.

'You sure it were here?' Jon asked me. I didn't even

bother answering him, but pulled Duggy's bloodstained leg through the privet to prove my point.

'Sometimes I don't like you very much, Kez,' he said. I lifted my hand and he flinched, as if he thought I'd hit him. But I was just touching his shoulder, trying to calm him down. He had a point. I didn't like me-sen much right then, neither. According to Mark it were just another side of the business, but I knew I couldn't ever think that way me-sen.

We dumped the bike skewed across the grass bank near the hedge. It clanked heavy to the ground. Jon argued we should put it on the road but I didn't want to risk causing another accident. I felt bad enough as it were. It were about five-thirty in the morning and we needed to sort things fast. Driving a yellow Boxster with its roof cut open was likely to get us noticed.

We came back a different route so's I could do Beechdale Road chicanes. Jon called me heartless after what'd happened, but it were my tradition. The top speed I'd managed without crashing was about fifty-five. It were a big challenge, weaving in and out of the beautiful wedges of concrete. This mate of Jon's reckoned he'd done sixty but I didn't believe him. I'd been riding with him and he wasn't as good a driver as me. He cared too much about mashing his-sen up in a crash. I was half-hearted that night though and only managed fifty. Before I knew it, we were driving down Lindfield Road. I was getting tired, the MDMA waning in my bloodstream.

I drove through a great gaping hole in the fence at Broxtowe Park and onto the grass. There were a load of burnt out cars. The place made me think about an elephants' graveyard, like I'd seen on The Discovery Channel. It'd always been a graveyard of sorts. When I was little it were Cinderhill tip, and there were piles of stinking old fridges and babies' prams with huge metal sprung suspensions. I didn't know what they'd done with all that junk – buried it, I guessed. Now it were where cars came to die. I had a beer bottle I found on the street on the way, and a bit of hose I carried round for just this kind of shit. I drove the motor right into the carcass of another, which creaked, and bits of sooty metal fell to the floor. I wrenched out the CD player cause I could get good money for that.

Jon was asleep so I pulled him out the passenger seat and made him walk a safe distance away. His snoring stopped, and he muttered, but didn't exactly wake up. I thought I might have to leave him there to sleep it off cause it wasn't going to be easy to drag him home. I opened up the petrol cap. Underneath the cover there was another seal what locked with a key but I found Duggy's flick knife, still in my back pocket, and managed to force it off. I pushed one end of the pipe down inside the petrol tank and sucked on the other till liquid hit my lips. The first time I did this I got a mouthful, which wasn't very pleasant, but I'd come a long way since then. I connected the hose to the bottle and filled it up.

Jon was snorting in his sleep on the grass nearby. I went into the pocket of his leather jacket and pulled out his lighter. I found his Rizlas too and rolled one up to make a fuse. I took my homemade bomb and lit it, chucked it at the car. The flame ripped through the soft top and leather seats like they was made of butter, the air smelled like an animal melting. The yellow paint on the outside of the car blackened and crackled and charred black. I watched the Boxster burn. I walked over to where Jon was lying and spread me-sen next to him. His arm reached out and squeezed me into him. I was dozing, slipping in and out of sleep. I felt the burn of the fire on my face and the soft heat of the morning sun on my bare legs. I let me-sen slip away.

Jon's loud snoring woke me up about midday. We were lucky we weren't picked up, lying next to a burning car. Maybes the police came by and thought it couldn't of been us being as we were lying blatantly next to the burnout. Maybes the police didn't come by no more if they could help it, went places there'd be less trouble to deal with. I was wide awake but my head felt fucked up. My fingers were spread across my face to keep the sun off. I pushed them away a bit and the backs of my hands came into focus.

I stared at my hands in that post-pilled blur you get, when you feel like you haven't slept for weeks. I noticed there were veins making my skin stick up, and thought this were interesting at first. I looked at my fingers for a bit, then turned my hands over and noticed the same thing was happening with my wrists. I wondered then if this was summat what was supposed to happen or not. I sat up and looked at my arms, lumps of vein sticking up on the surface. Blood vessels bulging, pushing up mounds of my sickly, pale skin. 'Stop, fucking stop,' I said. I rubbed the veins to try and break up the clots I was sure were forming. I shook Jon awake.

'I think summat's wrong wi-me,' I told him. His eyes opened but I could see nowt were going in. Jon always took ages to wake up. I shook him harder then slapped him.

'I think summat's wrong,' I said.

'What the fuck yer bugging me for, gell?' he said, swatting me away like I was a fly or a gnat.

I showed him the swellings on my arms and hands. He shrugged. 'It's probably nowt,' he said. This was hardly the kind of comment to put my mind at rest. Jon really was crap at this stuff.

'Will you come wi-me to casualty?' I said.

We got the thirty-five bus from the Co-op to the Queen's Medical Centre. We didn't go home and change or wash even and I wondered if it were obvious I'd been out all night. I checked me-sen out in the bus window as it pulled alongside the shelter. My hair was frizzy and matted up, and looked a bit like Jon's dreads. I pulled out some grass what'd stuck to me and threw it on the pavement, smoothed my fingers through my ponytail to try and pull out the lugs.

I registered at the casualty reception desk, hoping I was wasting their time. I'd read about this reaction you could get to E, summat what made your blood clot up all over your body. Maybes Jon was right that I read too much. I showed the reception guy the swellings on my arms.

'Could be an allergic reaction,' he said.

'Can an allergy cause this kind of thing?' I asked him.

'An allergy can cause anything,' he said. But this guy knew fuck-all, not a minute of medical training to his name. 'Area Four,' he said.

I walked round the corner and found Area Four. There were a load of people standing and sitting round with minor injuries, twisted ankles, torn ligaments. I wondered if he'd sent me to the right place. I looked at the form he'd given me. Lower arm complaint, it said. But it wasn't like I'd banged it or dislocated summat. I thought I might of been dying cause of blood clots in the lungs and they'd sent me to the fracture clinic.

Jon went off to get some coffee and I stood waiting for

a nurse to come so's I could hand over my form and get a place in the queue. My brain was sending sparks of panic down my spine and all over my body. The electricity crackled through me, making me want to shake my limbs and run for help. I tried not to freak out.

There was this old man in the cubicle I was stood opposite. He had a big cut on his head, an oozing red orb like the sun first thing that morning.

'I want ter go-ome,' he said. 'There's nowt wrong wi-me.'

'You've had a bump to your head and you're on warfarin and you don't remember it,' the nurse told him.

'Have I had a fall?' he said. She nodded. 'Oh,' he said. He screwed up all the little muscles he could find in his face, making the wound leak more blood.

Some woman came in and wheeled him over beside me. He was grinning his head off. I wondered how she knew him. Perhaps she was his daughter, or one of his neighbours, or a warden from his sheltered complex. I loved that idea, sheltered housing. My estate was the opposite of sheltered. In some ways the shit-coloured brick things we lived in might as well not of had roofs.

'I want to go home,' the old man said again. 'There's nowt wrong wi-me.'

'You can't, Dad. You've had a fall,' she told him. It disappointed me to find out the connection.

'Have I had a fall?' he said. 'Oh.'

I wondered what warfarin were, this drug he was on. Seemed to me it trapped the old sod in a grinning déjà-vu loop, like I sometimes got when I took mushrooms. I wondered if I could steal some from the hospital and sell it on. Then I remembered my swelling veins, my clotting blood.

At last a nurse came in and I handed her the piece of paper. I hoped the queue in front was not too long and sat down. I stood up again.

'You're in deep shit,' I told me-sen. Jon showed up then with two coffees. I took one sip from the plastic cup he gave me and felt sick. I dumped it, full, in the bin nearby. One of the orderlies told me off but I gave him a right dirty look and he shrivelled away from me.

'Miss Hill?' the nurse called, after a long time. She looked up from her clipboard with a sewn-on smile. I staggered over. She walked into a booth and offered me a seat opposite her. I fell into it.

'What seems to be a matter then?' she asked me.

'It's my veins,' I told her. I showed her the swellings on my arms and hands.

'Were you sitting out in the sun today? Did you get too hot?' she asked me.

I nodded, not just cause I had, but I also knew ecstasy made your body heat up. Summat else I'd found out through my reading.

'It's vasodilation,' she said. 'Your body's way of cooling you down. It's absolutely nothing to worry about.'

'Are you sure?' I asked her. 'It cun't be nowt else?'

'No,' she said. 'Look, my hands are the same.' She held them out for me to inspect, thick blue wires ran up to her fingers like summat out of a plug.

'It's just—' I stopped. I was thinking of telling her I'd took some pills the night before but I said nowt. Then I said thank you and rushed out the booth. And I realised that it were the drug what caused this but it wasn't blood clots, just paranoia. I'd never had it before no matter what I'd took, but I'd seen it happen to Jon loads of times. I couldn't believe I hadn't worked it out. I couldn't believe

Jon hadn't pointed it out to me. I walked over to where he was standing drinking coffee with a face as blank as brown paper. I knocked the cup from his hand.

'Hey,' he said, 'what were that for?'

I didn't tell him but stormed off, furious with him for being too thick to tell me I was being paranoid after all the times I'd nursed him through it. He really was a tosser at times.

I stood at the bus stop waiting for a thirty-five to take me home. Jon asked me a couple more times what he'd done, but gave up when he didn't get no answer. He knew me well enough to shut it.

I'd never got paranoid before, not with mushrooms or speed or owt so I wondered why it'd happened this time. Then the facts rushed through me, pumping from my heart out to my arms and legs. I'd killed Duggy. In my bullshit self-absorbed state of paranoia it'd gone right to the back of my mind. And now it hit me again, and it were physical shock as I remembered that look he gave me, his face as he flew out the car. Summat was wrong with what I'd done, I didn't know what.

I thought proper about what'd happened for a minute. It were bad enough that I'd got him standing up and shoved on the brakes so he got threw out. But then revving up the car and aiming it at him full throttle so's he didn't stand a chance, that made me feel sick to the core, and I'm not just using the word to describe being churned up or owt, but proper physical. I walked over to the bin beside the bus shelter and threw up in it. I looked up at Jon as I wiped my mouth with the back of my hand. His eyes were screwed up like he was trying to remember summat. I scared me-sen for a minute with the thought the nurse might of been wrong and I was really poorly after all, and thought how I should of told her I'd took some pills. I wondered what the fuck Mark Scotland was on with his rules about revenge, and what was necessary for the business, which fucked up god made him an authority on any of this shit.

Duggy's funeral was at Bramcote Crematorium. Turned out he was local, from some village on the way to Derby. He might as well of been from a different planet to us, though, them few miles made a shitload of difference. His mam and dad and his mates spoke with a snobby accent, and I guessed Duggy did too, once upon a time, before he'd had an assignment what'd sent him after us. Loads of people from the estate went, cause he'd made some friends. When we heard how many people were going we decided we'd better too, else it'd look bad being as he was staying with us and all that when it happened.

Mark looked out of place wrapped up in his funeral suit, with his patchy shaved head and his mad-looking eyes. He wasn't big enough to look like a bouncer, the way a lot of hard blokes do when they put on a suit. What he looked like was a bloke out of one of them Ska bands what'd been popular just a few years before. I looked rough as you like, as if I'd been crying loads, which was a handy way to look given the circumstances. It were cause I'd not slept proper at all the week before. I just kept playing the thing over and over in my head, what'd happened. My eyes stayed stuck open when I remembered how he'd looked at me when I was pressing on the brake. The once or twice I'd nearly dropped off I'd woke up with a violent start and that feeling like you're falling down a well and it'd all flooded my brain again.

Jon'd wanted to come to the funeral as well, said he'd

liked Duggy and wanted to pay his respects. I was worried about what he might say to people but I couldn't stop him coming. I told him to make sure he kept his mouth shut and he gave me that 'what you going to do about it' look again, but I knew it were all front by then. Jon was soft as shit.

It were a cremation they'd decided on. I'd never been to one me-sen. Mrs Ivanovich'd been cremated, but my mam wouldn't let me go to that, said I was too young and it were morbid. If only she knew the half of it. Not that she cared whether I was too young a few years on when Frank started me running drugs. Not if it meant she got commission in the form of the shit what she needed.

The coffin sat on this aisle while they talked about Duggy for a bit, went on about what a great bloke he was. Promising student, they said. They didn't say owt about his police job, and I guessed that was cause he was doing undercover work, stuff what wasn't finished. They wouldn't of wanted to draw our attention to that, I thought. I assumed the student stuff must of been some kind of cover. He'd certainly not seemed to be studying owt or going to no college when he was with us and he was older than normal university students, about twenty-five or summat.

Then there was this music and the conveyor belt started up, and Duggy rolled off in his coffin like summat on a supermarket conveyor belt. I wondered what happened behind the curtain. I know now it's nowt but I didn't then. I assumed that was where they burnt him, there and then. I didn't know they'd take the body off to an industrial furnace in another part of the crematorium and fire him with blue heat so's everything disintegrated into small bits. I didn't know when they handed the 'cremains' to the relatives they'd be more than dust. There'd be bits of bone and melted hair sitting in the ashes. I found out all that after.

We went outside the chapel and looked at the wreaths. There were loads. There was this one made of these little white flowers what reminded me a bit of daisies. It said DOUGLAS in big letters, his proper name of course. The letters were like great big daisy chains. I used to make daisy chains, on the park in the middle of the close when I was much smaller. Before Uncle Frank came along. Me and Trace and Jaqui, we used to wear them round our necks like garlands, wrapped in layers on our wrists, and pretend we were rich ladies in big houses. Thinking about them times made me miss my friends from junior school a bit, even if they'd let me down badly that time. Trace'd moved away a few years before, but Jaqui was still living on the estate and we said hello when we saw each other but that was it. I'd seen Trace once, in the middle of town with her boyfriend. She was pushing a pram and looked away when she saw me, but I knew she'd recognised me. Saw it in her eyes, noticed she'd looked away deliberate, the bitch. They weren't the same kids who'd sat on the park covered in daisies with me, anyway, and neither was I. It's amazing what you can do when you're little. You can stand in the middle of Whitwell park wearing clothes close to falling off you with holes in them, and the daisies round your head can be a crown. And you're a princess. You're a fairy. You can magic up whatever you want and it'll last for ever. Course, then your mommar runs off, your 'uncle' Frank comes along and has you selling 'happiness' and people beat you up, they're so desperate to get hold on it. But till all that happens, you believe it. That you're a princess or a fairy. Being a kid's a bit like being on pills without the tightening of your jaw and the staying up all night. Without the brain damage they reckon ecstasy gives you.

Some of Duggy's mates were stood round talking, wondering how comes he'd landed up riding a kids' bike through the country lanes near Eastwood. They knew he'd been living on that side of town, one of them said, but he'd been secretive about why. I bet he was, I thought. This Hoorah Henry type said summat then, about when they were at college together a few years before, how Duggy'd always been the brightest, and how sad it were. How Duggy'd been doing a PhD and was writing a 'thesis'. I didn't know what this thing was, a thesis, and I tried to earwig without no one noticing. Mark stood dead quiet next to me but I knew him well enough to realise he wanted to do one. I wasn't having none of it though and dug my feet into the floor. Duggy's mates went on for a bit about his potential and that, and how he would of made a contribution, all that kind of crap. Then they started talking about his project, 'the big one', this one bloke called it.

My head was going all over the place as I realised what they were talking about. It were like being on mushrooms, listening in to that conversation, cause nowt really made sense and the whole world felt all blurred and out of shape. I caught bits of sentences.

'Upbringing and roots of crime.'

'Criminal personalities, home environment rather than a lab or in prison.'

'More authentic. Genuine reactions.'

Just snippets like that, without no clue who'd said what. But I got enough to work out what'd been going off. If I'd been thinking real straight I would of been pissed off with Duggy for using us like we were lab rats or summat, but all's I could think about was how wrong we'd got it when we thought he was police.

It all made sense: the stuff in the notes and on the tapes. That was what Duggy's look'd meant, that was what I saw in his eyes before he flew off. You've got it wrong, Kerrie-Ann. It were clear as the midsummer sky to me now. I looked up at Mark. He squeezed my hand and looked straight ahead. No reaction, that meant. Keep it steady Kez, he was trying to tell me. I looked at them flowers. DOUGLAS. It were true, he was a student. A perfectionist. Not a nasty traitor bastard like what we'd thought. Words came back to me, stuff I'd read. Psychopath. Sociopathic tendencies. Borderline person-ality. It were true. I felt my knees go a bit weaker. I didn't want to stand there with all them people no more.

'Let's go, Mark,' I said. But this time he didn't want to move, problies thought it were too obvious or summat. He stood stock-still and squeezed my hand again. But I wasn't having none of that neither. I wriggled my hand out from under his and walked off. I couldn't hang round. I'd be sick or say summat or even faint and give me-sen away.

'Kez!' Mark called after me. I felt a strong urge to run away from my name, specially that version, the one people always used to get what they wanted, right back to Mam and Uncle Frank when I was about nine. Mark didn't follow me but Jon did.

'D'yer want ter go home?' he asked me. And I nodded. And he put his arm round me and we left the crematorium, and walked down the hill back towards home. And it were all right, with Jon there, warm beside me and helping me walk the three quarters of an hour it took to get home.

TWENTY-FOUR

When I got back from the funeral I went to bed for a bit, even though it were the middle of the afternoon. I curled up under my quilt, lay there and fell asleep. I was knackered, I can tell you, and what I'd learned'd somehow settled my head, like I'd needed to work it all out before I could relax. Once I knew I was totally in the wrong, and knew why, well, I slept like a baby. It didn't make no sense. I woke up when Mark came home and slid into bed beside me. He felt cold, even though it were hot outside. I thought it must be summat to do with whatever he'd put inside his body that afternoon, and I couldn't even guess what that'd be, not the way Mark went on. I lay there wide awake but I didn't say owt, and kept my eyes tight shut. I didn't want Mark to know I'd woke up. Once I heard him snoring I got out of bed.

The black clothes I'd wore earlier were lying beside the bed. I pulled them on over my nightdress quiet as I could and snuck out the room. The door creaked on its hinges as I left and I checked over at the bed, looking for signs of Mark stirring. His chest moved up and down under the quilt, steady. I walked away from the room on the soft pads of my feet, making no sound. I didn't feel tired no more. My eyes felt stuck wide open, glued, like I'd never sleep again. Like I'd took summat.

I went to the 'gram in the dining room and took out some cash. The right amount. Not enough so's it'd be noticed. Enough so's it'd begin to add up, sooner or later. I took these slips of paper out my bra, the premium bonds I'd bought, and put the cash inside instead. I'd buy some more bonds the next day. I was going through this routine once a week now, my special savings scheme growing quick. I went to a different Post Office each time, so no one thought owt on it.

I grabbed a torch and went outside. There was a slight chill in the air, and it looked like it might rain later, a thunderstorm or summat. It'd been hot as owt for days and the air felt ready to crack open and scream. I went to the little pots, lined up down the end of the garden, next to an aborted vegetable patch Jon'd started and lost interest in. I moved the plant pots what marked my spot. I dug, with my hands, scooping out the earth, grabbing as much of it as I could and flinging it aside. It felt good, the warm dry soil in my palms. Like sand. I thought about Duggy, how he'd be fine and dry and warm now, like this soil was. Cooling down from what they'd done to him this afternoon. I thought about Phil, stuck under tons of this stuff down Wilford Hill. I was crying but all I knew about it were the water on my face, covering my cheeks, running away and making a small trail of mud near my knees.

I felt the handle of the suitcase underneath me and pulled. It wouldn't come at first and I needed to clear more of the soil from round it before it'd budge. I levered it out and looked at it. I opened it and took out some money belts I'd bought, added the bonds. There was almost enough there now, it'd only be a few more weeks. The moment couldn't come soon enough, that were the only problem. I thought about my other treasure buried down there and pulled more soil out, grabbed the glass bottle. I pointed the torch at it. The words glistened in the light. Flammable. Volatile. Toxic. Words what described me, my life. It struck me then I could drink some, down it. It wouldn't be rank. It hardly smelled at all, a bit nutty, nowt worse than that. I could take a few big swigs and go back to bed, never wake up again.

I looked at my options. The suitcase. The bottle. It were a simple choice. Made more simple when I thought of Jon. The suitcase option meant I'd take him with me. The bottle'd be going it alone. I couldn't of left him behind to be brought up and used by Mark, maybes killed if he got in the way. I was never going to allow it. I chose the suitcase. But I didn't throw the bottle away. I buried both my options and flattened the soil, covered it back up with the empty pots to disguise the disturbance. I'd once had plants in them pots, big ones what never flowered, with palm tree leaves. But I didn't water them enough and they died, eventually I emptied out the soil and dead plants and dried up roots and put them on the pile of rubbish at the back of the garden.

I was low as I'd ever been after Duggy got cremated. Morbid, mortified, all them words what begin with m and are to do with dying. Inside I felt summat'd died, a part of me what I'd never get back. And I was tired. So tired. I didn't want to do owt. Mark and Jon both kept saying how I'd feel better if only I got out and enjoyed me-sen.

They thought I could grab hold of the sides and pull me-sen up from this big black hole. But I didn't want to, see. I wanted to sink under it, the black inky sea, lie back into it and breathe it in. Drown. I wanted to feel worse, not better, and that was the truth of it. I lay about in bed most of the day, wide awake and thinking about what I'd done. When I did get up I didn't shower or owt, not till Mark said I reminded him of my mam and I asked what he meant. 'Sitting there looking like a tramp wi-grease dripping from yer hair,' he said. And so I had a wash. That was about as much pride as I had, though.

Things were crap with Jon and Mark, and they kept arguing. I almost wished they'd gang up on me, the way they used to, Mark leading Jon astray a bit but at least not trying to hurt him. Mark got sick of arguing with Jon, and of my maudling round. He picked up the stash and some money and went off. Told me he was going to Birmingham to do some business, and if anyone came for stuff, to send them to this bloke we knew in Bilborough. I nodded.

'Yer want me to leave owt fer yer?' he said. And I shook my head. I wasn't no addict and I didn't feel like partying.

Mark being away improved my mood a bit. At least it felt like Jon was safer, and I slept a bit better. This one morning, Jon walked into my room, happy as Larry. He whistled as he walked over. He sat down on the edge of my bed and touched my forehead, like a mam does to a sick kid.

'Nah. Nowt wrong,' he said.

'What yer talking about?' I said.

'I'm not having this, Kez. Yer getting up today.' He made me sit up and he put summat in my hands. It were this voucher thing, inside a card, for the hairdresser's in town. 'It's yourn, to get yer-sen done up so's yer can feel better.' He smiled at me. 'And later, I'll score some pills for the pair on us.' Poor old Jon, thought you could solve owt with a nice thought and some good drugs. But he was optimistic, and it were cute. I couldn't help but try and do what he wanted.

The weather was all dash and bluster that day, total English crap. There were dead umbrellas everywhere. They were all over the pavements like a plague of daddy long legs hatched too early. They poked, all spiky, up from bins. It were quite hot but the air felt foreign, full of water like it gets inside a greenhouse. The rain sobbed down on the glass front of the hairdresser's the whole time I was there. This shampooist gell talked crap to me about going out and holidays and stuff. She asked me what I did and I lied, said I was a student. I would of liked to tell her the truth, see the look on her face. I'm a drug dealer, one of them evil rats what prey on your kids, and the other week I killed someone. Would she back off and run out the room? Or would she do what she did when I said I was a student, pick my hair up and drop it again in the water, and say 'lovely' and ask me if the water was okay? The rain sobbed and sobbed on the window, mirroring my mood. I could imagine putting my fist straight through the perfect membrane what separated us from the street, cracking wide open the stupor of the day. I didn't do this but, instead, thought about the pills Jon'd promised to get for that night.

On the bus home I studied the collection of mardy-looking people who got on. The woman in her thirties with wet hair stuck to her face like it were melted there. The mam with two rowdy kids, shaking her umbrella and trying to fold up a pushchair, holding a baby at the same time as making sure the other kid didn't end up under the wheels of the bus. She was about my age, eighteen or nineteen at the most. It were no kind of life.

The bus stopped and I got off. It'd stopped raining. I walked up Coleby Road towards the Six Ways Centre. I used to go there, hit a plastic ball across a table, talk to the good-looking youth worker, before Uncle Frank came along and I was too busy helping him out. But someone'd mashed up one leg of the tennis table, bent the other at a mad angle, and the youth worker'd married a gell with a cut glass accent he'd met at university. Me and the middle-class nobs I was attracted to. Maybes that youth worker was where it all started. I noticed as I came by that the windows of the youth centre were covered in that metal boarding the council used. A gang of lads stood round the fence, dressed like gangsta rappers. One of them spat on the grass. I turned the corner into my street and didn't look back. I was wary since that kid'd laid into Mark with the knife. They might of been school kids, dressed that way so's no one bothered them. And they might not.

I walked in the house and could smell Jon's spliff. He smoked them like cigarettes them days, and I'd given up trying to stop him. He'd decided his dad was a Rasta but, let's face it, no one could be sure of that. My slag of a mam wasn't round to ask, of course, but I wonder if she would of had a clue to tell him one way or the other if she had of been.

'Did yer gerr-em then?' I asked him, as I walked into the kitchen. My hair felt nice, and I felt okay. Not good, but okay for a change, and I fancied getting on one and having a laugh.

'Course,' he said, showing me some pills in the palm of his hand. I took one and had a good look at it.

'How much they cost?' I asked.

'Tenner. But the bloke says it's a double dose. Look how thick they are,' he said.

'Double stacked more like,' I said, taking one look at the tab and clocking it as PMA, the stuff we'd used to get Phil back. I'd read the other nicknames for this after Phil'd died. 'Killer' was one of them, and let's face it we'd proved that to be true. 'Jon, you can't drop that shit,' I told him.

We still had some mushrooms what Mark hadn't bothered taking. Jon hunted them out and I put some pans on to boil. I threw the shrooms into the pots. The potion bubbled on the hob and filled the room with a wet metal smell. As the water boiled we broke the law, turning the contents of our pot from toadstools into class-A drugs. Magic. As I filled a mug and passed it to Jon, in the eyes of the law I was dealing. Good job the eyes of the law weren't there then. If I'd got caught giving my brother this particular cup of tea, in theory I could of gone down for life. That made me laugh. All the other stuff I'd done, and someone in an office somewhere thought this was just as bad.

We sat at the table chatting, waiting for the effects of the tea to kick in. I wished my bro hadn't been such a tosser and'd got us some decent pills. But I still loved the nob.

I felt for the hallucinogen in my system. You have to work with them, drugs, believe in them, like ghosts or telepathy, or they don't work proper. If you fight them, especially stuff like shrooms and acid, that's when it all goes tits up. I leant back in my chair and waited to be took over, like I was a medium in a spiritualist church. And it were the same cause I knew I'd soon be speaking in tongues and seeing visions.

'Some monks tek MDMA,' I told Jon. 'I read about it somewhere. They reckon it brings-em closer to God.'

'You read too much, Kez. It freaks me out,' he said.

'D'yer think Moses was on acid?' I say. 'All them burning bushes what spoke to him and tablets handed down on mountains. Pills more like,' I said.

Jon laughed and I joined in. Our giggles bounced round the kitchen and rebounded off the walls.

I liked the way I felt. All silly and funny, like the world was a great big joke. It wasn't as good as ecstasy, not nearly. MDMA. I used to believe it opened up bits of the brain you couldn't usually use. I still think that, even if it leaves you damaged for good after. At least it's not like alcohol, a general anaesthetic, folding you inwards, making you numb so it doesn't hurt when you hit things, when you get hit, turning you into Superman with two left feet and two left hands, a superhero with the powers of judgement of a two-year-old. That's the most dangerous drug, which is why I don't bother drinking.

We sat round giggling for a while, till the shrooms took us further. I could see this huge moth on the wall, like summat out of Mrs Ivanovich's jars.

'Look at that moth,' I said to Jon.

'It in't a moth,' he said. 'It's a hole in the wall.'

I looked again. 'It's a hole in the wall,' I said. We both laughed.

We were sat opposite each other on our kitchen table, a cheap bench designed to go in a garden really, made of wood what'd been padded out with paper and other crap, covered in formica. It were cut and stained all over. We played slapsies and I won, slapping Jon softly round the face to celebrate my victory and making him laugh. I got up to fetch more tea, poured us another cup each. We sipped it.

Jon decided it'd be a laugh to tape us while we were tripping. He fetched the security camera and got it rolling. He was interviewing me.

'Miss Hill, you're a famous actress now,' he said, putting on this posh accent. He sounded like Robert. He sounded like Phil. I answered his silly questions with silly answers, but my voice echoed round the room. I could see the moth again. No matter how hard I looked at it then, it were a moth, not a hole in the wall. It took off from the wall, flew towards me. I stood up and waved my hand at it, tried to grab the thing.

'Vhatt can you see now, Mees Hill?' Jon said, putting on a German accent. He had a gift for talking in voices, did Jon. I kept grabbing at the moth. Then it flew at my face. I tried to push it away. It kept flying at my face. I was pushing at it and pushing at it and it kept flying at my eyes, trying to get into my mouth and nose. And I was screaming and waving my arms all over trying to get rid of this moth.

Jon put the camera down and grabbed hold of me. He pulled me tight to him, told me nowt was there. 'Close yer eyes, Kez. It in't there,' he said. I did what he told me, but I could still see the bastard thing, flying at me inside my head. Jon held me and kept saying, 'There's nowt there, Kez, nowt at all.' It took ages for it to fade and he squeezed me and told me it were going to be all right the whole time. It were a good job too. If he hadn't of been there I might of jumped out the window or summat, with this moth thing throwing its-sen at me the way it were.

I was calming down and Jon was still stroking my hair and I loved him so much for being like this with me. He walked me up the stairs, taking the video camera with us, making me laugh as he filmed our crappy house, and said stuff about the history of the stairs and the door, things he made up. He put me in bed and tucked me in. Stroked my head. Then he backed out the room, camera still running. He was saying stuff as he left the room, a running commentary on what was going off, but I couldn't make out the words. I shut my eyes.

I could see a line of silver like a mercury thread. It wrapped its-sen in a spiral, spinning out further and further. Then a new thread made a square shape what shot round and round till it filled up my whole head. There were a triangle then and it splintered, sending smaller triangles off in all directions, like glass breaking. Then I was asleep and dreaming, counter clerks from the dole office turning into moulded plastic aliens. In my dream I had a fit, shaking and dribbling all over. I had to fight through layers of consciousness to make it to the surface awake. I was awake but couldn't move, then I woke up and found worms on the end of my bed. Sitting up in my room, I waved my hands at the worms and screamed for Jon, then I woke up. Sitting up in my room, I had another fit, and then I woke up. I wondered if I'd died and gone to déjà-vu hell.

I woke up again, with a proper dry throat. I grabbed for the bottle of water I kept by the bed. But my hand found summat warm in its path. I sat up. I thought I was still asleep then, and would wake up again. I was waiting for that to happen when Mark woke up.

'You alright baby?' he said. And summat about how it sounded made me know I was awake. Mark was back. I'm not sure why that was such a surprise to me. But as I got used to being awake again, summat felt wrong. I couldn't put my finger on what. I sat up and Mark tried to pull me back down again, held me close and cuddled me. But he was holding me too hard. I felt trapped and didn't like it. I pushed him off. He resisted for a bit, then he let me get out of bed.

I got up and went downstairs, put the kettle on. The place seemed quiet. I couldn't explain. As the kettle boiled and I scalded my teabag, I realised what was missing. Jon was a nightmare snorer, so loud he often made downstairs vibrate with it. You could hear him loud through the thin wall what divided our room from his. It kept me awake sometimes but mostly I liked it, it told me he was there, and all right. But I hadn't heard him snoring, not at all that morning.

I slammed down the kettle and rushed up the stairs, taking them two at a time. I pushed Jon's door open. His quilt was shoved down the bottom of his bed. There was no snoring. No sign of him at all.

TWENTY-FIVE

It were like Jon'd disappeared into the air, abra-cadabra. And I knew straight away he wasn't coming back. It were like it wasn't just his physical body'd gone, but summat more fundamental. Like he'd never existed. It didn't stop me looking for him though. First in the house, checking the corners of every room in case he'd curled up in a ball and fell asleep like a cat, the way he used to when he was little. But he wasn't small enough for nooks and crannies no more, he was as big as a full grown man.

I searched the estate then, round the close to start with, and spoke to all his mates. None of them had a clue where he was, and I know they would of told me, out of being scared if nowt else. I went out into the rest of the estate, following the roads round and round in circles the way they was built. It were like when you're looking for summat you've lost, a watch or a ring. You know it's there, right in front of you, and you keep looking straight at it, but you pass it by without seeing owt. You're too busy searching to see what's right in your face.

When I was convinced he wasn't on the estate, I stole a car. An old thing, this battered up Escort, cause it were easy to get into. You could of done it with a hairclip – they built them old cars so vulnerable to it. I spose they didn't have to worry about them getting nicked so much back then. I drove round and round Nottingham in the thing, street after street, looking up and down the pavements. I don't know what I was expecting exactly. To see Jon walking along, happy as Larry, waving at me as I pulled the car over and saying, 'Ey-up mate, I've just been out fer a walk.' It were all wrong cause I knew Jon wouldn't of done summat like this to me. He was a good lad that way, never stayed out overnight without telling me he was going to, or ringing to let me know. And he wouldn't of run off. He knew what I was planning in that regard so there were no way he'd be mucking round.

Days turned into a week and still there wasn't sight nor sound of him. I felt sick to the stomach at the thought of what might of happened. That kid came to mind, the one what'd got stabbed and was found in the bin. His killer'd tried to chop him up, dispose of the body, but hadn't got the stomach for it. If he'd managed, would the kid of disappeared into the air, like Jon? Had Jon met the same man, but the bloke'd got used to the gore of it? Had he come across someone who'd 'learned to deal with that side of the business'? It crossed my mind it were a hell of a coincidence that Jon'd disappeared the same night Mark came back from his 'lickle holiday'. It made me cold to think of it, what Mark was capable of doing, even to someone like Jon he'd known forever. I didn't want to believe it were possible, but I couldn't stop torturing me-sen about it all the same.

After a fortnight I decided I didn't have a choice. I

couldn't sleep no more. Every night I lay there looking at the ceiling, or staring at the hammer Mark wore round his neck. Thinking what damage it could do to someone's skull. My eyes were rimmed red from lack of sleep, and from crying, in secret of course. I couldn't of cried in front of Mark, the way he looked at me if I did made me feel small as owt. So, when I felt the tears come on, I ran off. To the bathroom, or to Bek and Duggy's room, left like a shrine full of all of the things they'd both kept there before it all went fucked up. I'd lie on the mattress and smother my face with the quilt, and scream and cry, without no noise coming out the room. I fell asleep like that this one time. Mark came and found me, picked me up and carried me through to our room, kissing my tear-scorched face. He kissed my eyelids, which were all swollen and tender. It felt dead nice and woke me up.

'Yer bin crying?' he said.

'No,' I said.

'Yeah yer have. Yer was doing all them breathy sighy things what you always do when you've had a sob,' he said. I heard me-sen making the exact noise he was talking about and he smiled at me. 'S'alright, yer allowed to cry for yer brother running off. I wan't ever the same after me dad took off wi-Jason,' he said. Uncharacteristic, I thought, a long word what came into my head from nowhere, cause Mark almost never mentioned what'd happened with his brother. Jon would of said I read too much if I'd used that word in front of him, and I smiled at that thought, and did another one of them sighs come sobs. I thought about telling Mark I didn't think Jon'd run off, ask him to help me find out what'd happened. But I was thinking more and more it might of been Mark who was responsible. If I was right, and

Mark thought I might of cottoned that, I doubted he'd hesitate before doing summat to me an-all. So I kept my mouth shut.

I went to Broxtowe police station to report Jon missing. It went against the grain going to the pigs, it really did, but it were Jon and I was sure summat bad'd happened to him. This woman was at the desk. She looked up at me as I stood at the front of the queue. I could tell the way she eyeballed me she thought I was a junkie.

'Yeah?' she said, looking bored.

'Me brother's gone missing,' I said.

'Right.' She picked up this pen, looking even more fed up of the whole thing. 'How old?' she said.

'Thirteen.'

'You thought he might of just run off?' she asked.

'Course. I've looked fer him but they're in't no sign.'

She raised her eyebrows at me, which I noticed were badly plucked, making these strange half circles of an even thickness above her eyelids, like summat a clown might paint on deliberate. 'Where's yer mam?' she said.

'Gone away.'

'Dad?'

'Mine or me brother's?' She didn't looked shocked at this. 'It dun't matter anyways. Never met neither on-em,' I told her. The eyebrows danced a bit again then.

'You next-a kin?' she said. I nodded. 'Name?' she asked me.

She went through this list of questions then. When I'd last seen him, had I checked the hospitals, what about the ones in Derby and Leicester, was he into joyriding, drugs, gells? This came out as one long question. I told the cow that Jon was a normal teenager, for round here. She raised her eyebrows again and I thought to me-sen how she ought to have them done proper if she was going to draw attention to them all the time.

She took me into this room and asked me to wait. This older copper came in, he was about in his forties. He sat down and offered me a cup of tea. I said no. I didn't want to spend no more time there than what was necessary.

'Right, Miss Hill,' he said. 'We've got all the information about yer brother, and we'll do as much as we can about it.'

'Summat's happened to him,' I said.

'Wi-all due respect, that in't very likely. More probably he's just run off, or found some gell and shacked up there for a bit,' he said.

I shook my head. 'He wun't do that, not wi-out ringing or summat. I know he's been hurt. Or worse.'

'Miss Hill, nine times out-a ten, when teenagers go missing they turn up a month or so later right as rain,' he told me. But I kept shaking my head at him, and had to pull in the muscles hard round my mouth so's not to cry. He must of clocked this. 'Is there summat yer not telling me?'

'I'm telling you everything you need to know. Me brother's gone missing and summat bad's happened to him,' I said.

The police bloke sat there without saying owt for a few moments. Then he leaned forward on his chair. 'We'll do our best,' he said, tapping at my hand. But I didn't believe him. He thought I was a sad smackhead, and my brother too problies. People like him made assumptions about everyone off my estate. I got up and walked over to the door. I turned and gave him a right dirty look as I left, and he rolled his eyes.

'I'm not a junkie,' I said.

He smiled, one of them cocky wanker grins. 'Did I say yer were?' I was opening the door then and he said, 'Have you thought, Kerrie-Ann, that he might not want ter be found?' It were strange, to hear him use my name like that after calling me by my surname the rest of the time. I didn't turn back towards him. I slammed the door and carried on walking. Summat cracked inside me.

Mark, I thought. Fucking Mark Scotland. Like Duggy'd said, the man was a psycho and'd manipulated me. All this Phil stuff, then with Duggy as well. And now Jon'd gone and it were summat to do with him, I knew it were.

I didn't go home. I marched up the road towards Strelley Village instead. There was a chill in the air by then, not much, but enough so's I could see the steam of my breath in front of me. It reminded me of when I was little, them toy fags we used to buy, and how we used to pretend we were really smoking them on days like this.

I went up the churchyard. There was no one about cept for them as were tucked away inside the Broad Oak drinking beer. And them tucked up under the soil, course. I lit a fag and sat on the wall, breathed in the smoke. It were proper blustering around me, nasty cold droplets of rain being whipped up and into my face, but I was so fired up inside I hardly felt it. I put my feet on the wall and looked round me. Them old gravestones what you couldn't read no more, they could put the wind up you, they really could. It reminded you how short life was, and how long you'd be dead for.

I went for a wander round the graves, looked at the old ones first, then into the newer part of the yard. I read what it said and wondered how people'd died, specially the young ones. Road crashes, cancer, overdoses, what'd killed them in their prime like that? In my head, I saw the corpses underneath where I was walking, beginning to rot and mould and get ate by God knows what all. In the oldest graves, the skeletal remains, cold and white as painted china, empty eye sockets what stared up for good into the dark few inches above them. It freaked me out, and I decided there and then I wanted to be cremated like Duggy. I wondered about Jon. For the first time it struck me, he was probably dead. I wished I could be certain, one way or the other. It sounds stupid, I know, but it's almost worse when someone's missing. There's summat about being human what makes you want an ending. Closure, like the boggers call it in America. But it's true.

I walked home then, less angry but well upset instead. I came in the door and called to Mark, but there was no answer. I went upstairs and found him, spreadeagled on the bed, white and motionless. I thought of how he didn't look that different to the corpses I'd imagined down Strelley. I went downstairs and put the telly on. I flicked through the channels, but there were nowt on cept this boring football match, Arsenal versus Tottenham. I sat there thinking about Jon, what might of happened to him. About the corpses up the road at Strelley. I closed my eyes and remembered the last night I was with him. I could almost see him, sat with me at the kitchen table, videoing. I was wishing the inside of my head was like a videotape so's I could play it back, get clues as to whether he was thinking about running off. Then I realised I could play back what'd happened for real. It were all on tape cause Jon'd put it there.

I went to the front door, to the stand where we normally put the camera. It wasn't there. I had a good look round the kitchen to see if it'd been left round there somewhere, but there wasn't no sign of it. The next sensible place to look would of been Jon's room, I spose, but I didn't want to go in there. The day he'd gone I'd searched it top to bottom for clues as to where he'd be, and why he'd gone. I hadn't been exactly looking for the camera, so I couldn't of sworn it wasn't there, though I was sure I would of noticed it. I could remember how the room'd been. Random things strewn across the bed. It smelled of spliff, and of Jon of course. It didn't look the way someone'd leave a place if they'd got plans to go off somewhere. It were too depressing to look round it and see he'd took nowt with him, it didn't give me much hope. I didn't want to be reminded of all this shit, so I had a look round the front room first. I rooted through things, then pulled the sofa out. The camera was sitting there on the floor. The light wasn't flashing, the battery dead as the people in the churchyard.

I took out the tape and put it inside the adapter thing so's I could play it on the video. I pressed the button. And there was Jon, sitting with me at the kitchen table, in fuzzy but glorious colour. We were laughing like mad. All's you could see of Jon was his arm, and his hand some of the time. But I could hear his deep voice as he moved the camera round the room and we both talked shit and laughed our heads off.

There were this close-up of my face he'd done what scared the hell out of me. The look in my eyes mostly, all glossed over and drugged up. But how pale my skin looked too, white as death, white as Mark when I'd seen him a few minutes before. I didn't look no better than one of Mark's cronies, no better at all. I was too skinny as well, arms and legs like the greenstick trunks of new trees. I looked like the sort of gell I'd clock and assume was a junkie. No wonder they'd done that down the police station. It were like watching someone else. The gell in the video kept laughing at nowt, as if in preparation for the sick joke life was about to play on her. Then she freaked out. It took all the strength I'd got to carry on watching. You don't ever want to see yer-sen like that, I'm telling you.

Me and Jon and the camera climbed the stairs. The film shot between floorboards, and the old peeling wall-paper, and my arm or leg or belly, and we stumbled upstairs, and Jon garbled on about this and that. In my room, Jon must of put the camera down, cause all's I heard was muffled sounds of us talking, and saw the bottom of the divan bed, all blurred on the screen. Then me again, sleeping, and Jon going on about me looking all peaceful and being quiet for a change instead of nagging. None of the words he said sounded like summat you'd say if you knew you were off that night.

He went downstairs then, still filming and talking crap. As he got to the bottom of the staircase, in front of the door, it opened and Mark came in. Jon was filming him, and you could tell Mark wasn't happy about it. He screwed up his eyes at Jon and told him to fuck off. He went through to the living room but Jon didn't fuck off, he followed him instead. I thought how he should of known better, but then he was out on it so I doubt he was thinking straight. Mark sat down on the sofa.

'This here's Mark Scotland, infamous scary drug dealer who's so-ard he think it's a-right to pick on his gellfriend,' Jon said. My heart beat faster hearing this. I wanted to scream at him not to goad at Mark, but course this'd happened two weeks before and there was as much point telling Jon as they'd be yelling at Romeo not to down that poison.

'Fuck off, Jon,' Mark said, rolling up a doobie and waving his arm across his face as if to say 'no photos please'.

'But no, Mark. Audience'd like to know if yer think it's a-right to go round walloping gells one, or if yer just think it's okay when it's me sister,' Jon said.

Mark's face went all scary then, that way it did, like summat wild on the attack. He came at the camera like a fucking mad thing, arms and legs all over, laying into my brother, who was giving it summat back as well. They fell onto the sofa as they were fighting. I was shaking as I watched, scared witless of what I might of seen next. But the camera flew out Jon's hands and behind the sofa, and all's you could see then was the out of focus pictures of the flower pattern material it were made of. I could hear stuff though. Screaming and shouting. How's I could of slept through it were a mystery to me. I spose it were all them Lucy in the Sky with Diamonds dreams what I'd had that night. I'd tried to wake up, over and over, I remembered that, but I'd been too deep gone. I wanted to stop the tape, turn it off before I found summat out what I didn't want to know. But I couldn't, see. I needed my ending too bad.

I didn't get it though. All's I heard was a wild yelp from Jon, and another shout, then the sound of summat heavy falling, and doors slamming. Then silence. It could of been Jon being hit over the head with a hammer, and dragged out the room, and Mark slamming about mad with him still. Or it could of just been a fight, and Jon storming off in a temper, careering out into the night taking nowt with him. It were impossible to tell. I rewound and played the tape a few times, but I got no further trying to work out what'd gone off. There was no blood on the bare floor, or the sofa. Nowt to make me think Jon'd been

249

hit with the hammer in that room. If this was what'd happened, then Mark'd done a proper job of cleaning up after his-sen.

It didn't matter though. Dead or alive, I knew I wasn't going to see my brother again. I could tell by the sounds on the tape how much my psycho boyfriend'd scared him. Mark, the bloke who reckoned he loved me more than owt else in the world. Fucking liar. It might of been true a few years before, way back whenever. But if he could attack my brother like that, then he was full of shit. All's he cared about was his-sen, and getting his next fix, nowt else mattered. If he'd really loved me he would of took care of Jon, like he did that time I was away.

I played Mark's face over and over, the way he'd come at Jon like the psychopath Duggy'd described in them notes he'd made. It were a face of pure evil, all snarled up with hate and focused on destroying summat I loved. Tears streamed down my face. I didn't care if Mark saw me cry then, I couldn't of cared less what he thought of me at all. I knew it were important to make sure he didn't realise I'd seen the tape, though. For a few weeks I'd been filling the suitcase. As well as putting premium bonds in the money belts, I'd packed clothes and other stuff I wanted too. I was ready to go any day. I'd been taking more risks to get it sorted since Jon'd gone. I took the tape out the player, then out the case thing, and put it back in the camera, threw that back down behind the sofa where I'd found it.

I went upstairs, looked at Mark laying there, all peaceful. There was a bit of colour coming back in his cheeks then, and I knew he wasn't as out on it as he'd been. I thought about taking the hammer and smashing his head in, then getting my suitcase and running off. But I didn't have the guts for it, and that was the truth. Besides, he was too close to waking up by then and it'd just as likely end up being me who'd got their head mashed up. I had some other ideas though, to do with the poison what was buried in my garden. I was full of ideas about that.

TWENTY-SIX

My tongue was bleeding from biting on it, but I said nowt to Mark about the video I'd found, and what'd happened with Jon. Every time my brother's name came up in the conversation, crunch, teeth into tongue. It would of been stupid to say summat at that point, with everything ready for me to get away. Specially when Mark went to pains to tell me it'd all be alright, like he knew everything in the world. It were the faking what pissed me off the most. What he'd done to Jon was bad enough, but pretending he knew nowt was taking the piss. Making a big deal of reckoning Jon'd be all right, only a right wanker'd do shit like that.

We were sitting watching telly one night. I was fidgeting, and kept going in and out the kitchen fetching stuff. A glass of water. Then crisps, though I didn't even eat them. I made a cup of tea for the pair on us. I just couldn't sit still.

'What the fuck's up wi-yer, Kez?' Mark said.

'I just got the fidgets,' I said. It were a word we used to

describe the moods Mark got into from time to time, and it wasn't typical of me. Mark frowned at me, side on.

'What you bin taking?' he said.

'Nowt.'

'You an't been at me smack, ay-yer?' he said.

'No,' I said. I didn't say owt for a minute, stared at the telly. 'What if I had?'

'Yer don't want ter gerr-inter that Kez, I'm telling yer,' he said.

'Halle-bloody-luia,' I said. Mark half smiled, and took a gulp of tea. He burped dead loud.

'You're disgusting,' I said.

He answered with another loud belch. God knows, given all what'd gone off, why it bothered me, but I had to leave the room. I went upstairs and opened the window, leaned out and breathed in the air. I could smell bonfire, and heard a firework go off in the distance. It were only October, so problies kids fucking about. My heart flipped at the thought it might of been Jon. He'd always liked fireworks, since he was well little. He'd learned how to set them off when he was nine, Mark'd showed him. I watched over the park for a while, hoping to see his dark shadow heading back towards the house. He'd be chewing summat, a match or toothpick or whatever he could get his hands on. Spitting bits of it sideways onto the concrete. Swaggering. I could see him clear as if he was really there. Course, he wasn't.

I went downstairs then. Mark was probing behind the sofa.

'What yer looking for?' I said, as if I didn't have a clue.

Mark pulled out the video camera, all full on it. 'Da-daa!' he said. 'I've been looking fer that all over.'

'Din't know we'd lost it,' I said, sitting down and chewing my nails like the camera wasn't no big deal.

'Yeah, I was messing wi-it when I were out on it, the other day. I cun't remember for the life on me where it'd gone,' he said. He let out a shot of laughter. 'Must of bin well out on it.'

'You must of,' I said. I stopped talking then, cause the words going through my head were wanker, bastard, liar, cunt, and I would of said one of them out loud if I'd of opened my mouth. Then I sat up. 'You don't think they might be summat on the tape what'd help wi-Jon,' I said. I said this all earnest, I deserved an award for my acting, I really did.

'What d'yer mean?' he said.

'Well it might of recorded him going off. Or summat happening ter him,' I said.

'Nah, I checked the tape before, when I were messing wi-it,' he said.

'I thought you was out on it,' I said.

'I wan't that out on it,' he said. 'Anyways, the battery's dead. They'll of been nowt recorded on it for weeks,' he said.

'But you was messing wi-it the other night,' I said.

'There in't nowt on it,' he said, raising his voice and turning sharp towards me. I held a hand up in front of my face. He gave me that scary look for an instant, then turned away. He stared straight ahead at the telly. 'That were two week ago. The tape would of run out-a space. It would of recorded over owt what were there be-now,' he said.

I shrugged. I'd backed me-sen into a corner. To say owt else would of given me away. Saying nowt might of as well. 'I just want ter know what's happened,' I said. I think there were this little part of me wanted Mark to tell me about the row. Confess he'd upset Jon and my brother'd ran off cause of it. That'd mean Mark wasn't a total lying wanker, and Jon wasn't dead. 'What d'yer think's happened ter him?' I said.

He turned round on the sofa to face me, looked straight at me, all serious. 'I wish I could tell yer, Kez. I swear down, I do. I can't work out why he would of ran off but teenagers are all fucked up, yer know that.' I didn't say owt and looked straight back at him, right into them big grey eyes. They didn't give him away, not one bit. I wondered how much he could tell from my expression. I was thinking liar, wanker, nob, thinking them words hard like I thought my hate could of melted him. He was talking again then, stuff what went in my ears but I hardly heard. Every word he said made my neck prickle. 'He said summat ter me Kez, night he left. You was in bed and I saw him down here. He was pissed off that I'd hit yer, and said he were sick of having ter live under the same roof as me. I got the feeling then he meant summat more, like he was planning to go off.'

'And you just lerr-im?' I said.

'He din't go nowhere, not while I were up. I wun't-a let him,' Mark said.

I had to turn away from him then. Otherwise I would of spat in the wanker's face. My eyes stung. Mark took hold of my chin and turned my face round so's I was looking at him. It were like he was even going to decide what I looked at.

'C-mon, Kez. He'll be back when he's sulked enough. He's just tryna put us through it,' Mark said. But summat about the way he said it didn't ring true. Maybes he wasn't such a good actor after all.

'What if he dun't? What if summat's happened ter him?' I said.

Mark shrugged. 'You mithering on ter me in't going ter mek much difference,' he said. And I could of smacked him one. The only thing what stopped me was the thought of the suitcase buried in the garden. And the poison. It wasn't worth starting a fight with Mark. I was too close to what I really wanted and he'd took enough from me.

It stood out to me, that afternoon, how easy he found it to lie. I mean, I wasn't exactly being open and honest, I know that. But that was hard for me. I wanted to blurt out everything I knew, and it were only the sight of the hammer round Mark's neck stopped me. I knew him well enough to pick up little signs he was bullshitting, the way he looked to the right, and chewed at his nails, for starters. He was a better liar than Bek – the signs weren't so extreme, but they were there. Still, he sat calm as you like, looking me in the eye without no emotion, pretending he hadn't threw his-sen at my brother like a wild animal the night he disappeared.

His focus'd moved, he was watching the telly now, all intense on that. He'd got the fidgets, and kept glancing at the clock, and I knew it wouldn't be long before he needed his next fix. Them days when he took stuff, he didn't look high after. There'd been this time when he had. I can remember exactly how it'd been. It were like his whole skin were smiling, and his eyes glowed like cats' eyes in the middle of the road. But now he only looked relieved, like some doctor'd told him a lump he'd found was just a cyst.

'What d'yer think I should do about it?' I said.

'Bout what?' he said.

I looked right at him. He was sat forward in his chair, eyes straight ahead, focused on the next fix, that was all. Nowt else mattered. He'd genuinely forgot the whole of our last conversation, the one where I was all het up about what might of happened to the only family I had. That was it then, the moment I decided he was going. I would put the nob out of his misery, cure his addiction for good.

Mark was no better than an insect, a nasty piece of garden mush, and I was going to kill him just like I'd kill a beetle, caught in a jar.

Back when Mark'd wanted Phil out the way, he'd told me these rules about revenge. Once I'd decided I wanted my own back on Mark, I wrote them down in a notebook, just to remind me what he'd said. I wrote the title 'The Scotland Method' then three sentences.

Revenge should be quick.

It were quite funny to see this, written on my Silver Jubilee notepad in the girlie bubble writing we'd all culti-vated at school. I wondered what 'quick' meant. A week, a month? Mark hadn't specified. I was planning to get mine just as soon as I could pluck up the guts. That'd have to be quick enough.

You need to see your revenge for it to work.

It wouldn't be dramatic, Mark Scotland's death. He wouldn't go out with a bang, like what Duggy had, and it wouldn't be as ugly as Phil Tyneside's sticky end. And the way I was planning it, I couldn't stand in the room with him unless I wanted to suffer the same. But I could watch it. I had just the equipment for the job. One afternoon when Mark was out, and I knew he wouldn't be back till the night time, I took down our security camera from the front door. I wasn't worried he'd miss it, and thought if he did I could tell him it'd been nicked or summat, and say it were ironic, a word what usually shut him up.

I balanced the camera on top of the wardrobe and hid

it under one of the spare blankets so's just the lens poked out, and you would never see that unless you knew it were there. This bloke round the corner'd swapped me this video extension lead for a few grams of speed. It were a long thing what stretched all the way downstairs. I trailed it under carpet, where we had it, and beneath the floor boards where we didn't. I plugged it into the telly downstairs, and tuned it to the video camera. I looked at the picture. It missed the bed, pointing too low. I went upstairs to adjust the camera, shoving some pillowcases under it, but ended up with the top of the wall and some ceiling on screen. It took a few trips up and down stairs before I'd got it sorted. Then there it were. Mine and Mark's bed, perfectly framed. Like I was planning a dirty movie or summat. But that wasn't what I was planning.

Make sure the fucker knows it were you.

This was the hardest by a long way. There were no way I could make Mark so vulnerable to me that I could tell him. If he found out it were me before he was dead, then I'd cop it as well. He'd make sure he took me with him, no matter how weak he was. I decided it wasn't all that, this rule. Maybes I could ignore it. Would have to.

I'd dug the poison up from the garden. It were just a matter of waiting till the right moment. Mark'd have to be wasted on heroin for it to work. It were the only way he'd not work out what was happening to him, not wake up. As I switched the channels back to the TV, I hoped he'd come home wasted that night. The longer this sat round all set up, the more likely it'd be that Mark'd cotton on. In a practical sense, that first rule was all important.

He came home wasted that day, but it were from booze and not heroin. He'd had some smack, earlier in the night, then got pissed. He had all sorts of other shit in his system too. A line of coke. A bit of speed to keep him awake. When he's like that he twitches, and notices stuff he wouldn't normally. It were dark outside and I hadn't expected him to see that the camera was missing, but he did.

'What yer done wi-the camera, Kez?' he said as he came in the door.

I had my answer, about it being stolen, but then I thought, what if he found out what I'd done with it? If I said it must of been nicked and then he saw what I'd set up he'd know summat dodgy was going off.

'I needed it for summat,' I said.

'Fer what?' Mark said.

'A surprise,' I said.

He sniffed up hard, and adjusted his-sen on the sofa. 'We got any beer?' he said.

'Don't know. Don't drink it,' I said.

He laughed. 'Yer might as well do, Kezza duck, all the shit you put in yer system the odd pint in't goin-ter crack it.'

I ignored him pointedly, staring at the telly. *Coronation Street* was on.

'This is shit,' he said.

I shrugged. 'I like it.'

'Let's put a video on. *Pulp Fiction* or summat,' Mark said.

I prickled. 'I'm watching *Corra*,' I said, too quick.

'C'mon baby, since when've me and you argued like middle-aged pricks about whether to watch *Pulp Fiction* or *Corra*,' he said, getting up from the sofa and laying right across the floor, playing with the video controls. The batteries in both remotes'd gone ages ago, and we'd never bothered fixing them. It were less effort to lean across from our chairs or spread across the floor to change channel, size of our front room. As he reached for the TV buttons I felt sick, and I nearly gave me-sen right away, my instincts being to run out the room and hide. But I held firm. He flicked channels. There it were, our bedroom on the screen. Mark turned to look at me. 'What's going off?'

I smiled. 'I was hoping we could use it fer that special movie, the one you was talking about when we first got the camera,' I said.

Mark carried on staring at me, and I grinned at him but it felt well fake, more like a grimace. His face didn't change for so long I didn't think I could hold the smile no more. Then he grinned. He threw back his head and laughed. It went off in slow motion. 'Now yer talking, baby,' he said. He walked over to the sofa and grabbed hold on me. He picked me up. I was skinny as owt and feather weight, and it seemed like I flew into the air under his arms. He was skinny too, but still strong despite that. He swept me out the room and up the stairs. I didn't point out he hadn't pressed record.

We never made love them days, me and Mark. We had sex, fucked each other from time to time. It depended what type of muck he'd took. If he was coked or rushed with speed, he wanted to manipulate me into awkward positions, tie me up and play-act fantasies. If he'd took smack he wasn't interested in doing much more than picking his nose or sleeping. He didn't drop pills very often them days. Maybe it wouldn't of made much difference in any case. He was so messed up who knows.

He threw me on the bed and started pulling at my clothes. I lay back and tried to kiss him but he laughed, and pushed me over onto my front, pulled up my mini skirt.

'Yer a dirty lickle slapper like yer mam,' he said. And he pushed my face into the pillow. 'Is that nice and comfy?' he said. 'Yes?' And he pushed me harder. 'Now?' I made a muffled sound from inside the pillow. 'No?' A pause. 'Good.' I couldn't see what he was doing behind me, all's I could hear was his clothes rustling round. Then I felt him push up inside me. He thrust hard over and over so's my messed-up screams went straight into the pillow. Having me half suffocated must of really turned him on, cause he'd cum in about a minute. He groaned and fell off me, and I could move my head away from the pillow and breathe again. I gasped for air. 'That'll look nice on film,' he said. I didn't say owt. I was just glad I'd got away with the video shit.

It were two afternoons later he came home wasted and went to bed. I checked he was proper gone, dropping things in the room and banging loud as I could to make sure he was as dead to the world as I needed him to be. He didn't stir. I went downstairs and found the potassium cyanide.

To make a killing jar for an insect, you need to put a layer of plaster in the bottom, and soak it with a tiny bit of liquid. Just a drop on cotton wool's all you need. I knew, cause Mrs Ivanovich'd told me.

To make a killing jar for a person you needed a lot more. I knew this too. Mrs Ivanovich'd told me.

She didn't set all that up her-sen, course not. She was too weak, in too much pain with arthritis in her arms and legs and back. She couldn't of lifted all them bowls of poison, placing them on top of the 'gram, beside her chair. At that point, she couldn't even get her-sen upstairs to get a bath. 'You need a couple of washing-up bowls to be sure,' she'd told me.

'I don't want to get found and put into one of those home places, Kerrie-Ann. We've got to make sure,' Mrs Ivanovich'd said. I'm sure she thought I understood but I swear down I didn't, not till I saw her laying still and stiff and cold as a dead fish the next day. Then I knew what she'd made me sort for her. All's I thought at the time was I was helping.

'It'll stop hurting me if you do this, Kerrie-Ann,' she'd said.

I was five for fuck's sake. Course I didn't understand what I was doing. But I did this time.

'This'll mek yer all better,' I said to Mark, as I placed a washing up bowl beside the bed. 'All better,' I said, putting the bucket next to it. I thought about pouring the stuff all over the quilt cover, but I didn't. I don't know why, cause it wouldn't of woke him, not how out on it he'd got his-sen.

I kissed him then, and drew back. The kiss what'd send him to sleep, like the reverse of sleeping-fucking-beauty. There were nowt beautiful about neither on us though. 'This is goin-ter mek you feel all better, baby,' I said. I took the clingfilm I'd brought up from the kitchen, and pushed and pulled it round the edges of the window where they let in cold air and would of let out the fumes. This was another little detail Mrs Ivanovich'd had me deal with all them years back.

I took one last look at him from the bedroom door. He looked nice and peaceful. I could almost imagine him as the kid I'd first known. But I knew it were a fake peace, virtue of stuff he'd injected. I could see his works sitting on the dressing table, in a glass of water. They was sat there like a normal bedside thing, false teeth, or a glass of water to drink if you woke up. You'd get a nasty shock if you drank this water. It were misted with blood, a vivid red snaked through the water out the end of the syringe. It made me sick.

I closed the door, and used the rest of the cling film to seal that as well. I went downstairs then, and turned on the telly.

There was a perfect image of Mark on the screen, asleep on our bed. His head was at the centre of the picture and as he breathed the pillowcase moved underneath his mouth. I watched. I pulled my eyelids wide for fear I'd drop off and he'd wake up. I was ready to sprint, without even the money bonds if need be, away from Mark's vicious streak. But he didn't wake up. The only movement on the screen was his breathing, up and down. It were narcotic. Soporific.

It were a lullaby.

TWENTY-SEVEN

I dreamed I was crawling along the garden on my stomach. But the grass towered round me, and I was tiny and could swim in the mud. I couldn't work out what was going off, then I tried to look at my hands. But I didn't have no hands, or legs ner nowt else for that matter. Just a long green body, wiggling through the mud. I knew then I was a caterpillar and things made sense. Sometimes, when I'm asleep, I know I'm dreaming. But I didn't. You'd think you'd realise cause of how silly it all were. It sounds stupid, but this dream felt like real life.

I was chewing up leaves and chewing up leaves till I heaved on them. I couldn't of stood to sink my teeth into one more. They tasted like grass smells when the council get the mowers out. I decided it were time to cocoon. It were like I'd had some sort of practice at being a caterpillar before, cause I knew it were time to spin me-sen into my own little prison and wait till my wings came. I spat out brown goo, and wrapped it round me and round me. The world went brown, then black, but still I kept winding me-sen up in gooey mess. I knew it were worth it, see. Cause when I'd finished changing I'd be gorgeous. I'd be able to fly.

In my dream, I slept then. Funny, how you can sleep in a dream. But I did. I slept and slept till I could feel wings sprout from the side of me, feel them grow and get sticky and restless. Like I'd practised it all before, I knew when I was ready, and I woke up. I fluffed my wings, but course, I couldn't move nowhere. I was dying to see what colour they were, what patterns were on them, but it were dark as the inside of a wardrobe. I pushed then, thinking if I didn't get out I'd run out of air. I pushed and struggled, and it were all sticky and messy round me and I wasn't getting nowhere. But I knew if I didn't keep going I'd die, suffocate stuck there in a cocoon I'd made me-sen. So I kept kicking and flapping till I saw a small pinch of light. I pushed my eyes through the hole, then my shoulders, then I could open up my wings. They were red. The colour of blood from an artery. I was an Admiral. A leader, summat to admire.

Then I hit glass. I felt the wind knocked out on me and fell to the floor.

I was operating on insect logic and couldn't see no glass, so I thought I might of imagined it. I took to the air again, tried to fly off to go suck nectar from flowers. But I was into the glass again soon as I got any rhythm going.

I tried all the different directions I could but each time I hit this invisible wall and fell down with a thud. I was trapped.

I sat up sharp on the sofa, my breathing funny. My arms and legs hurt like wanno.

In front of me, on the telly screen, was Mark. Sleeping

like an infant, all tucked up and peaceful. But it didn't tell the full story, the one where he was being poisoned. Breath by breath, beat by beat of his traitor heart. My own heart felt like a trapped butterfly, it fluttered in my chest like it were trying to escape. I wasn't sure how much of this was down to the dream I'd just had, and how much was cause of what I was doing, how I was killing Mark. The bloke I'd lived with ever since my mam ran out on me. The only person I'd been able to rely on over the years. I told me-sen not to think that way. He'd beat up my brother, or worse, and at the very least he'd made him so scared he'd run off from me for good. Mark had it coming.

But I could only remember that when I looked away from the telly screen. I wondered then if Mark knew me better than I'd realised. If that rule about seeing it when you're taking your revenge was there for his own protection. Perhaps he thought if I looked at him as I was harming him I wouldn't be able to go through with it. But I wasn't going to fall for that shit. I flirted with the idea of him waking up, scaring me-sen with what he'd do to me. Trying to make sure I remembered why this was happening, what he was like, but it were hard to keep it in mind. He looked so peaceful.

I told me-sen it were an artificial peace. He'd paid for that contentment, God knows how much an ounce for the shit he got, but he'd once told me it cost more than gold. Then he'd laughed and said how he couldn't work out why gold was worth so much, it wasn't like you could snort it or smoke it or owt. That was the junkie talking, the bloke I hated. I could see him, in my mind's eye, and I could see me making faces at him, full of contempt. But the thing was I couldn't feel it. The look on his face reminded me of when we were first together.

I shook my head to try and get rid of that image. I stared at his left arm riding visible above the sheet. The tracks running down it. I looked right at his badly shaved head. I searched in his face for signs of the animal I saw on the video, laying into my brother like a vision of evil. But there wasn't no signs of this in the man what slept on my video screen. Maybes it were a trick of the light, or summat to do with the slight blur of the picture, but all's I could see was a little boy. On his bike, doing wheelies on Cinderhill tip. Smiling at me from under floppy blond hair. Talking bollocks after a shared hit of speed. Climbing through attics to get stuff out a house the police'd got surrounded.

I tried to remember the first time I'd seen him without them bangs what fell into his eyes and softened the harsh lines of his face. It came to me, a picture of a lad coming down the stairs. Behind him, my little brother, all pleased with his-sen for growing dreadlocks. Me, picking up the little boy, holding him and saying thanks over and over to Mark. God, I wished I could still pick up that little boy now, hold him tight and protect him from all the crap in this nobhead world. But I couldn't deny it, Mark'd looked after him then. So it didn't make no sense that he'd of hurt him. No sense at all. I watched Mark's chest, up and down, up and down, waiting for it to stop. I sighed. Did I want it to stop?

I tried to focus on the needle, sitting there in a cup of water beside the bed. It made me feel sick but didn't do as much as I'd hoped to turn me back against him. He was a fucking addict, I told me-sen. A sad fucking case with nowt going for him, and no loyalty to owt but the needle and the spoon. I searched for that feeling what usually haunted me when it came to his addiction. To any junkie for that matter, starting with my mam. Contempt it were. A raw nasty feeling what made you want to cut someone. But no matter what I thought about, what picture I brought to my head to try and hate Mark Scotland, to despise him as a junkie and a wanker, I couldn't. I felt sorry for him, that was the truth.

He wasn't stupid, not Mark, not by a long way. He'd of been dead years before if that'd been the case. Dead or in prison. You can't afford to be owt but sharp and snide in our line of work. He'd been good looking too, before he got too thin and his skin went all nasty from the rubbish he was shooting up and snorting and doing God knows what all with. He was caring too. I thought about his tender side, the times he'd held me, and the way he'd kissed away all the tears after that shitty abortion.

The things he would of done for me. Scary things, like setting light to some kid cause he'd beat me up. Making sure Tyneside got what he deserved. These things, shit what'd made me angry a few hours before, they had this other status now. Like he was some sort of hero who'd looked out for me. I couldn't help but think how stuff could of been so different for Mark. If he'd been born into a family like Tyneside's or Rob's, people with a bit of money and respect for themselves, he could of really been summat. He could of saved lives instead of taking them. Done summat important for a living instead of cutting heroin with other shit and selling it on.

He'd always looked out for me. Carrying me home after I'd got beat up that time. The state I was in, watching Mark breathe and thinking he might stop any second, in that state I kidded me-sen I could remember it. Being swept up in his arms and carried all the way home. Course, I couldn't really recall this. I'd been out cold the whole way home and hadn't woke up proper for days after, partly cause Frank'd pumped me up with heroin. I thought then how it were a miracle I hadn't ended up like Mark, hooked on it.

And I realised the memory of being swept up and looked after wasn't owt to do with that time he brought me home. It were when he thought we were making a dirty video a few days before, and he'd took me upstairs and we'd had the only kind of sex he seemed to enjoy these days. I couldn't get my head round all the different Marks what came into my head. It were like he was fifty different people.

Then I did summat I wouldn't ever of predicted. I needed peace, that was the problem. And I knew where to get peace, if I wanted to. Always had. I remembered vividly how it'd felt, after I'd got beat up, how the world melted into a happy shiny place and I had no more worries at all.

I went to the 'gram and took out some of Mark's grade one stash. I went through the routine I'd seen him do, so many times, over and over till he didn't even feel good when he did it no more. I used to wonder if it were the routine of taking smack what people loved so much, the rigmarole of melting the powder on a spoon, of sucking it up with the needle. Of strapping up your arm and pressing on the veins to find one what hadn't collapsed with it all. The pinch of the needle and that cold rush down your vein, then the hot rush to your head. Course, I knew heroin was addictive as you like, second only to nicotine they reckon. But it struck me there were summat comforting about the mechanics of a fix an-all.

I took a fresh set of needles Mark'd fetched from the exchange. He was clean living like that at least. He never shared his works. Wouldn't of dreamed of it. I took a couple of pinches of white powder. It looked like icing sugar. I knew for a fact Mark sometimes used that to cut it with. I'd seen him do it. I wondered what effect that had, shooting up sugar. You'd get some kind of hit, I guessed. You only had to look at kids when they'd ate a lot of sweets to see that. I tied up my arm, looked for veins coming up to meet the headrush I'd soon have. I added a squeeze of lemon juice and some water to the spoon, like I'd seen Mark do so often, and heated it over one of the lights on the hob. The smack dissolved, then the mixture on the spoon rolled and bucked.

I dipped in the tip of the needle and pulled back the syringe. I watched it fill with the hot liquid, then dumped the spoon on the worktop and smiled. I placed the needle beside my skin, next to the vein what was standing up to attention begging to be used.

I pushed the syringe down. What's supposed to happen next is you see your blood rush into the tube, streaking through the thick clear liquid like candy cane. And you push and all the blood and heroin and whatever other shit your dealers cut your stash with goes rushing back into you and you roll back your eyes. When you do it the first few times it's like having an orgasm. As time wears on, and your veins get all cracked and used up, and your head gets used to the rush of it all, it's not like cumming at all. It's more like going to the toilet.

What actually happened was the liquid rushed down my arm and onto the floor. I never put the needle tip anywhere near that blood vessel, never mind in it. Never really intended to. I wanted to see how close I'd come. I wanted to know if I'd do it.

I walked back to the living room. There to greet me on

the screen was another experiment, another way I was testing me-sen to see how far I could go. But this one wasn't so cut and dried. I was much more serious about carrying it through.

All these times Mark and me'd had together came into my head. That first time when we'd halved an E, and he'd said we were drug brothers. It does bond you, rolling together, specially when it's summat you've not done before. We walked up Aspley Lane, into the sunset. And I thought, 'This is the best feeling ever.'

I looked at Mark, tried to work out if his breathing was more laboured. Was he going yet? Slipping away? I couldn't tell. My eyes went all prickly and my mouth was loosening. I wanted to cry. I told me-sen not to feel sorry for the tosser. But that was it, see, I didn't feel sorry. That wasn't what I was feeling at all. Summat warm was running from my heart, through my veins. It were a little bit like how you got on ecstasy, loved up. I'd been wrong that my brother was the only person I'd loved proper. What they say about blood being thicker than water, maybes that's true. Maybes there's other stuff what's thicker than the pair of them.

My thoughts flew back to the day we'd took that E. To the last thing I remember before my brain was changed for good. Me and Mark, behind some bushes somewhere, him wanting to move our relationship on quicker than I did. Where'd we been before that?

Romeo and Juliet in a school playground, that was it. So romantic. I'd wanted to shout and scream at Romeo when he thought Juliet was dead. She's not, I would of screamed, if it'd of made any difference. She's just pretending. But you can't make no difference in a play. There's been times I've thought the same about life, that it's like that play and you can't change owt. Course, that's right about a play, and the past, but it's not the same if you're talking about the future. You can change next year, next week. You can make all the difference to the next few minutes.

I went upstairs and ripped the clingfilm off the window frames. I flung the windows wide open. I picked up the bowl, then the bucket, and chucked the cyanide out onto the back garden. It wasn't going to be no good for the plants and insects, but it were the quickest way to get rid on it. I couldn't feel that bad about it, cause I felt great about not letting Mark die.

I was still going to run off. I couldn't stay. It were only a matter of time before I'd succumb to the same painkillers Mark used to make life bearable, and that were against everything I believed. I couldn't stay and become another sad junkie, one of them wasted zombie people what worshipped Mark cause he sold them a mixture of opium with icing sugar and the odd load of washing powder. Brown, they called it, cause, depending what it were cut with that could be the colour it were.

Mark'd kill his-sen sooner or later, I knew that. The way I saw it, he had no more chance of getting out alive than that beetle in Mrs I's jar all them years back. He'd end up going OD on the smack, or get so wasted he choked on his own nasty vomit. But that was down to him. He had plenty of choices, just like I had. I couldn't carry on screaming at Romeo from the crowd. Telling him not to take the poison. Not when he never took no notice.

I stood at the door, watching Mark sleep. He shivered a bit, and pulled the quilt tighter round his-sen. He turned onto his back and started snoring. I knew I didn't have long to sort my shit out then. He was coming up to the surface, a bit slower than usual thanks to what he'd been breathing in when he slept. On the dressing table was one of my rainforest books. I'd brought it up a few nights before to have a good look at. I took the book down off the dresser and jammed it under the door, made sure it wasn't going to slip closed when I went out. I didn't want to leave the book but I didn't have room to take it with me. If I loaded the bag up too heavy I wouldn't be able to run with it if I had to.

I looked over at the bed again. Mark made some gargling noise in his sleep, then he snored again.

'Goodbye,' I said. It didn't seem a big enough word for what I was doing.

TWENTY-EIGHT

It were dark as mud outside, and cold. The kitchen window lit up the garden a bit so's I could find the spot where my suitcase was buried. As I moved the plant pots, they felt heavier somehow, filled with the lead weight of what I was on with. Bile rose to my throat for about the fifth time in ten minutes, and I was sure I was going to be sick. I swallowed back the burning and dug with my hands. The soil was muddy and cloying. It were all compacted and I couldn't move it quick enough.

I went to the outhouse to fetch a shovel, but when I pulled on the door it were locked. I swore, then went in the back door to fetch the key. It wasn't hanging on the rack with the other keys where it were supposed to be. I looked round the kitchen, through the drawers and under the stuff on the table but it wasn't nowhere to be found. I swore again, and clonked stuff about. I really felt like I was going to be sick, and my hands were shaking. I felt cold, clammy. And tired. I'd been up half the night watching Mark sleep. But I came to my senses and realised banging about wasn't going to find me the key, and it might find me a load of trouble instead if Mark woke up.

I went upstairs then, looked round mine and Mark's room quick, then the other bedrooms. Even the bathroom, though there wasn't no reason it'd be there. I couldn't find it nowhere and could of screamed with frustration. It struck me then that it might of been hid somewhere. That there might of been summat in the shed Mark didn't want me to see. Fear made its way down my neck and up my arms.

I crept back into our room, searched through the drawers quiet as I could. I found the key, hiding among Mark's boxer shorts. It were cold to the touch, and a right fear shot through me with the chill as I picked it up. It were all I could do not to fall right down the stairs in a dead faint, but I made it out to the garden again. I knew it'd be getting light soon, and I was shitting me-sen that Mark'd wake up and find me.

I pushed the key into the lock, my hand shaking so hard I couldn't hardly hold onto the bogger. I managed it, but had to push up hard on the handle to straighten it flush so's the lock'd move. I pulled the door wide. The smell from inside hit me hard. It were rank, the dried blood smell of a butcher's shop but worse. It were the stink of rotting flesh. I didn't doubt it.

I retched as I walked in. The smell was too strong, and I threw up on a rusted up old lawnmower what was sitting there. I pushed past all the junk so's I could find what was causing the stench. It were one of them situations, the ones where you don't want to know, you really don't, but you have to find out. Maybes it went back to that closure bullshit.

At the back of the outhouse, where the toilet used to

be, I could see a black lump of stuff, but it were too dark to make out much more. I remembered we had a torch in there somewhere, and pulled it out from under some gardening tools. I fought my way past all the crap piled up in front, then shone the light over what was there. It were wrapped up in bin bags. The last thing in the world I wanted to do was pierce and rip them open. But I had to. I needed to know.

As I shone my torch inside the bags and saw what was in them, I let out a yelp. I was sick again then, too quick to move out the way, and I got it all over my shoes. I tried to wipe it off with a bit of the bin bag, then realised what I was doing and threw the manky plastic down.

In the bags were bits of cut-up dog. Fuck knows what Mark was playing at. Maybes it were practice, training for his stomach. I didn't want to know. I just wanted to go. To get out this shed, and this garden, and this estate, fucking Nottingham and this messed-up life where you could find a butchered dog in the back of your shed and be relieved.

I grabbed the spade as I left, and didn't bother locking the door. I dug hard into the ground where my suitcase was, shovelling mud at a rate. Behind me I could hear the outhouse door banging in the wind. I prayed this wouldn't wake Mark up but I was too out on it to go back and shut it proper. Didn't have the heart to go nowhere near that shed again if the truth be known. I dug and dug like it were some kind of race to empty the ground. I glanced up at the bedroom from time to time, checking there wasn't no one watching me. One time, I thought I saw the shadow of a shaved head in the upstairs window and turned sharp to look. But it must of been some kind of hallucination cause when I stared hard, it'd gone.

I slammed the shovel into the soil round the top of the suitcase. I pulled on the handle hard and the thing began to move. It stuck a third of the way up and I gave it another big tug. It flew out like the soil'd given birth to it. It were there, my way out. I opened up the case and took out the money belts. I strapped them to my body, all the way down from my chest to my hips, wrapping me-sen up like a mummy and pulling my clothes back over the top. I zipped up the bag. My heart was thumping in my chest, hard and scary like when you've overdone it with the speed. I felt frozen. I couldn't go nowhere, I thought. I'd have to tell Mark what'd gone off and hope he'd forgive me. I needed to get out the garden, though, before he saw me and the mess I'd made and came to sort me out. I didn't want to end up in bin bags at the back of the outhouse.

The hole I'd used to get in and out Mrs Ivanovich's garden when I was little was still there. I pushed the suitcase through it and followed. The garden was well different now. It used to be full of grass and wild flowers – Mrs I said it helped with her work, attracted the bugs and creepy crawlies. Now it were cropped as Mark's head, with similar clumsy bald patches. There was a kids' slide and swing set. It made me sad that. There was that park in the middle of the close, but I knew these things'd been bought so's the neighbours' kids didn't have to use it. The park was always covered in broken glass, and the swings mashed up or pushed round and round the frame so's you needed an adult to get them down. Then there were the needles, the discarded works of the people what put food on our table. I could of sicked all that food up, there and then, at the thought of it. It were so different when I was little, even though no time'd passed since in the scheme of things. I used to play on that park all the time, no worries.

I virtually lived there that long hot summer before Jon was born, even slept overnight under the climbing frame and didn't get no hassle.

This estate wasn't getting no better, that was for sure. I wanted kids of my own one day. That was one thing I'd learned from that abortion if nowt else. And I didn't want them here. I didn't want them to come out me half-Mark, part animal like what he was. I grabbed the handle of my suitcase. It surprised me how hard it were to pull and I thought about leaving it behind. I could do, if I had to, just dump the bogger and run for it. That was why I'd strapped the money bonds all over me-sen. I stood up and looked at the back of what used to be Mrs Ivanovich's house. It were exactly the same as ourn. Just like all the other shithole houses on our shithole estate. The walls were mud brown and brought to mind pictures of English slums in history books. There was this bit of ground what was concreted right next to the house. Mark and me'd used ourn to have barbecues a couple of times when we were pretending to be a normal couple. There were this waste pipe shot out from the back of the kitchen. I could see our neighbours were up cause water was pouring out on it. Behind me was their outhouse, a place what used to be the property's only toilet before they modernised us all. Some of the sheds still had the old toilets sitting in the back, not used in all them years. I didn't know about Mrs Ivanovich's, but it wasn't the case with ourn. It might of been useful for Mark if it had of been. He could of used it to flush things away. I shuddered at the thought.

I was woke up from my daydreams by a loud knock behind me. I jumped and turned. The man from next door was standing at his kitchen window, banging on the glass and making signs at me telling me to clear off.

'I'm fucking going,' I said, with an enthusiastic two-finger salute thrown in his direction. And I meant it too. I pulled my suitcase behind me. Its wheels snagged in the grass, but it moved more smooth when I got onto the concrete. I headed to the jitty what divided the two houses. This cat was licking its-sen clean in the alley, and I made it squeal and dash away as I trundled my way through at a rate of knots. The wheels of the suitcase made a hell of a racket on the concrete ground. It must of sounded louder to me being how I was dead aware Mark'd be close to waking up.

The jittyway opened up to the circle of houses. My heart lurched at the thought I was going to walk away from the close when I'd spent my whole life there. It might not of been the best place in the world, but it were home, and about all I knew. As I headed up the right-hand curve, I saw that arsey cow from next door but one come out to get the milk. She gave me a dirty look, like she always did. But then she clocked my suitcase and did a double take. She stared at me. For a minute I thought she might shout Mark and tell him I was on my way off. Course, she didn't. Why would she? She looked me in the eye, half friendly.

'Good fer you, duck,' she said. And we exchanged smiles for about the first time ever. I knew I was doing the right thing when someone like her confirmed it to me. I couldn't feel it though. Not quite.

I made my way round the close, up to the road at the end. That summer I'd been daydreaming about, this little gell'd got killed on that road. She'd got knocked over by a lorry. That was a memory almost as vivid as the lady-birds. They'd been a right fuss about it, and none of my friends were allowed out to play for weeks.

I cut through the estate, pulling my suitcase behind me.

I didn't dare look back. It struck me how it were much easier than I'd thought it were going to be, leaving. You just had to put one foot in front of the other and keep doing it over and over, and resist the urge to run back where you've come from. I thought about places I might go, tried to take my mind off the idea I was going, and off the cold flush I felt on the back of my neck, put there by the thought Mark might grab me from behind any minute. Before I knew it I could see the houses on Strelley Road. Soon there were bus stops, and a supermarket, the nursery school, and a load of other signs of the real world beyond my estate.

I stood at the thirty-five bus stop, outside Strelley Co-op. I did look back then, staring at the end of Lindfield Road expecting Mark's screaming shaved head to appear there any second. I wasn't wearing a watch, so I didn't know much about the time cept it were early. There wasn't no point checking the timetable. When you can't keep a track like that, waiting seems longer, like for ever cause you aren't there yet and that's all you've got to measure against. I thought about where I'd go, to cheer me-sen up. The Amazon rainforest was a bit of a grand idea, I thought, and I wasn't sure you could live there. I might have to find a town nearby to live in, somewhere close enough so's I could walk or cycle to the edge of the forest. Perhaps I'd be able to see it from my window, and the same butterflies would fly past as nested in the trees. I could go round Brazil, travel a bit too. See Rio at carnival, look for the right place to live.

Mark didn't appear round the corner. The bus came and I got on it, dragging my suitcase after me. I stood there with these bond things what were worth a fortune strapped all over me, scrambling for change from my pockets to pay the driver. It made you laugh.

'Where to, duck?' he said.

I put my coins in the machine. 'The Amazon basin, please,' I said. And I grinned at him.

He joined in with my joke. 'I can tek yer as far as town be-Radford,' he said. 'Maybes you can get yer connection from there?'

I nodded and we both laughed a bit. My ticket chugged out the machine.

'You really going ter the rainforest?' he asked me.

'Maybes,' I said.

'Good fer you, duck. Better-n hanging round here yer whole life waiting for summat interesting ter happen,' he told me.

I went and sat on a seat near the front, one with plenty of legroom so's I could keep my bag with me. I hugged the case. I thought how funny it were, what the bus driver'd said. It definitely wasn't for lack of stuff happening that I was off.

It were getting light. I watched the sky round my fingers as I leaned against the window. The edge of my skin glowed blue. I'd seen dawn happen a shitload of times, you do when you're a pillhead. The sun splitting open and leaking all over the sky. Laser beams of light what pierce through bits of cloud. I reckon if you showed me any sunrise, I could tell you the exact time of year it'd happened. It were the first winter dawn I'd seen that year and it were special. Not everso dramatic or owt like that. Not brazen and bloody like a summer's morning when you're due a baking day. But bright and clear, the sky hanging high and open way above me. The light felt like cool water on my eyelids, bathing them and taking away the soreness from not having much sleep.

The bus wasn't moving yet, sat still cause the stop was

a timing point. Every now and then the engine shuddered, like the way a kid lets out the odd sob when they've
finished bawling their eyes out. I'd forgot about the idea
Mark might come for me. The pale clean sky'd soothed
away all that shit.

Then I turned to the window and he was there, his face
inches from mine. He banged on the glass. My stomach
jerked right up into my chest and I jolted in my seat. The
driver did summat what changed the noise of the engine
and I knew we'd be moving any minute. I stared at Mark.
The first thing I looked for was his hammer, where it were
usually hung, against his chest. But it wasn't there. I looked
for it in his hands.

If you'd asked me what Mark'd do if he caught me up,
I'd of said mashed me up with his hammer, or had a go
at stabbing me or grabbed me by the hair and dragged
me all the way back to the close. But there wasn't no sign
of his hammer or a knife, and he didn't try to get on
the bus. He looked me right in the eyes and mouthed
some words at me. I didn't get it at first, couldn't read his
lips.

The bus began to pull off and I shrugged at Mark. He
screwed up his eyes, frustrated. He jogged beside the bus
as it moved, exaggerating the movement of his lips until
I got it. 'I love you,' he said. 'I love you, I love you, I love
you.'

They reckon you feel love in your heart but that's
bollocks. True love, the type what strikes you down and
makes you change for ever, you feel that kind of love in
every fucking organ inside you. Liver, kidneys, heart and
spleen. Every tiny cell what makes up your brain and your
spine, your bones and blood and muscles. It keens through
you.